**Here's what critics are saying about
Gemma Halliday's Wine & Dine Mysteries:**

"I rank *A Sip Before Dying* as one of my favorite fun reads.
I say to Gemma Halliday, well done. She wrote a mystery
that encompassed suspense flavored with romantic notions,
while giving us a heroine to make us smile."
—*The Book Breeze Magazine*

"Gemma Halliday's signature well-written story filled with
wonderful characters is just what I expected. All in all, this
is the beginning of a great cozy series no one should miss!"
—*Kings River Life Magazine*

"I've always enjoyed the writing style and comfortable tone
of Gemma novels and this one fits in perfectly. From the
first page, the author pulled me in...when all was said and
done, I enjoyed this delightfully engaging tale and I can't
wait to spend more time with Emmy, Ava and their
friends."
—*Dru's Book Musings*

"This is a great cozy mystery, and I highly recommend it!"
—*Book Review Crew*

"I could not put *A Sip Before Dying* by Gemma Halliday
down. Once I started reading it, I was hooked!!"
—*Cozy Mystery Book Reviews*

BOOKS BY GEMMA HALLIDAY

High Heels Mysteries
Spying in High Heels
Killer in High Heels
Undercover in High Heels
Christmas in High Heels
(short story)
Alibi in High Heels
Mayhem in High Heels
Honeymoon in High Heels
(short story)
Sweetheart in High Heels
(short story)
Fearless in High Heels
Danger in High Heels
Homicide in High Heels
Deadly in High Heels
Suspect in High Heels
Peril in High Heels
Jeopardy in High Heels

Wine & Dine Mysteries
A Sip Before Dying
Chocolate Covered Death
Victim in the Vineyard
Marriage, Merlot & Murder
Death in Wine Country
Fashion, Rosé & Foul Play
Witness at the Winery

Hollywood Headlines
Mysteries
Hollywood Scandals
Hollywood Secrets
Hollywood Confessions
Hollywood Holiday
(short story)
Hollywood Deception

Marty Hudson Mysteries
Sherlock Holmes and the Case
of the Brash Blonde
Sherlock Holmes and the Case
of the Disappearing Diva
Sherlock Holmes and the Case
of the Wealthy Widow

Tahoe Tessie Mysteries
Luck Be A Lady
Hey Big Spender
Baby It's Cold Outside
(holiday short story)

Jamie Bond Mysteries
Unbreakable Bond
Secret Bond
Bond Bombshell
(short story)
Lethal Bond
Dangerous Bond
Bond Ambition
(short story)
Fatal Bond
Deadly Bond

Hartley Grace Featherstone
Mysteries
Deadly Cool
Social Suicide
Wicked Games

Other Works
Play Dead
Viva Las Vegas
A High Heels Haunting
Watching You (short story)
Confessions of a Bombshell
Bandit (short story)

MARRIAGE, MERLOT & MURDER

a Wine & Dine mystery

GEMMA HALLIDAY

Dedicated to Nick, my buddy with the snacks.

CHAPTER ONE

———

"Everything has to be perfect," I muttered to myself for what was probably the hundredth time that day. It was a Friday afternoon, and I was prepping Oak Valley Vineyards, my family's small winery in Sonoma, to host our first wedding since I'd taken over its management. While I'd been lucky enough in the last few months to book a couple of private parties at our large outdoor venue overlooking the picturesque vineyard—and even most recently hosted a Food and Wine Festival—I can't say that any of the events thus far had gone off without a hitch. Or ended up bringing in the kind of revenue that Oak Valley sorely needed to avoid being gobbled up by the corporate giants of the region. But I had hope that our future as a wedding venue looked rosy, as the first couple in over a decade to rent our space for their nuptials would be arriving for their final walk-through and rehearsal.

Hope I tried to hold on to as I glanced at my prerehearsal checklist. *Table linens for the reception—check. Centerpieces arrived—check. Chairs set up for the outdoor ceremony—check.*

"You okay, Emmy?" my best friend, Ava Barnett, asked, leaning on the bar top in our tasting room.

"Sure, why?"

"You're muttering to yourself again." Ava grinned at me.

I couldn't help smiling back. Ava had known me since childhood, and if anything could counteract my nerves, it was her optimistic spirit and easy-going vibe. Both of us being only children in our families, we'd been more like sisters than just friends, some saying we even looked alike. Though, while we were both the same age (twenty-nine. Ish.), Ava's long blonde hair had a thickness and shine to it, while mine tended more toward frizzy or, on a good day, wavy with a chance of curls.

Ava was also a few pounds lighter than I was, due to her love of the outdoors and my love of all things chocolate and/or bacon–covered. And while my style was usually more jeans and T-shirts, Ava always looked fresh and fashionable in her collection of boho dresses and skirts. Today's outfit: a long, semi-sheer floral skirt paired with an opaque mini underneath and an off-the-shoulder blouse that looked both easy and elegant at the same time.

Ava had graciously offered to take the day off from running her downtown shop, Silver Girl, where she sold her handmade jewelry creations, to help me prep the winery for the big day.

"I just want everything to be perfect," I told her in defense of my muttering.

"I know. And it will be. The bride and groom wouldn't have booked your space for their ceremony if they didn't love it," she reasoned. "And what's not to love? A wedding at a charming hillside vineyard in the heart of Wine Country is something that most girls only *dream* about." Her smile widened. "This is a total fairy tale scenario."

"As long as you don't mean one of the Grimm Brothers' variety," I countered, stooping to pick up a broken piece of cork off the floor behind the bar. "We have less than an hour to finish putting up the decorations before the wedding party gets here."

"Which Conchita is already working on," Ava reminded me.

"But the altar still needs some last minute adjustments," I added.

"Which Hector promised he would do in the morning," Ava responded.

"And what about the Eddie Factor?"

Ava grinned. "You got me there. There's nothing I can do about the Eddie Factor."

Eddie Bliss was my lovable but completely inept winery manager who, no matter the occasion, always seemed to break, drop, or spill something. I made a mental note to keep him busy elsewhere when our guests made their arrivals. Like possibly Alaska.

"But," Ava offered, "maybe I can have him help Jean Luc with the—"

"Stop right zere, *mademoiselle*!"

I looked up to find Jean Luc, my sommelier, emerge from the back door as if on command. He was tall, slim, and wore a sculpted black mustache to rival any cartoon villain's. "Zee Eddie is to be nowhere near zee pouring during zee event!" he said, his French accent thick.

"You have my word," I assured him quickly. "But the bride and groom will be here soon, and I'll need them to confirm that we have their order correct before the reception tomorrow. Could you grab the bottles from the cellar that we talked about yesterday?" I asked, mentally checking off the next item on my list.

"Of course." He bent forward in a slight bow that bordered on comical, though his mustache twitched as he walked away. "Though I *still* zeenk it's a travesty that zey want to pair Pinot Noir with zee lobster," he muttered under his breath, just loud enough for me to hear. "A Chardonnay would be much better."

I felt my mouth curve into a smile again as I watched him go. Having grown up in the Bordeaux region of France, my sommelier knew his wine pairings better than most guests— possibly even better than I did, though I had been trained by the CIA. (Though, not *that* CIA. The Culinary Institute of America.)

"He's not wrong," I said, winking at Ava. "But it's what the groom requested." And considering we were in the low-to-no tourist season here in Sonoma, when many small wineries went from struggling to belly up, whatever the guests wanted, the guests got! Case in point: the decor the bride had requested, going with a floral fairy tale theme that had been a challenge to pull off in Northern California in the winter. I'd had to enlist the help of no less than three local florists to find "spring" flowers in January.

While Jean Luc was in The Cave, as my grandmother had affectionately dubbed our wine cellar, Ava, Conchita, and I made quick work of the few remaining items on my list, ensuring that every wisteria garland, tulip bouquet, and calla lily cascade was perfectly placed. I was just setting the last centerpiece on one of the tables when I heard tires crunching the gravel in the parking lot outside.

"They're here!" Ava exclaimed, her blue eyes wide with excitement. She scurried around one of the reception tables to peer out the window.

I didn't respond, too busy trying to quash the nerves bundling in my stomach. I risked a quick peek in the mirror behind the bar counter to check my reflection. My own blonde strands were a bit on the frizzy side today, and I found myself wishing I had a brush handy. I quickly combed through a few tangles with my fingers and rubbed away a small smudge of mascara beneath one of my pale blue eyes. A quick smile showed me that my lipstick thankfully hadn't smeared on my teeth. So I at least had that going for me.

Here we go, I thought as I turned away from the mirror. I took a deep breath to ease the tightening sensation in my chest. Then I squared my shoulders and pasted a wide smile on my face as I marched out into the bright afternoon sun to greet my clients.

Two cars had pulled to a stop in the gravel lot at the top of our oak tree–lined drive. A distinguished looking older gentleman climbed out of the driver's side of the first car, a shiny black Mercedes. The man was tall but thick around the middle, with a full head of silver hair and dark eyes that crinkled at the corners as he squinted in the sunlight. He stepped around to the passenger side and held out his hand to a woman with sandy blonde hair in an elegant, knee-length black dress and pearls. Based on their sophisticated appearance, I presumed they were Mr. and Mrs. Somersby, the bride-to-be's parents.

Parked next to the Mercedes was a flashy red Jaguar. Four figures climbed out of the little sports car to join the middle-aged couple in the gravel lot. Though I'd never seen the tall man and the woman who seemed engrossed in her phone who emerged from the back seat, I did recognize the man with dark, slicked back hair who slid out from behind the driver's seat, as well as the pretty, slim-waisted brunette in a lacy, cream-colored dress who came to stand next to him. She took his hand with one of hers and waved cheerfully to me with the other.

"Hi, Emmy," the brunette called, flashing me a bright smile.

I returned her wave. "Hi, Juliet," I replied with the same enthusiasm.

Alfred Campbell and Juliet Somersby were the bride-and groom-to-be, and their happiness this weekend was my top priority. Money aside, it was a true pleasure to help the young woman celebrate her big day. In my interactions with Juliet leading up to this weekend, I'd found her to be sweet, genuine, and the complete opposite of the bridezillas I had originally feared when venturing into weddings. She was classically beautiful in a way that reminded me of Anne Hathaway, with shoulder-length brown hair, long lashes, and wide doe eyes, and while I knew her trust fund meant she'd never had to work a day in her life, she served on the board of several charities, her latest being a project to help provide warm clothing during the winter months to the homeless in San Francisco.

Juliet's bubbly personality and excitement for her nuptials were infectious, and I couldn't help but grin as the happy woman pulled her fiancé toward me from across the parking lot. Ava stood next to me as the engaged couple and their guests closed the gap between us.

"I can't believe the big day is finally here," Juliet said, her tone giddy. She released her man's hand and stepped forward to give me a hug. "Thank you for everything, Emmy. I just know that tomorrow is going to be perfect."

That made one of us.

"No thanks necessary," I told her. "It's worth it just to see the smile on your face." Of course, the check that would soon be hitting my bank account didn't hurt, either—especially since it would allow me to make payroll for another month. "I hope you'll recommend Oak Valley Vineyards to your friends whenever they're ready to walk down the aisle," I added.

"Of course we will." Juliet beamed at me. She turned and swept her arm toward the older man and woman. "Emmy, these are my parents, Edward and Meredith Somersby."

I stood up a little straighter as I regarded the older couple. They were footing the bill for the weekend's festivities, so I wanted to make a good impression. As I'd learned from

Juliet, the Somersbys hailed from Atherton, an exclusive area just south of San Francisco that dripped with old money. Edward's grandfather, Joseph Somersby, had founded a chain of luxury hotels that spanned the West Coast, which was why it had come as a surprise that Edward's only daughter, Juliet, had chosen to book her ceremony at my vineyard instead of one of their several locations that boasted breathtaking views of the Pacific Ocean. Not that I was complaining, of course—locking in a high-profile family like the Somersbys for Oak Valley Vineyards' debut wedding was sure to attract the attention of more potential clients.

As long as everything goes well, that anxious voice in the back of my head reminded me for the fiftieth time.

I ignored my doubtful inner monologue and offered Mr. and Mrs. Somersby what I hoped was a cordial smile. "I'm so pleased to meet you both. I'm Emmeline Oak, owner of the Oak Valley Vineyards. You can call me Emmy." I shook Edward's hand when he offered it.

"A pleasure," he said stiffly. Mr. Somersby squinted at the Spanish style buildings behind us that made up the main inner workings of the winery. They'd originally been built by my great-grandfather, but generations since had added on and improved here and there. Edward nodded to himself as if indicating that the venue's appearance met his approval. "If you don't mind, I'd like to see where my money's going," he told me, lifting his chin. "Can you give us a quick tour of your establishment?"

"I'd be delighted," I replied, nodding politely. I'd spent my childhood playing in the old building with its tanned façade, stone accents, and a tiled terra cotta roof, and I was proud to call it both my place of business and my home.

I gestured to Ava, who was still standing beside me. "First, I'd like for you to meet my friend and associate, Ava Barnett. She'll be serving as my assistant wedding planner this weekend. We're here to make this a memorable experience for your whole family, so if there's anything at all that we can do for you between now and tomorrow's festivities, please don't hesitate to ask."

"Nice to meet you all." Ava gave the group a friendly wave. "Congratulations, Juliet and Alfred," she said, offering the younger couple a bright smile.

"The pleasure is all mine." The groom flashed a blindingly white smile Ava's way. "You can call me Freddie." He took Ava's hand and pumped it up and down, his grip on her fingers lingering just a tad longer than might have been necessary.

I tried not to judge the groom too quickly. Most of my dealings had been with Juliet, and I'd only had the opportunity to meet Freddie Campbell a couple of times—both of which had been brief. He was classically tall, dark, and handsome, but beyond that I knew very little about him or his background. Juliet had said he was some sort of entrepreneur, but it was all kind of vague.

Freddie released Ava from his grip and took a step back, sweeping his arm toward the other man who had arrived in the Jaguar with Juliet and him. "This is my best man, Baker Evans."

Baker was a few inches shorter than Freddie and quite a few pounds heavier—a fact accentuated by his round features and small, dark eyes set behind thick glasses. His dress shirt strained against his belly, his dark hair shaggy in a way that spoke of the need for a haircut more than a fashion choice, and his nose sat slightly crooked in a face that was marked with the scars of teenage acne. He gave Ava and me a curt nod and a shy smile.

Next to him, the final member of their party, a woman with short black hair in a stylish pixie cut and a phone that seemed attached to her hand like an appendage, cleared her throat and looked impatiently at Freddie.

The groom's polished smile lost some of its sparkle. "And this is Natalie," he added, his tone going just a tad flat.

"Natalie Weisman," the woman said, stepping forward to shake first my hand and then Ava's. "I'm Freddie's cousin. *And* I'm also one of Juliet's bridesmaids," she emphasized, nodding toward Juliet. "I told Jules here that if Freddie was really going to throw in the towel on bachelorhood and settle down, I want a front row seat."

Out of the corner of my eye, I saw Juliet stiffen. Edward and Meredith also stared at the woman in silent disapproval. I had the impression that the Somersbys weren't fans of Freddie's outspoken cousin—not that it seemed to bother the woman. Natalie continued to look at Juliet with a taunting smile. "Poor Julesy. Doesn't know what she's gotten herself into with this one."

"Well, then," I said, hoping to break the sudden tension in the air. "Now that we're all acquainted, Ava and I will walk you around the property before the rest of the wedding party arrives for the rehearsal. Right this way, please." I motioned for the group to follow me into the tasting room.

Ava and I spent the next forty-five minutes escorting the engaged couple and their entourage around Oak Valley. We showed Juliet the rooms where she and her bridesmaids would do their hair and makeup for the ceremony, as well as several of the more scenic locations around the property that were perfect for taking wedding photos.

My ten-acre plot of land boasted a breathtaking view of the countryside and also featured a charming terrace courtyard in the back that was bordered by thriving rose bushes. Despite the dismal state of our finances, I was proud of how well Hector had managed to maintain the landscaping. I was hoping that tomorrow I could convince the wedding photographer to cut me a deal on a few promotional images of the property to post on our website and social media pages.

"Ooh!" Juliet squealed when we stepped out onto the second-floor balcony, which overlooked the vineyard, bathed this time of year in warm hues of orange and gold. She squeezed Freddie's hand. "We have to do some pictures up here! I feel like I'm in a scene from a romantic movie." She exhaled a happy sigh. "The view is absolutely breathtaking."

"Breathtaking," Freddie agreed smoothly. Though I couldn't help but notice that the only "scenic view" he was taking in was that of Ava's backside as she leaned on the railing.

I wasn't the only one who noticed the groom's wandering eye. I flicked a glance toward Edward Somersby and found him scowling at his soon-to-be son-in-law. Behind him, Freddie's cousin, Natalie, smirked at the groom.

"Yoo-hoo!" A man's lilting voice echoed up the stairs from the tasting room. "Is there a blushing bride in the house?"

Juliet's eyes lit up. "Andrew!" She released Freddie's hand and started across the balcony, heading for the stairs that led back down to the first floor. "The rest of the wedding party must be here," she called over her shoulder.

I checked my watch. The rehearsal was scheduled to begin in twenty minutes.

"Perhaps we should head outside to the ceremony space?" I suggested. I followed Juliet toward the stairs, and the others trailed after us.

A tall man with red hair and freckles was leaning against the tasting room bar. At the sight of him, Juliet shrieked and skipped across the room to fling her arms around his neck. "I'm so glad you finally made it!" she cooed.

"Dahling, I wouldn't miss it for the world!" the newcomer told her, his voice laced with a slow drawl.

"Can you believe I'm getting *married* tomorrow?" Juliet giggled.

The man sent a glance over Juliet's shoulder, his gaze settling on Freddie as the rest of us walked toward him. His brows bunched. "No, baby girl. I really cannot," he replied, and I thought I detected a hint of disdain in his tone.

Juliet released the man and turned around to face the rest of us. "Emmy, this is Andrew Phillips, one of my best friends from college. He's—" Her forehead wrinkled. "You know, I'm not really sure what to call him. He's not exactly a brides*maid*." She giggled.

I closed the gap between us and shook Andrew's hand. "Nice to meet you. I believe the official term for a man in the bride's party is the bride's attendant or bridesman," I explained. I glanced at Freddie and his best man, Baker. "Though, I do know that all the men in a wedding party were originally referred to as bridesknights." To prepare for my role as wedding planner for the weekend, I'd pored over a few chapters of a book about wedding history and traditions, and I'd gleaned several interesting tidbits.

"I think I'll stick with groomsman, thanks," Baker said.

Andrew grinned. "Oh, not me, honey. I'll be a knight. Very medieval chic."

"How about a toast before we head outside for the rehearsal?" Freddie suggested. He looked at me. "You have champagne?"

"Of course." I nodded to Jean Luc, who was stationed behind the bar, and made a mental head count of the group. "Seven glasses, I believe."

"*Oui*," Jean Luc agreed and pulled several slim flutes down from our glass fronted cabinets. Fortunately, we'd chilled several bottles of champagne in preparation for the wedding party to arrive. While I was excited to showcase our own varietals at the dinner, I knew bubbly was the toasting beverage of choice for the occasion and had purchased several cases from a local winery who specialized in sparkly wines.

Once Jean Luc had the glasses poured, I quickly distributed one to each person in attendance.

Andrew gave a low whistle of appreciation as I moved through the group, his gaze fixed on Jean Luc. "Speaking of knights, I think I just found my Prince Charming." He leaned close to my ear. "*Who* is that Hottie McTottie in the tight pants?" he asked, inclining his head toward the Frenchman.

I stifled a laugh. "That's Jean Luc Gasteon," I replied. "He's our sommelier."

"French and a hottie." Andrew licked his lips and reached over to grab Juliet's arm. "Girl, is he just my type or what?"

"He *is* cute," Juliet agreed.

I didn't have the heart to tell Andrew that he wasn't Jean Luc's type, which, from what I had gathered, was waifish French women with refined palettes and an appreciation for a good glass of Bordeaux.

I handed Andrew his champagne and then offered a flute to Juliet. She held up her hand and politely waved me off. "Oh, no thank you," she said, giving me a demure smile. "I really shouldn't."

"Why not?" Natalie teased. "Do you already have a bun in the oven?" She eyed Freddie, a wicked grin curving her lips. "What do they call that, cuz—a shotgun wedding?"

Juliet tensed, and her smile evaporated. "No—it's nothing like that," she stammered, sounding embarrassed. "It's just that I'm a total lightweight, and I want to have a clear head for tomorrow." She dropped her gaze to her feet, frowning.

"Give her a break, *cuz*," Freddie said, admonishing his cousin. He placed a protective arm around his bride-to-be. Luckily her tension seemed to drain at his touch.

I glanced at the Somersbys, who'd been silent throughout the exchange. Edward was still scowling, and Meredith wore the same placid expression she'd had since exiting her Mercedes. What either of them was thinking was a mystery.

"Perhaps we should say a few words to our friends and family," Freddie said, addressing the room. He beamed in the faces of his future in-laws' stoic presence.

"What a good idea," Juliet agreed, her smile back in place as she stared up at her groom.

"Thank you all for being here with Juliet and me as we begin this happy new chapter of our lives together," Freddie began. He glanced at his fiancée before returning his attention to the others. "We're both honored that you've chosen to bear witness to the commitment that we're making tomorrow. So, let's raise a glass to all of you."

The members of the little group lifted their drinks—everyone except Edward Somersby. He continued to frown at the groom while the others clinked glasses and then took sips of their champagne.

Freddie took a long pull from his own glass and then set it down on the bar. He turned to Juliet and gently gripped her face with one hand, tilting it upward to so that she was looking at him. "After tomorrow, it's just you and me, babe," he said, kissing her lightly on the lips. "Nothing is going to stand in the way of our happy ending."

CHAPTER TWO

———

"Emmy? Are you in there?" Ava's voice accompanied the soft knock on my office door the next morning.

I quickly finished applying my lipstick and checked for loose strands of my hair, which was pulled back in a sleek, professional-looking bun. Rising from my desk chair, I smoothed a wrinkle in my purple silk blouse and tucked the bottom into my gray pencil skirt. Then I hurried over to the door and opened it.

"What do you think?" I asked Ava as I let her into the room. "Does this outfit say 'awesome wedding planner'?" I held up my headset and clipboard as I twirled around in a slow circle.

She grinned. "Girl, it screams it," she said, giving me a thumbs-up. "You look fab."

"Thanks." I beamed at her and then turned back to the desk and grabbed a second headset, which I held out to Ava. "I got one for you, too. You'll need it so we can communicate during the ceremony and reception."

"So official." She took the earpiece from my outstretched hand and offered me a latte in its place. "Okay, boss lady," Ava joked, "put me to work. Let's get this wedding party started!"

I sent her to wait out front for the servers we'd hired for the reception dinner to arrive while I made my way to the rooms where the bridal party was getting dressed. According to the schedule I'd printed for myself (and that I'd already triple checked, of course), the ceremony was set to begin shortly, and I wanted to make sure Juliet had everything she needed before she walked down the aisle.

"Juliet, it's Emmy," I said, knocking softly on the door. "Can I come in?"

"Sure," she called in response.

I turned the doorknob. "I just wanted to see how everything was coming along—" I stopped short when my gaze landed on the bride, who was standing with her back to me as she faced the floor-length mirror on the opposite wall.

Juliet was a picture of elegance in her sleeveless white gown with tiny pearl beads and feathered accents woven into the bodice. Her dark hair was braided and pinned back in an elegant updo, secured with a pearl encrusted barrette. Even her makeup was flawless.

"Wow. You look gorgeous," I told her, and I meant it.

Juliet beamed at me through the mirror. "Thank you." Twin spots of rosy color appeared on her cheeks. "I feel like a princess," she added with a giggle.

"And you look like one too, baby girl," Andrew cooed from beside her.

Juliet continued to stand still while Andrew and one of the bridesmaids tied the silk ribbons on the back of her dress. In the opposite corner of the room, Natalie was seated on the black leather loveseat, looking disinterested as she sipped a mimosa and scrolled on her phone.

Andrew finished tying one of the ribbons and then straightened, glancing at the self-absorbed woman in the pixie cut. He gave me a dramatic eye roll. "Clearly we've been all hands on deck here getting ready."

I grinned, though Andrew's sarcasm seemed to be lost on Juliet as she nodded enthusiastically. "Mom and Dad were both in earlier too—they wanted to see the dress before the ceremony."

I checked my watch. "The bridal party should begin lining up for the wedding procession in about five minutes," I told Juliet and her entourage. I met her gaze through the mirror. "I'll go find your father and make sure he's ready to walk you down the aisle."

"Perfect! We'll be outside in just a few minutes," she promised as I slipped out of the room.

I made my way over to the meadow where the ceremony was to be held, behind the winery's main building. Hector Villarreal, my vineyard manager, had built a gorgeous wooden gazebo for the occasion, placing it at the far side of the meadow, with the backdrop of the vine covered hills behind it. The entrance to the structure was decorated with garlands made of delicate white flowers and bright green vines, and several dozen white folding chairs were set up to face the ethereal scene. We'd worked hard to create a picturesque location for the ceremony, and I had to say, the end product was not too shabby.

Guests had already begun to arrive. Some had taken their seats, while others milled about and greeted one another. I spotted Edward and Meredith Somersby standing among the crowd, chatting amiably with another couple near the back row of folding chairs.

As I walked up the stone path toward them, I navigated around several guests starting to trickle toward their seats as the big moment neared. In fact, one tall man with sandy blonde hair practically ran into me, his eyes so focused on the phone in his hand he barely noticed me.

"Sorry," he mumbled, gaze shifting from me to the screen in rapid succession.

"No problem," I told him, mentally rolling my own eyes at how attached to their screens some people were. I said a silent prayer that he at least put it away during the ceremony. One thing I could not control would be a trilling cell phone in the audience as the bride and groom said their nuptials. I tried not to let that thought stir up a new bundle of nerves as I approached the Somersbys.

"Sorry to interrupt," I said, going for a courteous tone as I reached the couple, who were still engaged in a conversation with a pair of guests. "But it's almost time for the ceremony to begin." I met Edward's gaze. "Would you mind following me to meet up with the bride?"

Mr. Somersby nodded. "Of course." He placed his hand on the small of his wife's back and leaned over to give her a peck on the cheek. Then he bid farewell to the man and woman they'd been chatting with and turned away, falling into step beside me.

"Are you ready to give your daughter away?" I asked in an effort to make small talk.

Edward scowled. "To Freddie? Not at all." He sighed. "But I suppose I don't have much of a choice in the matter, do I?"

I paused, not quite sure how to answer that question. "She seems very much in love with him," I said carefully.

His expression softened. "I know. I just want my little girl to be happy."

"Well, she appears *very* happy," I said, hoping to ease some of his uncertainty. "I just saw her a few minutes ago in the bridal suite, and she was practically glowing."

"She usually is." Edward beamed. "My Juliet is an angel."

My heart warmed. It was clear the man truly loved his daughter.

We fell silent as we passed the three groomsmen, in their matching gray tuxes, making their way to line up beside the pastor at the entrance to the gazebo—Baker and two men who'd been introduced to me the previous day as old high school friends of Freddie's.

I found Natalie, Andrew, and the two other bridesmaids—one a petite blonde and the other a slender brunette with a chin-length bob and blunt bangs—grouped together under a sprawling oak tree just outside the main building. The women were dressed in sleeveless chiffon gowns in a gorgeous plum color, and Andrew wore a silk shirt of the same deep purple hue with gray dress pants and a matching gray bowtie. He was helping the bridesmaid with the bob with last minute adjustments to the flower pinned in her hair, and Natalie was engrossed in something on her phone, fingers typing away as she generally ignored her surroundings.

Juliet glided up behind the others just as Edward and I reached them.

He beamed with pride as he wrapped his daughter in a warm embrace. "Are you sure you want to go through with this, pumpkin?" I heard him ask in a low voice. "There's still time to change your mind. Your mother and I would support your decision, of course."

"Stop it, Daddy!" Juliet pulled away and gave him a playful slap on the arm. "Of *course* I'm sure. I've been waiting for this day my whole life." Her brown eyes shone with excitement. "I'm about to marry the man of my dreams."

Edward gave a small grunt in response, though it didn't sound exactly approving.

"Emmy." Ava's voice crackled in my ear.

"Excuse me," I said to Juliet and her father, taking a step away from the group before I answered.

"I'm here," I replied into the headset, adjusting it so that I could hear her better. "What's up?"

"Small snag."

Those nerves I'd been trying to squelch all day came back full force. "How small is small?" I asked in a hushed tone. I glanced to the bride and her father, who were waiting impatiently.

"Can you meet me by the tasting room entrance?" she asked, the urgency in her voice not making me feel any better.

"I'm on my way," I told her. I pulled the headset down around my neck as I walked back over to Juliet and the others. "I just need to run to the tasting room for a moment to check on something," I said, keeping my tone even.

"Is everything okay?" Juliet asked, a frown forming between her slim eyebrows.

I pasted on my most reassuring smile. "Of course. Just dotting our *i*'s and crossing our *t*'s," I said with maybe a little too much chipperness to be believed.

Edward Somersby frowned at me. Then again, I was starting to think it was his default expression.

"I'll be back before the ceremony begins," I promised and then quickly hurried away before anyone could question me further.

I spotted Ava as soon as I rounded the corner to the tasting room entrance. She was waiting for me in the doorway, leaning against the threshold and nervously tugging at a strand of her blonde hair.

"What's wrong?" I asked, though I was afraid to hear the answer.

Ava chewed her lip. "Just promise you won't freak out, okay?"

"Words like that don't exactly inspire calm or confidence," I replied, feeling my palms grow sweaty. A dozen worst case scenarios crashed through my head. "Did the photographer not show up? Did the band cancel?"

"No." Ava quickly shook her head. "The photographer is here, and the band is unloading their gear in the parking lot." She sucked in a breath. "But I can't find the groom."

I closed my eyes and thought a dirty word. "Please tell me you're joking."

"I wish I were." She grimaced. "Emmy, I've looked practically everywhere, but I can't find him."

"I saw the groomsmen taking their places. He's not with them?"

She shook her head.

I frowned, mentally chastising his best man for not keeping better tabs on Freddie. "You tried calling him?" I asked, flipping through the pages on my clipboard until I found the contact sheet that contained the phone numbers for every member of the wedding party.

"Several times," Ava responded.

"And?" I asked, punching the number into my own phone just for good measure.

"Goes straight to voicemail."

I pursed my lips together, listening to my phone give me the same results. "He's probably got it shut off for the ceremony," I reasoned.

"Smart. *If* he was at the ceremony," Ava pointed out.

"He's not in the groomsmen's room? Maybe making last minute adjustments?"

She shook her head. "First place I looked. He's also not at the bar downing liquid courage, not greeting guests, and not at the altar next to his best man like he's supposed to be."

I could hear the growing concern in her voice that matched my own feelings as I remembered his wandering eye the day before. "You don't think he could have done a runner, do you?" I asked, hating to even voice the thought out loud.

Ava bit her lip. "I thought of that, but his car is still here." She hiked her thumb over her shoulder toward the parking lot.

"Then he's got to be here somewhere," I concluded.

Ava's brow pinched. "What do you want me to do?"

I swallowed. "All right. Let's just try to stay calm and figure out where he went," I said. I closed my eyes and took a few cleansing breaths. "Okay, go fetch the best man," I instructed Ava. "And then stall the ceremony for as long as you can. I don't want the bride to suspect that anything is wrong."

"Got it." Ava gave a quick nod and took off around the corner.

I entered the tasting room and nervously paced the floor as I waited for her to return with Baker Evans. I prayed Freddie would not leave that poor girl at the altar. I couldn't bear the thought of how heartbroken Juliet would be if he'd decided to bail on her at the last minute.

After a few minutes that felt like an eternity, Baker finally poked his head through the doorway. "Your assistant said you wanted to see me, Miss Oak?"

"Yes, please. Come in," I told him.

"Is there some sort of delay?" he asked, glancing at his watch as he stepped fully into the room. His gray suit was a tad too tight for his frame, and his hair had been slicked back from his face in a way that only served to accentuate his round features.

"Uh, sort of," I hedged. "Have you seen Freddie?" I asked, trying not to sound as frantic as I felt.

He shook his head. "No—not since I left the bed and breakfast a couple hours ago."

"A couple hours ago?" I blurted out, the franticness starting to rise. "You mean he never showed up at the groomsmen's room at all?"

Baker had the good grace to look sheepish. "I know it's kinda in my job description to keep tabs on the groom, but when I left he said he'd be right behind me."

"A couple *hours* ago," I emphasized.

He shrugged. "I figured he just needed a little alone time before taking the plunge, right?" He grinned at me as if I was in on the joke.

"Right." I forced down the lump of panic that filled my throat. "So, you haven't seen him at all since you arrived at the winery?"

"No." Baker frowned. "Why?"

I inhaled slowly and then pushed it back out. "We're having trouble locating him," I admitted.

The frown deepened. "You mean he's missing?"

I nodded. "He didn't say anything to you about..." I paused, not sure I should even float the idea. "...getting cold feet?"

But thankfully Baker shook his head. "No. I mean, why would he? Juliet's great."

"She is great," I agreed. "And she's waiting very patiently right now. Are you sure you have no idea where Freddie could be? He didn't mention anything to you?"

But the man just shrugged. "Sorry." He paused. "Do you want me to help you look for him?"

I sighed and shook my head. "No, actually, I want your help stalling the ceremony. Ava's with the bride, but if you could just reassure the guests that we're, uh, just experiencing a slight delay but we'll be starting shortly?" Which I hope sounded a lot better than *we've misplaced the groom.*

Baker nodded curtly then turned back toward the meadow.

I took a deep breath and tried to think. If Freddie's car was there, he had to be on the grounds somewhere. Retracing Ava's steps, I double checked that the red Jag was, indeed, in the parking lot. I even looked in all the windows on the off chance Freddie was taking a pre-wedding nap in his car. Negative. I had much the same result rechecking the groomsmen's room, the side lot, and the kitchen, where I was happy to at least see servers had shown up. Conchita, my house manager, was dutifully instructing them on how to describe each of the canapés she and I had spent the last week preparing.

But no sign of the groom.

Getting desperate, I even checked the men's restroom. No Freddie.

I was just about to give up and admit we'd really truly lost him, when my headset crackled to life again. "Emmy?" Ava's voice asked.

"Tell me you found him?" I pleaded into the microphone.

"No, sorry," she responded. "But one of the bridesmaids—the one with the brunette bob—her boyfriend said he thought he saw a couple people heading toward the terrace a little while ago."

The back terrace was where I normally held small dinner parties and more intimate events, though for this occasion we'd decorated it with potted flowers and lush greenery to provide a spot for wedding party photos to be taken before the reception.

"Was one of them Freddie?" I asked the obvious question, already backtracking toward the terrace.

"He wasn't sure. But I thought it might be worth looking."

"Absolutely, thanks," I told her, jogging in my heels down the small stone pathway that led to the courtyard. My heart was pounding in my chest as I rounded the shrubbery. Short of casing the vineyard behind the meadow where the ceremony was being held, we'd checked everywhere else on the property with no sign of Freddie. I mentally crossed my fingers that I'd find him on the other side of those bushes.

But as the terrace came into view a moment later, I regretted that wish.

My body froze, and I opened my mouth to scream, but no sound came out.

Lying in the middle of the roughhewn stones, sprawled facedown and unmoving, was Freddie Campbell. And judging by the bottle of expensive champagne on the ground beside him, covered in blood, he would not be saying his vows that day. Or any day.

Freddie Campbell was dead.

CHAPTER THREE

———

The next hour went by in a chaotic blur of emotion, reaction, and panic. After my initial shock had worn off at seeing the grisly scene in our terrace courtyard, the scream I'd been cultivating did, in fact, rise out of me. Loudly. In a shrieking violence that summoned Ava in seconds flat. Luckily, she'd been clearer headed than I and managed to keep most of the guests away from the scene and instruct someone to call 9-1-1.

It seemed like forever before the police arrived, but in reality it was probably only minutes before the air was filled with sirens and flashing red and blue lights. As much as that had not been the way I'd envisioned the afternoon going, I was grateful when they arrived and took charge of the scene, as I was still shaking when they started corralling guests into separate areas of the winery to question them as witnesses.

Witnesses.

The words stuck in my brain, rolling around like a terrible song I couldn't get out of it. A man had been killed on my property. Not just killed—murdered. In broad daylight. And now all of my wedding guests were witnesses.

While I was reeling, I couldn't even imagine what Juliet was going through. My own screams of shock and fear at initially finding Freddie's body were nothing compared to the gut wrenching sobs that had escaped Juliet as she heard the news. She'd collapsed into her father's arms, and I'd been thankful that she'd had so many loved ones around her to care for her. My heart had ached for her as I'd watched her parents whisk her away to the bride's suite. I resisted the urge to break down and cry myself, instead pushing emotion aside and numbing myself to the proceedings long enough to give my version of events to a uniformed officer. She'd politely sat me in one of the chairs we'd set up for the ceremony and taken silent notes as I fumbled through my monologue.

I was repeating the entire story for the second time, and had just gotten to the part where I'd seen the bloody champagne bottle again, when I looked up and spotted a familiar face in the frenzied crowd.

Deep assessing eyes, dark brown hair just a little too long on his neck, premature five-o-clock stubble on his chin, even though we were nowhere near the hour. Detective Christopher Grant of the Sonoma County Sheriff's Office, VCI Unit (Violent Crimes Investigations).

His tall, broad-shouldered frame filled the back doorway of the winery, and he was dressed in jeans and a robin's egg blue button-down shirt. A dark gray tie hung low around his neck as if he'd just loosened the knot, but his eyes were keenly scanning over the scene until they found mine and locked on.

In a couple of quick strides he was by my side, dismissing the uniformed officer with a curt, "I'll take it from here."

The younger officer must have heard the authority in Grant's voice, as she quickly shut her notebook and stepped away, leaving Grant looming over me, shading me from the midday sunshine that was struggling to shine through the gloomy situation.

"Emmy," he said softly. "You okay?"

I nodded, not trusting my voice to stay steady. Grant and I had something of a history, though how I'd label our relationship I'd be hard pressed to say. Flirtatious sounded a little too juvenile for the way my body responded to his presence, but to say we were dating felt like it was jumping the gun—especially considering we'd only been on one proper date thus far. And it had ended in a chaste kiss at the door.

Okay, maybe not *totally* chaste, as I'd been pretty sure every hormone I owned had been on fire after his lips left mine. But beyond smoking hot kisses, I wasn't sure what emotion Grant had invested in me. Or, to be honest, how invested I wanted to get in him. He had a dangerous streak that I'd only seen hints at, but it was real enough that he'd been transferred under a cloud of suspicion from the San Francisco PD to sleepy Sonoma County.

Though, I guess even sleepy Wine Country still had its murders.

"Can you tell me what happened?" Grant asked, pulling a chair from the row to my right and sitting to face me.

I licked my lips. "I, uh, found the groom. Dead. On my terrace." I shuddered, thinking I'd never again enjoy an after dinner glass of Zinfandel there.

"I'm sorry," he said. "You were alone when you found him?"

I nodded. "It was awful," I admitted in a small voice. I'd been trying not to dwell on the horror of discovering a corpse in my courtyard, but now that I was alone with Grant, my guard began to slip. My lip quivered as I pictured the prone figure on the stone tiles and the champagne bottle that had been intended to toast his nuptials—not be used as a murder weapon.

He must have been able to sense my distress, as Grant reached out and took my hand, squeezing it reassuringly in his larger one. "You sure you're all right?" he asked again.

No. "Yes." I took a deep breath, mentally putting on my big girl panties. "Pretty shaken up, but I'll be okay."

"Good." Our sweet moment over, his expression hardened as his professional demeanor slipped back into place. "So, tell me exactly what happened. What were you doing before you discovered Mr. Campbell's body?"

I took a calming breath. "I was looking for him," I replied matter-of-factly. "It was time for the ceremony to begin, and Freddie never showed. His car was here, so I knew he had to be somewhere on the property. I didn't want to cause the bride concern if she found out that we couldn't find him, so I asked Ava and the best man to stall while I tried to locate him."

"The best man. That would be—" Grant checked his notes. Paper ones. Unlike most of the officers sporting electronic tablets, he had a small spiral notebook tucked in the back pocket of his jeans at all times. "Baker Evans?"

"Yes," I replied, the no-nonsense conversation actually helping me clear my head. "He said the last time he saw Freddie was when Baker left him to come to the winery a couple of hours before the ceremony."

"They came in separate cars?" Grant clarified.

I nodded. "I guess so. I mean, Freddie's car was in the lot, so he must have driven here."

"But no one saw him at the winery?"

I went to shake my head, but then I paused. "Wait—the bridesmaid's boyfriend!"

Grant's gaze jumped up from his notebook to meet mine.

"Ava said the boyfriend said he saw a couple of people walking toward the terrace. That's why I went to look for Freddie there."

"Did he say he saw Freddie?"

I licked my lips. "Not specifically, no."

"When was this?"

"I-I don't actually know when he saw them," I admitted. "But as soon as Ava told me about it, I headed for the terrace."

"Got a name for the boyfriend?"

I shook my head. "But he's dating the bridesmaid with the bob."

Grant made a note, his pen scratching against the paper. "Where was the rest of the wedding party at the time?"

I tried to think back. "Well, as far as I know, all the guests were already seated and waiting for the ceremony to begin. The other groomsmen were in the gazebo with the officiant, and the rest of the bridal party was waiting near the back buildings to make their entrance."

"What about the bride?" he asked next.

I frowned. "What about her?"

He met my gaze, and I could see the hazel flecks in his deep brown eyes buzzing with intensity. "Where was Miss Somersby leading up to the ceremony and the discovery that the groom was missing?"

"She was with the rest of the bridal party. And her father," I added. "Edward Somersby. He was waiting to walk her down the aisle."

"What about before that?" he pressed.

"Before?"

"Yes, where was the bride before they stepped outside to make her entrance?"

"Um, in her bridal suite. We cleared out some storage space and turned it into dressing rooms for her and her bridal party."

"How many in the party?" he asked, jotting down notes.

"Not a lot. Just Natalie, the groom's cousin, her bride's attendant, Andrew, and the one with the bob, one of Juliet's girlfriends from school." I paused. "Why?"

But instead of answering my questions, Grant moved on to another one of his own. "And they were with her the entire morning?"

"I-I really don't know. I mean, everyone was getting ready. There was a lot going on." I paused again, reading between his lines. "Are you asking me if Juliet has an alibi?"

He pinned me with a hard look that said that was exactly what he was doing. "I'm just establishing everyone's whereabouts at the time of death."

My insides clenched at the word death, visions of Freddie's body washing over me again. "So they know when he was killed?"

Grant sighed. "Approximately. ME will know more once he gets him on the table, but liver temp indicates that he expired sometime between ten and noon."

Which was a pretty big window. The bridal party had been with hair and makeup since early that morning, but the groomsmen had only been scheduled to arrive at ten. With everyone rushing to get ready, I doubted anyone could really be accounted for the entire two hours. And it wasn't as if we'd had security guards checking invitations. Anyone could have walked onto the property dressed as a guest, and no one would have said a thing. I held on to the thought that this *could* have been some random act of violence as I watched Grant scribble more notes.

"There's no way Juliet did this," I told Grant.

"You were with her?" he pressed.

"No, but she's just not the type."

Grant sighed and set his pen down. "Emmy, anyone can be the type to kill if the circumstances are right."

"No," I said, shaking my head. "You're wrong." I hesitated to argue more, as I knew Grant had, in fact, been pushed to kill once. It was the reason for his transfer, though I'd never quite gotten all the details. But I knew Grant had shot a man, and after Internal Affairs concluded their investigation, Grant had been reassigned.

However, a wedding party was a far cry from the dangerous streets of The City.

"You don't know Juliet," I told him.

"Do *you* know her?" he pressed.

"Not that well," I admitted. "But she was in love with Freddie. Like, stupid crazy in love. Why would she want to hurt him?"

"Juliet's father seemed to think Freddie had a bit of a wandering eye."

I frowned. "Mr. Somersby said that?"

Grant nodded. "According to the officer who interviewed him, Mr. Somersby said Freddie was even checking out 'the blonde at the wedding rehearsal,'" he said, reading the quote from his notes.

"Not me. Ava," I clarified. "And, yeah, he might have been checking her out a little."

One of Grant's eyebrows rose my way.

"A *very* little," I emphasized. "But, come on—all guys check out Ava."

The corner of his mouth turned up in a half smile. "*Most* guys," he countered.

He was right. I'd never seen him checking out my best friend. One point for Bad Cop. But I didn't let his sexy smile distract me.

"Even so, it's hardly grounds to kill him right before the wedding ceremony," I argued.

Grant shrugged. "You're right. *If* Freddie stopped at just checking out other women."

I bit my lip. He had a point there. I could imagine that if I'd found out that my intended was sleeping with someone else moments before my wedding, I might have been tempted to swing a champagne bottle or two near his head.

"When was the last time you saw Juliet?" he asked.

"I left her with her father and the bridal party." I glanced up at Grant's face, trying to read just how serious he was about pointing the finger at the bride. Unfortunately, the hazel flecks in his eyes were still and stoic, giving nothing away. "Look, with all the preparations, I'm sure Juliet wasn't alone for more than five minutes all morning. Talk to the bride's attendant. He'll tell you."

Grant nodded. "I will," he said, though it held more of a threat than promise.

He stood, reaching out a hand to steady me to my feet, his eyes a little softer as they met mine. "You sure you're going to be okay?"

"I'll be fine," I said, actually feeling much calmer now.

"Good." He inclined his head toward the tasting room, where the uniformed officers were still taking statements from the last of the wedding guests. "We'll be here for a bit longer. I'm going to ask that the wedding party stay in town for the weekend, but everyone else should be cleared to leave soon."

Leave. With the shock and horror of finding Freddie, the thought of the cancelled wedding hadn't even hit me until then. Someone had to send the band and servers home and do something with the hundred uneaten dinners and several dozen canapés. Not to mention break down a never used ceremony space and discuss the financial obligations of the event with the grieving father of the bride.

The overwhelming weight of it must have shown on my face as Grant's eyes softened with concern again. "Call me if you need anything," he said.

I nodded, forcing a smile. "I will. But I'll be fine."

He gave my hand a quick squeeze before walking away, making strides toward the tasting room to interrogate my wedding guests as witnesses.

And possibly suspects.

* * *

I spent the rest of the afternoon on autopilot, checking my emotions in favor of rolling up my sleeves to take down what would have been a lovely wedding. I sent the photographers, servers, and band home, and Ava, Conchita, and I packed up what we could salvage of the food—storing what could be reused in our freezer and packing the rest for Conchita to take to a shelter in town on her way home. At least someone could enjoy the Lobster Tails Thermidor that evening.

As soon as Grant had spoken with the bride, the Somersbys packed up to leave, understandably to help their daughter grieve in private. I'd mumbled my condolences to Juliet, though I wasn't sure she even heard me, her entire being still in a state of shock. She had hugged me back, though, when I'd put my arms around her for a comforting squeeze before she left, and I told her to call me anytime. While I knew she had the support of her friends and family with her, somehow I felt responsible for making sure she was okay.

Pity surged through me as I watched Andrew and Juliet's father help her to the black Mercedes, still dressed in her wedding gown, her tastefully done makeup streaking down her cheeks in smudged trails.

"What about the cake? And the doves? And the presents?" she sobbed, her mind clearly spiraling with grief. "I just wouldn't feel right keeping any of them."

"Oh, honey." Andrew took both of Juliet's hands in his. "You don't need to worry yourself with that sort of thing right now. We'll handle it all later."

She nodded. "Who would do such a thing, Andrew? Who would hurt Freddie?" she asked, her voice small.

Andrew shook his head. "I don't know, baby girl."

Juliet dissolved into tears again, shoulders sagging as her head dropped down. Andrew wrapped her in a comforting hug, and another pang of sadness ran through me as I watched her weep into her friend's shirt.

The rest of the wedding guests left as soon as the officers dismissed them, everyone in more of a hurry to leave than they'd been to arrive. Not that I blamed them. They'd come for a wedding and ended up at a crime scene. Needless to say, I didn't think any of them would be hurrying back to Oak Valley for a weekend tasting anytime soon.

By the time the last of the uniformed officers had left and the bulk of the wedding items had been stowed away, the sky was dark, and I was mentally and physically exhausted. I hugged Ava good-bye, thanking her for all her help that day, and made my way to my cozy two-bedroom cottage at the back of the property.

When I'd come home to take over the winery, I'd moved back into the same cottage my parents had occupied my entire childhood. I'll admit it had seemed larger then as a kid than it did now as an adult. The small building nestled among the centuries old oak trees had originally been built by my grandfather before I'd been born. It had been upgraded little by little with AC and modern electrical, so it was comfortable even if it wasn't palatial. In my dreams I could envision expanding the upstairs and adding a walk-in closet to the master bedroom, but my dreams were considerably larger than my bank account, so for now the guest room served as a fine overflow for my shoes and winter coats.

I grabbed a pint of mint chip from my freezer and settled on the sofa to let mind numbing TV take me away. Unfortunately, the first thing I saw as I turned my set on was my winery—a reporter in a windbreaker standing in front of it talking about the untimely death of Alfred Campbell at the "killer wedding on the hill."

The mint chip stuck in my throat as I listened to the reporter say the police were investigating but as of yet had no leads. While I wasn't sure it was entirely true, at least no one had mentioned Juliet, except to say the "bride-not-to-be" was grieving in private and had no comment.

Soured on TV, I flipped the thing off and crawled up to my big, comfy bed, where sleep sadly eluded me. The adrenaline and shock of the day's events caused me to toss and turn, resting only in short spurts before visions of dead bodies and crying brides woke me again.

If it was possible, by the time the sun streamed in through my bedroom windows, I felt even more tired than when I'd gone to bed. I groaned, throwing an arm over my eyes and contemplating just staying in bed that day. It was a nice thought. One I entertained for a good two minutes before the million things on my to-do list compelled me out of my sheets and into a long, hot shower.

I did a quick mascara and lip gloss thing before throwing on a pair of jeans, a T-shirt, and a pale lavender sweater. I attempted to tame my hair into something presentable, but three tries in, I gave up and pulled it back into an easy ponytail instead. I was just slipping my feet into a pair of suede ankle boots when a text came in from Ava.

I'm outside. I have lattes.

Before heading downstairs to the front door, I said a silent thank you to fate for sending me such an awesome best friend.

My boots echoed off the hardwood floor of the small living room as I crossed to the door, where I found Ava just approaching with two coffee cups bearing the logo of our favorite café, the Half Calf.

"Have I told you lately how much I love you?" I asked her, grabbing one cup and stepping back to allow her entry.

"Yes. But I don't mind hearing it again." She gave me a grin as she plopped down on my well worn sofa, tucking her legging encased legs up underneath her. She'd paired them with a cold-shoulder tunic top in the same navy color that served as a stylish backdrop for the silver crescent moon pendant around her neck. "How did you sleep?" she asked, taking the lid off her latte and blowing on it to cool the drink.

"I'm not sure I did," I told her truthfully, inhaling the warm French Roast scented steam rising from my own cup.

"Sorry, Emmy." She sent me a sympathetic smile.

I shook my head. "I'm really sorry for Juliet. I can't imagine what she's going through."

"I saw a CSI van in the lot already when I pulled in," Ava said. "The police have any leads?"

"None that Grant shared with me."

Ava paused, and by the mischievous look in her eyes, I could tell she was trying to read some meaning into those words. "So what *did* Grant share with you?"

"Nothing," I told her emphatically. Then I paused, sipping my drink. "Except that Juliet's dad told him Freddie might have had a thing for the ladies."

"Gee, ya think?" Ava said, heavy on the sarcasm.

I shot her a look.

"What?" Ava said, doing an innocent palms-up thing with the hand not holding her latte. "You can't tell me you didn't see the groom checking out my derriere at the rehearsal."

"You're right. I can't," I conceded. "And the police know about that too."

"Grant said that?" Ava asked, taking a sip from her steaming coffee.

I nodded. "He thinks it's motive for Juliet to want him dead."

"Get out! Juliet?" Ava shot me an incredulous look.

"I know, right?" I told her. "I mean, Juliet is a philanthropist. She collects blankets for the homeless. I don't see her murdering her fiancé over a wandering eye."

"Does Grant think that's all that wandered?" Ava asked, picking up on the same thought I'd had last night.

"Maybe not." I shook my head. "I don't know. All I know is, I don't see Juliet doing this."

"Wasn't her bride's attendant with her the whole time anyway? What was his name…Andrew?"

I nodded. "Probably."

"And her dad was there too. I know because he kept asking me how much longer until the ceremony started."

I groaned, thinking of Edward Somersby. I was supposed to have collected the final payment for the wedding last night, after the reception. Only we'd had a corpse instead of a ceremony, and clearly I hadn't had the heart to ask him for it. Or, honestly, even a clear enough head. "I have to collect a check from him for the nonexistent wedding."

Ava clucked her tongue. "Talk about awkward."

"I know." I paused. "I really wish I could just forget it, but the truth is even though the wedding didn't go on as planned, I still have expenses. The servers all showed up, the tables and chairs were laid out, and there are all the nonreturnable items—food, flowers, centerpieces."

"Champagne," Ava added. Then must have remembered how Freddie'd been found, because she visibly cringed. "Sorry."

"Yeah, I'll never look at a bottle the same way again," I agreed, taking another fortifying sip of coffee.

"Do you want me to go with you?" Ava asked. "To talk to Somersby?"

"Would you?" I immediately asked.

She grinned. "What are friends for?"

"I owe you one," I promised her.

"Well, make that *one* a bottle of last year's Pinot Grigio from the cellar, and I'll call it even."

"Done!"

CHAPTER FOUR

———

The Somersbys had rented out the Belle Inn Bed &
Breakfast, just east of downtown, for the wedding party to stay
in. The two story, asymmetrical building boasted a beautiful
front porch that wrapped around one side of the house and had
been a stately Victorian residence in its heyday. Now it was
flanked by mature maple trees and a couple of large palms and
sat across the street from a Starbucks, an indie bookshop, and a
café. I pulled my Jeep around the back and parked in the small
lot that bordered a well-appointed garden, and we followed the
pathway back around to the front entrance. While the vibe inside
was quaint and homey, a polished reception desk sat just off to
the right.

After we gave our names to the young, freckle-faced
woman behind the desk and listened to her end of the
conversation as she called up to the Somersbys' suite, she
directed us to wait in the parlor just to the left of the entry. I took
a seat on a high backed chair near the picture window, and Ava
sat opposite me, perching on the edge of a loveseat with ornately
carved arms and legs.

We didn't have to wait long, as Edward Somersby's
frame filled the doorway just a few moments later. While he'd
seemed an impressive patriarch on our previous meetings, today
his shoulders held a slump, and he seemed years older, his face
sunken and pale.

"Mr. Somersby." I stood, greeting him as he came into
the room, and Ava did the same.

He nodded to us both and gave a weak smile before
sagging into another high backed chair beside me. "You wanted
to see me?"

"First off, let me offer my condolences," I said, the words sounding hollow even to my own ears. "How is Juliet?"

He sighed deeply, shrugging. "Not well. As expected. She's been inconsolable. I don't think any of us got a lick of sleep."

"We're so sorry for your loss," Ava said gently.

"Oh, don't feel sorry for *me*," Edward replied with a scoff and a frown.

"Uh, we didn't mean to imply…" I trailed off, looking to Ava, not sure what to say to that.

Luckily, Edward plowed on. "That man wasn't good enough for my daughter. I always knew that." He sighed and rubbed a hand over his face. "But it kills me to see her in so much pain."

I nodded sympathetically. I'd only known Juliet a short time, and it was heartbreaking for me to see her in such a state. I could only imagine how it felt as a parent. "Please let me know if there's anything I can do to help."

He shook his head. "Not much to be done now but move on."

I had a feeling it would be some time before the grieving almost-widow would be moving on, but I kept that to myself.

"How long had Juliet and Freddie known each other?" Ava asked, her voice soft and comforting.

Edward's bushy eyebrows hunkered down in a frown, as if he was trying to remember. "Oh, about a year, I guess."

"That's not very long," I mused.

"No. It wasn't." He shot me a pointed look. "And her mother and I told her there was no reason to rush into marriage, but Juliet always has been headstrong like that."

"So, it was Juliet's idea to get married?"

"Oh, I don't know. I mean, Freddie proposed, of course, but who started the conversation? Well, it's really none of my business, is it?"

What he really meant was it wasn't my business. And he was right—it wasn't. I cleared my throat. "Anyway, I'm sorry to intrude at such a time, but there is the small matter of the funding for the…uh…event," I finished lamely.

Somersby blinked at me as if not understanding.

I did some more throat clearing. "I, uh, will see if I can get some of the fees refunded, but we do have to settle accounts still with our vendors. For the flowers, food, chairs..." I trailed off, hoping he'd catch my drift.

"Oh, yes. You want your check." His face was stoic, though his voice held an edge to it.

I licked my lips. "I know you have some...extenuating circumstances," I said, dancing around the dead body. "I talked with the band last night, and they're willing to only bill for travel expenses, not the full evening. And the officiant graciously waived all fees."

"Well, I suppose I should be thankful for small favors," he said, though I noticed he made no move to retrieve a checkbook.

I smiled awkwardly at him, wondering how many times I'd have to uncouthly ask for payment before it arrived. "Yes, well, I'm sure everyone understands what a difficult time this must be for you."

Though instead of looking grieved, Edward let out a sardonic bark of laughter. "Difficult? That Freddie Campbell has been more trouble than he's worth since the start. And his death is no exception."

"You really weren't a fan," I said, stating the obvious as I shot a look Ava's way. She seemed as taken aback at his open hostility as I was, a small frown forming between her slim eyebrows.

"No, I wasn't," Edward went on. "But in truth, I didn't know the man well enough to be a fan. And that was what I told Juliet, too. What did she really know about him? Where did he come from? Where did all this supposed money come from?"

"Supposed?" I asked, jumping on the word. "You think Freddie was pretending to have more assets than he did?"

But Edward blew out a long sigh and shook his head. "I don't know. I mean, he drove flashy cars and spent enough, but every time I asked him about his business, all I got were vague answers."

Which was what I'd gotten too. Then again, I hadn't actually pressed either him or Juliet for details. The truth was, considering that the elder Somersbys were footing the bill for the ceremony and reception, I hadn't really cared how the engaged couple earned their own paychecks. "Juliet mentioned he was an entrepreneur of some sort?" I said, remembering what she'd told me.

"Of some sort." Edward snorted. "Never did pin him down to more than that." He paused. "Not that it matters now, I suppose."

I bit my lip. With the police looking in Juliet's direction, I had a feeling every detail about Freddie's life mattered now. Maybe even more so to Juliet than it had before. I was almost hesitating to ask, but... "The police said you mentioned Freddie had an eye for the ladies."

Edward scoffed again. "Didn't you notice?" He turned to Ava. "I know you must have. His eyes were practically glued to you all evening."

"Were they?" Ava asked innocently. To her credit, she didn't even blush.

"I take it that was not an isolated incident?" I surmised.

"No. Hardly." Edward shook his head again. "And, again, her mother and I told Juliet as much, but she just laughed me off as being overprotective."

On that point I agreed. Edward Somersby did seem protective of his daughter. He'd struck me as that way before the ceremony that never happened too. I wondered... A protective father might do all sorts of things to preserve his daughter's happiness. Clearly Edward Somersby hadn't wanted Juliet to marry Freddie. Maybe he'd thought a dead groom was better than a cheating husband?

Ava must have been wandering down that line of thinking too, as she piped up from her perch on the sofa. "Do you remember when the last time was that you saw Freddie alive?"

Edward's forehead wrinkled. "Last night at the rehearsal dinner," he replied. "We left him at the restaurant, and Juliet rode back here with my wife and me."

"She didn't ride with Freddie?" I asked, remembering the couple had arrived at the winery for the rehearsal together.

But he shook his head. "No, Juliet didn't want Freddie to see her the night before the wedding. Tradition, superstition—

call it what you will." He shook his head as if he really didn't understand either. "Anyway, she stayed with Meredith and me in our room that night."

"And neither of you saw Freddie after that?" I asked.

He shook his head. "No."

"Not at all the day of the wedding?" Ava pressed.

"No. I assumed he was with the groomsmen."

"What about Juliet?" I asked, remembering Grant's line of questioning. "Did she arrive with you?"

But Edward shook his head again. "No, she and Andrew drove in together."

"So you came alone?" Ava asked.

"I arrived with my wife." Edward's frown was deepening with each question we lobbed his way, and I could tell we were on the verge of pushing it. "She and I were together all morning."

"You were together the *entire* time you were at the winery yesterday?" Ava said, pressing it just a little further.

"Yes. I mean, up until you came to get me for the ceremony," he said, nodding my direction.

"Your wife didn't leave you to check on Juliet at all?" I asked.

Edward looked up at me again and scowled. "No. We checked on her together. Why does it matter where I was anyway? Are you insinuating that *I* had something to do with Freddie's death?"

Oops. Yep, definitely over the verge.

"No, of course not," I backpedaled. "But the detective was asking me about Juliet."

Edward's eyes narrowed. "Juliet? Why?"

"He, uh, seemed as though he thought she might have had something to do with…" I trailed off, chickening out at voicing that thought under Mr. Somersby's scowl.

"That's ridiculous!" he said, practically shouting in the small parlor. "What reason could she possibly have to want Freddie dead?"

"His wandering eye," Ava reminded him.

Edward's mouth moved up and down a few times, but nothing came out as the realization must have hit him that he'd been the one to give police the motive. "Th-that's completely ridiculous," he finally repeated.

"I agree," I reassured him. "And Detective Grant is very good at his job. I'm sure his questions were just routine," I told him, but even I could hear the uncertainty in my voice.

Edward turned in his seat so that he was facing me. One of his bushy brows lifted. "Are you well acquainted with Detective Grant?"

I felt the warmth creep into my cheeks. "You could say that," I replied, choosing my words carefully. I could practically feel Ava smirking beside me.

"Well then, you can tell that detective to look elsewhere for that man's killer," he said hotly. "I assure you a *Somersby* did not have any hand in this."

The way he emphasized the word made me think he had some inkling who could have had a hand in it.

Again, Ava must have been on the same track, as she asked, "Who *do* you think might have wanted Freddie dead?"

"Believe me, I have no idea. But if the police are going to look anywhere, they should start with *his* family, not mine."

"Natalie?" I asked, remembering the one family member from Freddie's side who had been in attendance.

His eyebrows formed a frowning *v* again as he nodded in the affirmative. "Bad blood there, mark my words."

I thought back to the interactions I'd witnessed between the cousins. While Natalie had seemed to enjoy poking fun at Freddie, I'd taken it as just that—fun. "I thought Freddie and Natalie were close. Isn't that why Juliet asked her to be in the wedding party?"

Edward shook his head. "Having her in the wedding party was Freddie's idea. Why? I haven't the foggiest. From what I saw, their relationship was tenuous at best." His expression hardened. "They'd been at each other's throats since we arrived in town. Not only was it distracting, but it was upsetting for my poor daughter."

I was about to ask more, when a soft voice called from the doorway.

"Edward?"

I looked up to find Meredith Somersby hovering near the stairs. Her eyes were red, as if she'd been crying right along with her daughter, and the wrinkles in her face seemed more pronounced today, her entire being sagging just that much more. "Juliet's asking for you," she said softly.

Edward rose to his feet. "If you'll excuse me," he directed my way.

"Of course," I assured him, rising from my seat as well. "But, uh, about the account..." I trailed off, trying not to sound too indelicate.

He blinked at me again, as if he'd completely forgotten why I'd been there. "Oh. Right. Yes. I, uh, I'll get it to you soon."

Soon. I just hoped that soon was sooner than the soon when my bills were due to the vendors.

*　*　*

"Well, that was interesting," Ava said as we stepped outside into the sunshine again.

"Interesting that I didn't get the check?" I asked, my mind still on the money.

"No," Ava corrected, "that he threw Natalie under the bus."

I sent a questioning look her way. "You think that's what he was doing?"

Ava nodded, her blonde hair bobbing around her shoulders. "I mean, I can see why he didn't like Freddie, but why point the finger at Natalie? As far as I could tell, she was just along for the ride with this whole wedding thing."

"Maybe he was just pointing it away from himself," I mused.

Ava nodded. "Sure. Or away from his daughter."

"Juliet?" I asked. "You don't really think she could have anything to do with this?"

"No," Ava agreed. "But maybe Dad isn't so sure."

"Or maybe Natalie and Freddie really *weren't* on good terms." I thought back to the brief interactions I'd witnessed between the pair. It had been clear that Natalie had been goading her cousin, but killing him before his wedding? It felt like a stretch.

"Hey, think you could drop me at Silver Girl?" Ava asked, looking at her watch. "I've got a private client coming in at ten."

I nodded, getting into my Jeep. "Sure. I'll pick you up later to get your car." Ava drove a vintage 1970s olive green convertible Pontiac GTO, which was her pride and joy. Some people had kids, some people had pets—Ava had her GTO.

"You sure you don't mind?" Ava asked, buckling up.

I shrugged. "Will I mind taking a break from stalling our vendors for payment due to a death at the winery?" I asked, heavy on the sarcasm. "It'll be a heartbreak to leave that task, but anything for you, girl."

CHAPTER FIVE

————

After dropping Ava off at her shop downtown, I drove back to Oak Valley alone, thoughts of the grieving Juliet Somersby, Freddie Campbell's bludgeoned body, and the overprotective father who seemed to have no qualms about speaking ill of the dead all swirling in my head. I tried to push them out, instead mentally going down my to-do list again. Even if the wedding had gone off with the very big hitch of a dead groom, there'd be plenty to do to clean up after the event and return our winery back to normal.

Arrangements had to be made to pick up the chairs and tables, flowers had to be disposed of, the bride and groom's suites had to be cleaned, and in light of the haste the wedding party had understandably left in, there were still personal items and gifts left behind to package up and have delivered to the B&B. And then there were the dreaded calls I'd mentioned to Ava that needed to be made to put off the vendors just a little longer as I awaited payment from the father of the bride.

As I pulled up to the winery and noticed that the CSI van was still parked in our lot, I decided to get the least pleasant task over with first—the phone calls. On the upside, my office did provide a haven from the police technicians swarming our terrace, serving as a grim reminder of what I'd seen there.

Two hours later, I was several depressing calls into that task, when a soft knock sounded at my office door and Conchita stuck her head in.

"Emmy?" she called.

"What's up?" I asked, honestly grateful for the distraction.

That is, grateful until she spoke again and revealed just what the distraction was.

"Your detective wants to see you."

I felt my cheeks heat. "He's not *my* detective—" I started to protest, though I didn't get much further than that as Grant pushed past her into the room, his broad frame suddenly filling it.

"Emmy," he said, his tone even and authoritative, telling me this was not a social call.

"Grant," I countered, trying to sound just as detached and professional. Even though my voice faltered a bit more than his, the element of surprise catching me off guard. Feeling the height disadvantage of sitting at my desk, I quickly stood. Though even then he still towered over me by a good six inches, despite my high heels.

"I'll, uh, leave you two alone," Conchita murmured, beating a hasty retreat back to the kitchen. I didn't blame her. The steely look in Grant's eyes had me wanting to retreat as well.

"Are your CSIs finished yet?" I asked, breaking the silence.

"Almost," he replied. Then he shot me a look, mouth curving upward at one corner in a half smile. "But they're not *my* CSIs."

I felt my cheeks heat again, my eyes instinctively hitting the carpet to avoid his teasing gaze. So he'd heard that, huh?

"Did you need something?" I asked, clearing my throat.

"I did," he replied, thankfully letting it go, though the mocking smile was still there. "I wanted to ask you about this." He held up a small plastic bag with an official looking seal securing the top.

"What is it?" I asked, taking a step around my desk to get a closer look.

"Feathers." He set the bag down on the desktop.

"Feathers?" I picked it up, peering at the items encased in clear plastic. Sure enough—small, white feathers that looked like they'd been trampled in the dirt a bit.

"They were found on the terrace near the victim," Grant went on. "We're trying to ascertain where they came from. I don't suppose you have any fowl living on the property?"

As I turned the bag over in my hands, inspecting the fluffy white plumage, recognition set in, and I felt my stomach drop. I did know where these feathers had come from. And it wasn't a local bird. In fact, I was almost certain I'd seen identical feathers the day before…on the bust of Juliet Somersby's wedding dress.

"Emmy?" Grant prompted.

I took a deep breath and set the bag back down.

"No, no birds on the property," I told him. Even as my mind went into overdrive, trying to think of how pieces of Juliet's wedding dress had ended up on the terrace. She'd gotten dressed in the bridal suite. She'd come straight from there to the ceremony. She'd had attendants with her every second of the time between when she'd arrived at the winery to when Freddie had been found.

Hadn't she?

"Emmy?" Grant asked again. "Something wrong?"

I looked up to find him staring at me, mouth drawn down in a frown, the hazel flecks in his eyes working in a frenzy as they tried to read my jumbled thoughts.

Dang. I really needed to work on my poker face.

"Uh, no," I lied, clearing my throat again loudly.

"Do you know where these feathers came from?" he asked, his eyes intent on mine, as if he already knew the answer to that particular question.

I licked my lips. "You said they came from the terrace."

The frown on his face deepened, all traces of his previous humor gone. He was in Cop Mode now—all business. "How did they get there?"

"Search me!" I did an exaggerated shrug that did nothing to erase the suspicion in his eyes.

"Okay. But these feathers do look familiar to you," he said, phrasing it as a statement, not a question. Clearly the look on my face had told him that much.

I sucked air in through my nose, holding it a second before letting it out slowly. "Yes," I admitted.

I expected him to look triumphant, but instead he kept his stoic expression in place. "And?"

I let out another long breath of air, ruffling my hair with it. "Fine!"

He quirked an eyebrow at me.

"Look, you're going to find out sooner or later anyway," I reasoned. "They're from Juliet's wedding dress."

If it was a surprise to him, he didn't show it, simply nodding as he picked up the baggie again. "I see."

"But that doesn't mean anything," I quickly added.

He looked up at me again, one eyebrow still higher than the other. "No?"

"No," I said empathically. "I mean, wedding dresses are notoriously delicate. Those feathers could have come off of it at any time."

"At any time," Grant repeated. He nodded again, as if considering that possibility. Though whether he was serious or was just humoring me, I wasn't entirely sure.

"The Somersbys strike me as traditional," Grant said.

"What?" I asked.

"My understanding is that it's customary for the bride to stay hidden from the groom before the ceremony? That it's bad luck for him to see her in her dress before she walks down the aisle?"

"I guess," I hedged, not liking where this was going.

"So, did Freddie break with tradition and visit his bride right before the wedding?"

"No," I admitted. "I don't think he did."

"So, he wouldn't have been around her wedding gown enough to, say, transfer half a dozen feathers from her dress?" He held up the plastic baggie again with the evidence in it that looked more and more like it would be admitted at a murder trial.

I sighed loudly. "No. He wasn't. Not that morning."

"Which means if the feathers didn't get onto the terrace on Freddie, they must have arrived with someone else."

"Someone *other* than Juliet," I told him.

He cocked his head at me. "Was anyone else wearing white feathers to the wedding?"

I narrowed my eyes at him. "No. But that doesn't mean anything. They could have gotten there from…from…from flying out the window of the bridal suite and down to the terrace," I finished.

Grant's lips curled up into a half smile again. "Nice theory."

"Thank you."

"But, as you know, the terrace is on the opposite side of the winery from the bride's suite."

"Well, then…they got there some other way. Someone else must have met Freddie on the terrace. Someone who came into contact with the bride," I reasoned.

"Possibly," he hedged, his expression giving nothing away.

I crossed my arms over my chest. "Look, I don't know how these got on the terrace, but I know Juliet did not kill Freddie. She was in love."

Grant gave me a long stare, and I could have sworn it was laced with sympathy at how naïve he thought I was being.

I straightened my spine, giving him a challenging stare of my own. "Was there anything else, Detective?" I asked, doing my best at icy professionalism.

Only, instead of being affronted by it, he gave me that slow half smile again. His lips curling up enticingly in a way that was dangerous to my resolve. "No, Ms. Oak. That will be all." He turned to go but paused in the doorway and added, "For now."

The promise in those two little words sent a surge of heat to my cheeks.

And, if I was being totally honest, to other places of my body too.

* * *

After Grant left, I thought about calling the caterer to see if I could stall on paying off the last bill, but all I could focus on was the fact that Juliet was looking more and more like a real suspect in the police's eyes. I had to admit, the accoutrements from her wedding dress ending up at the crime scene was not good. I still thought there was another explanation—like possibly someone had accidentally transferred them or even put them there specifically to frame the bride—but the who and the how eluded me.

One thing was for sure though—this didn't look like a possible random act of violence anymore. Someone close to the couple had wanted the groom dead.

I gave up on paperwork and phone calls and went looking for Conchita, who was hard at work cleaning up the bride's suite. I dug in beside her, the physical labor a welcomed distraction as we packed up the few stray bits of clothing and makeup left behind by the harried bridal party and cleared away champagne glasses, empty bottles, and trays of brunch canapés the group had nibbled on while preparing for Juliet's big day. All of it had an air of sadness about it that was deflating. The room had been so full of such hope just 24 hours earlier. Now those moments would only serve as tragic memories for the bride.

I was just carrying the last tray of glasses back to the kitchen when I passed the tasting room. Two people sat at the bar, and I recognized both immediately.

The first was stocky, dark haired, and wearing a pair of thick glasses atop a slightly crooked nose—Baker Evans, the best man. He was sipping a glass of Pinot Noir and chatting amiably with the second man. If he was drowning his sorrows, he was doing a good job of it, as he chuckled jovially at something the second guy said.

Whom I knew only too well—David Allen, of the Allen-Price-Pennington family fame.

David Allen was tall and slim, all sinewy muscle, and wore a pair of fitted jeans and a black T-shirt. His dark hair hung loose, falling into his eyes that were equally dark and always seeming to hint at a private joke only he was in on. His immediate vibe was rebellious teen, though I knew he was at least my age—maybe older. He came from an ultra wealthy and highly dysfunctional family, and he spent his days enjoying his trust fund, smoking pot in the guest house of his mother's estate, and painting dark, thought provoking art.

And, on his off days, bothering me.

David looked up as I approached, giving me a wide smile. "Ems, my dear, there you are."

"David," I said, setting my tray of empty glasses down on the back counter. I nodded toward the full glass in his hand. "Enjoying our Pinot Noir?"

"Immensely," he told me, without even a hint of self-consciousness at taking advantage of our open tasting room policy.

I turned to my other guest. "Nice to see you again, Mr. Evans."

"Thank you. I, uh, hope you don't mind my mooching a glass." He gestured to his wine.

"Not at all," David jumped in before I had the chance. "Emmy is always happy to spare a sip for a friend, right, Ems?"

I forced the smile on my face as I ignored that comment and addressed Baker Evans. "Please, enjoy."

"Thanks. I, uh, came to pick up the wedding gifts. You know, for Juliet. She's…well, not really up to it." He ended the comment on a sigh that spoke volumes about how the last day had been for the best man.

"Of course. And please accept my condolences on your loss," I told him.

"Thanks." He looked down into his wineglass, all trace of jovialness having sobered. "It's, uh, hard to believe he's gone, you know?"

"I'm sure it's been a shock," I agreed, stating the obvious. I'd admit I was terrible at knowing what to say to grieving people. I'd been in my teens when my father had passed away, and I'd been so full of anger and resentment that nothing anyone had said back then had come even close to being comforting. And I had a hard time believing anything I was saying now was any kind of salve for the raw emotions those close to the murdered man were feeling.

"Yeah. A shock. That's a good way to put it," Baker agreed, giving me a rueful smile before sipping from his glass again.

"Baker here was just telling me what a fun guy our Freddie was," David said. "Sounds like I missed a heck of a bachelor party."

"Oh?" I asked. Thankfully, that was one aspect of the wedding I'd not been tasked to plan.

"Well, you know. Freddie knew how to have a good time," Baker mumbled, clearly not as comfortable discussing the proceedings with a member of the fairer sex as he had been with a stranger at a bar.

"How is Juliet doing?" I asked, steering the topic elsewhere for him.

Baker shrugged. "Honestly, I don't know. I mean, of course she's torn up. But I've just kinda left the Somersbys be, you know? Let her mourn in private with her family right now."

Which made sense. But, I noted, it also left Baker to grieve alone for his friend. I felt a pang of sympathy for the man. "How long had you known Freddie?"

"Wow, feels like forever." Baker let out a low, soft laugh, his eyes going to a far off spot in his memory. "Since high school. Man, we were always together then."

"That is a long time," David agreed.

Baker sucked in a breath, bringing his focus back to present. "Freddie kind of took me under his wing then. Helped me get into the right parties and stuff." He chuckled again, clearly reliving better times. "Of course, in exchange I helped him out with his homework." He grinned. "It was a win-win."

"Did you know Natalie then too?"

Baker frowned. "Natalie?"

"Freddie's cousin? Did she go to school with you two as well?"

"Oh." He looked down into his glass again. "No. No, she wasn't around then."

The way he said it made me think there was more to that story. Edward Somersby's insinuations that there was bad blood between Freddie and his cousin rang in the back of my mind.

"They must have been close lately?" I asked, probing carefully. "I mean, she's the only family he invited to his wedding."

Baker shrugged. "I'm not surprised she was the only one. Freddie wasn't close with any of his family. Divorced parents, remarriages, steps—it was messy."

"I understand all about *that*," David said, raising his glass in camaraderie. A statement that was not an exaggeration. When I'd first met David, his stepfather had been found murdered in my wine cellar. David had one of the messiest families on record.

"But Freddie *did* invite Natalie. In fact, she was even part of the wedding party," I pointed out.

"I guess," Baker said.

"So, Freddie and his cousin got along?"

Baker looked up from his wineglass. "What do you mean? Why wouldn't they?"

I paused, hesitating to repeat what I'd heard. "Well, Juliet's father just mentioned that they seemed to have a bit of a strained relationship."

He frowned. "Mr. Somersby said that?"

"In passing," I quickly covered, not wanting to seem as if I was spreading rumors. Which, clearly, I was.

But Baker just shrugged again. "I don't know. I never saw anything."

"Well, *I* couldn't help but notice that Natalie was teasing Freddie quite a bit at the rehearsal," I pointed out.

Baker blinked at me behind his thick lenses. "Sure. But that's just what family does, right? Rib each other?"

"So none of the ribbing had any merit?"

"Like what?" Baker asked with a sardonic laugh.

David shot me a questioning look over the rim of his glass. The smile on his face said he was enjoying watching this little interrogation play out.

"Well," I said, choosing my words carefully, "Natalie was teasing Freddie about finally settling down. Was he a bit of a ladies' man?"

Baker narrowed his eyes at me and pursed his lips, seemingly taking his time to figure out how to answer that one. Finally he settled on, "Freddie was no saint. He was a good looking guy. Charming. Women were drawn to that. So, yeah, sure, he'd been with a few women. In the *past*. But believe me when I tell you that he only had eyes for Juliet. She changed everything for him."

Something flitted behind Baker's eyes with that last statement, but before I could read what it was, he lifted his glass, obscuring his expression from view. Suddenly I wondered if the best man wasn't a little jealous of Freddie and Juliet's relationship. If he'd been that tight with Freddie since high school, he might not have been thrilled at now becoming a third wheel.

"You're sure Freddie never had interest in another woman?" I asked, thinking back to the way his eyes had seemed magnetically drawn to Ava at the rehearsal. "Freddie and Juliet never maybe argued about other women? Even ones in the past?"

But Baker shook his head. "No, the only ex they ever argued about was Juliet's."

"Juliet, the fiancée?" David clarified, playing catch-up. "She had an ex-boyfriend in the mix?"

Baker nodded, shifting his gaze from David to me. "Yeah. Surely someone told you about him?"

I shook my head. "No. Why would they?"

Baker let out a sarcastic laugh again. "Well, because the guy attacked Freddie just hours before he died."

"What?" This was news to me. "Did you tell this to the police?"

He nodded. "Sure. I told that detective all about it. That the guy hit Freddie at the rehearsal dinner."

That was one key detail Grant hadn't shared with me earlier. Though, whether it made Juliet look more or less guilty, I wasn't sure. "What happened?" I asked.

He shrugged. "Well, the guy showed up at the restaurant just as we were finishing dinner. He said he needed to speak to Freddie. Then the two went outside. Freddie was gone for awhile, so I went out to see what was up."

"And what was up?" David asked, leaning an elbow on the bar.

"He and Freddie were going at it outside."

"You mean they were arguing?" I clarified.

Baker nodded. "Loudly."

"About what?" David asked.

But he just shrugged again. "I don't know. By the time I got there, they were already in each other's faces. And the next thing I knew, the ex hauled off and hit Freddie. I had to pry them apart before someone got seriously hurt."

"And Freddie didn't tell you what it was about afterward?" I pressed.

Baker shook his head. "No. Just said the guy had a jealous streak and a lot of nerve. Said he didn't want to talk about it more than that. He didn't want the guy to ruin his wedding."

Which was understandable. "Did Freddie tell Juliet?"

Baker frowned. "I don't know. I mean, by the time anyone else came outside, the guy was gone."

"You get a name for the ex?" David asked.

Baker squinted up at the ceiling. "Jason? Jackson? Something with a *J*." He looked back at me. "Sorry, I don't remember. But I'm sure the police are looking into it."

I was sure they were too. But what lens they were filtering it through was another story. If Grant was sure Juliet had something to do with Freddie's death, his fight with a jealous ex-lover could have been the catalyst that pushed her over the edge.

CHAPTER SIX

———

"Well, it sounds like our Emmy's got another little mystery on her hands," David Allen said once we'd packed Baker and the haul of wedding gifts into his car and sent him back to town.

"What I have on my hands," I said as I watched Baker's taillights disappear down the oak-lined drive, "is a cancelled ceremony and a grieving wedding party. That's it."

"Really." One of David's eyebrow rose into his thick, dark hair.

"Really!" I told him emphatically.

"Then what was all that probing about the victim's cousin? What was her name, Natalie?"

I shrugged. "Nothing."

"Not buyin' it, Oak," he told me with a grin.

"I was just asking a few questions. That's all." I paused. "The police think the bride did it."

David nodded, as if agreeing with that assessment. "It usually is the wife. I guess she's the closest thing in this instance."

"Yeah, but I just think Juliet is innocent. For starters, she was crazy in love with Freddie."

"Crazy people do crazy things," David noted.

"Not *that* kind of crazy. She was devoted to him. No"—I shook my head—"I just can't see her doing this."

"Okay, so who *can* you see doing it?" David asked.

I opened my mouth to answer then realized he'd caught me. "Nice try. Like I said, it's not *my* mystery. I'm not getting involved."

David grinned. "Sure."

"What are you doing up here anyway?" I asked, putting my hands on my hips.

He gave me a look of mock innocence. "What? I can't come have a friendly drink with my favorite vintner?"

"Hmmm." I narrowed my eyes, giving him a noncommittal answer to that one. Mostly because I wasn't ever sure what David's definition of friendly was. I knew his name and family's social status opened just about any door in Wine Country, and I knew that he had acquaintances he often card sharked in the back rooms of the local golf club, and I knew he had family doing a stint in the state prison. But I'd yet to meet any of David's "friends." Which always made me wary when he used the word in conjunction with me.

"Maybe another time," I told him. "I've got to return Ava's car." I gestured to her GTO still sitting in the lot, bathed now in the pale pink hues of the setting sun just off the horizon.

"Cool. Meet you there," David said with a decisive nod toward the car.

"That wasn't exactly an invitation," I protested.

But David was already heading toward the white Rolls Royce he drove while his mother was off on an extended trip to Belize. "You bring the wine, and I'll pick up a pizza," he called over his shoulder.

I might have protested, but as my stomach growled at the thought of a hot, melty slice of pizza, I realized I'd forgotten to eat lunch that day. And my Zinfandel did go great with pepperoni. Having reasoned away my wariness, I ducked back into the winery to grab my purse and a bottle of last year's Zin, and said good night to Conchita and Jean Luc.

Then I hopped into Ava's GTO, only mildly worried I'd put a scratch on her baby and put two decades of friendship to the test. Twenty careful minutes later, I parked in the small lot behind Silver Girl, slipping into a slot near the door designated for *Resident.*

When Ava had opened the custom jewelry shop, with the help of a small business loan from her parents, she'd been lucky enough to be able to rent the loft apartment above the shop as well. While it vied with my place for the title of "coziest" abode in Sonoma, it was comfortably furnished in a hand-me-down eclectic way that perfectly suited her personality.

I gave a shave-and-a-hair-cut knock on the door, which was answered by Ava's voice calling from the other side.

"Come in! It's open!"

I did, pushing through it to find Ava and David already on her low burgundy sofa, a box of pizza open on the rattan coffee table in front of them. Ava sat with her long legs tucked up under her, and David had one arm casually draped across the back of the sofa and his legs splayed out in front of him, crossed at the ankles. He reminded me of a cat, lounging in such a way that he'd staked his territory.

"I brought wine," I said, holding up the bottle as I shut the door behind me.

"You rock!" Ava told me. "Opener's in the kitchen. Want me to get it?"

"I can find it," I told her, taking the few steps to the right to enter her tiny kitchen that smelled faintly of mint tea and patchouli incense. Truth was, I was almost as familiar with her kitchen as I was with my own. And, thanks to our frequent girls' nights where we binge-watched 90s rom com movies with a bottle of rosé, finding her corkscrew was an easy task.

I quickly opened the Zinfandel and joined the other two in the living room again just in time to hear the tail end of their conversation.

"…punched him before Baker could break it up," David said, obviously filling her in on what Baker had told us at the winery.

"Whoa," Ava said around a bite of pepperoni. "Interesting timing, right? I mean, the guy hits Freddie. Then the next morning he winds up dead."

"Or a coincidence," I said, grabbing a slice and sitting on the leather armchair opposite them. "Remember, Edward Somersby said Natalie and Freddie fought too."

"Yeah, but did she punch him?" Ava asked.

I shrugged. "Doubtful?"

"I'd love to know what the fight was about," David mused, chewing thoughtfully. "Freddie and the ex. You think it was over Juliet?"

"That would be kind of romantic," Ava said. "You know, like Colin Firth and Hugh Grant fighting over Bridget Jones."

"I'm sorry, call me old-fashioned, but bloodshed is never romantic," I said.

"Old-fashioned," David replied, goading me.

I resisted the urge to stick my tongue out at him. Mostly because I'd just taken a big bite of gooey pizza.

"What I'd love to know," Ava cut in, "is who the ex is." She wiped her fingers on a napkin bearing the pizzeria's logo and pulled out her phone. "Baker give up a name on the ex?"

"I think he said Jason," I told her.

"Or Jackson," David added. "He wasn't totally sure."

"Right," I agreed. "But something with a *J*."

I watched as Ava pulled up one of Juliet's social media pages, quickly clicking through to her friends list, and moved to look over her shoulder. She typed *Jason* in, but no one in her list showed up as having that name. Ditto *Jackson*.

"Maybe they're not friends anymore. She could have purged him. I mean, he was her *ex*," I pointed out.

"Maybe," Ava said. Then she switched to a screen that displayed all of Juliet's uploaded photos. "But maybe she didn't delete all the photos of him on her timeline."

She quickly scrolled through the past year or so, slowing when she got to older pictures that predated her meeting of Freddie.

I felt my heart clench as I saw dozens of pictures of Juliet's smiling face—at family functions, hanging out with friends, goofing off on vacations. She seemed so happy and joyful that I could hardly stand to think of her holed up at the B&B, grieving the death of her husband-who-would-never-be.

"There!" David said, stabbing a finger at the phone.

Ava stopped scrolling, pausing at a photo of Juliet and another man. His face was partially obscured by the camera angle, but he appeared to be giving Juliet a kiss on the cheek as she took a selfie.

"This was posted on Valentine's Day," David said, pointing to the date. "If she was seeing anyone at the time, it's gotta be this guy."

"Nice," Ava said, giving David a wide smile. "I'm impressed."

David did a mock bow at the compliment.

Ava hovered over the man's face, and a tag popped up displaying his name. Justin Hall.

"Justin!" I said triumphantly. "That's got to be our *J* guy."

Ava typed his name into the search bar and immediately got a hit, clicking through to his social media page.

As soon as she did, a photo of the man's face appeared, and I felt my heart leap up into my throat. "I know him!"

Both David and Ava turned to look at me.

"I mean, I don't know-know him, but I've seen him before."

"Where?" Ava asked.

"At Juliet's wedding." I thought back, remembering the man who'd bumped into me just before the ceremony had been scheduled to start. I'd taken his attachment to his phone for typical millennial fare then, but in hindsight he'd seemed distinctly distracted. Antsy, even. Though, now that I thought back, he hadn't any reason to be yet—the ceremony hadn't been delayed at that point. I told as much to Ava and David.

"You think maybe he was anxious because he had just killed Freddie?" Ava asked.

"I-I don't know about that. It feels like a leap," I hedged, looking at the photo of Justin Hall again. He looked about the same age as Freddie'd been, but while Freddie was classically tall, dark, and handsome, Justin had a rough-around-the-edges feel to him—his dirty blond hair a little on the shaggy side, the angles of his jaw harder set, and the look in his eyes speaking of a rougher life than Jaguars and champagne.

"What was he even doing there?" David asked. "I mean, I can't imagine inviting my ex to my wedding."

"I can't imagine you having a wedding," I joked.

"Ouch." David put this hand over his heart in mock hurt. "I'm a very romantic guy." He paused, sending a wink Ava's way. "Once given the chance."

I narrowed my eyes. Was David flirting with Ava? I watched as she laughed in response, swatting David playfully on the arm. They certainly seemed chummy.

"But you have a point," Ava said, pointing at the photo again. "What was Justin doing there? He'd just beat up the groom the night before—I can't imagine Freddie being too happy to see him there."

"Maybe he wasn't happy. Maybe they fought again, and this time Baker wasn't there to break it up," David said, stabbing a finger in the air to make his point.

"I don't know," I said, staring at the photo again. "Maybe Juliet invited him. Maybe they broke up on good terms?"

"Or maybe," David countered, "he was still in love with her and was there to stop the wedding. By offing the groom."

"It says here he's an artist," Ava noted, scrolling through his profile. She looked up at David. "Ever run into him at the gallery?"

I knew David often showed his work at the Salavence Gallery downtown. I'd been there on one or two occasions, and while the art was interesting, the price tags were way out of my range.

But David shook his head. "Sorry. Don't recognize him. But I do know that studio space he rents," he said, pointing to a post mentioning a piece for sale at the Art Initiative. "It's just off Broadway."

"Maybe we should check it out," Ava said, her eyes gleaming with a dangerously mischievous light I'd come to dub her Charlie's Angels Look. Whenever she got that look in her eyes, I knew she was envisioning the two of us as hot television detectives with cool cars and feathered bangs. Me? That look had my mind filled with visions of the two of us explaining ourselves to security guards, Lucy and Ethel style.

"No. No checking it out," I decided.

"But don't you want to know what really happened to Freddie?" Ava prodded. "I mean, it *did* happen at your winery."

"Thanks for the reminder," I mumbled. "And yes, I do want to know what happened, but I'm sure Grant will get to the bottom of it."

"We're still seeing *him*, huh?" David asked, his tone losing some of its mocking lightness.

"I'm not *seeing* him," I protested, feeling my cheeks heat. "I mean, I *saw* him. Once."

"How'd he look?" Ava sent me a wink.

I rolled my eyes. "You two are children, you know that?"

"Then indulge the children, and let's go talk to Justin Hall, huh?" Ava said. "Just talk."

"Please, Mommy, can we, please?" David teased, clasping his hands in a pleading motion.

I sucked in a big breath and was very proud of myself that I didn't call David any of the dirty names running through my head.

"Just talk?" I repeated to Ava.

Ava nodded. "Promise."

"Fine, I'm outnumbered anyway," I mumbled.

Ava clapped. David grinned.

I shoved more pizza into my mouth. I needed all the fortification I could get with these two.

* * *

After we'd finished off an entire pepperoni pizza and half a ham and pineapple, along with the bottle of Zin I'd donated to the evening, we all hopped into David's borrowed Rolls, and ten minutes later we were parked in front of a post-industrial warehouse in a gentrified area of the city. The old building had been converted into a space for commercial businesses, and various shop signs lined the sidewalk in front of it. I walked past a smoothie bar, a used bookstore, and a yoga studio before spotting the Art Initiative mentioned on Justin's social media.

As David had explained to us on the way over, it was a small studio that rented out space to several artists to create and show their works, sort of like a co-op. It was open to the general public, but most of the artists in residence were small time, not big enough to warrant their own showings in a proper gallery yet. As we pushed inside, the scents of turpentine, acrylic paint, and clay hit my nostrils, along with the slightly musty smell of old pipes and reclaimed wood.

A woman with purple hair stood in front of a large, floor to ceiling canvas, throwing splatters of paint at it in seemingly random patterns, and in another corner a man in a pair of stained jeans was molding a piece of clay on a potter's wheel. And against the far wall, I spotted the shaggy blond-haired guy in Juliet's photo, Justin Hall, paintbrush in hand as he carefully applied minute details to a canvas.

"Can I help you?" the purple-haired woman asked, having noticed our arrival.

"Uh, we're just here to look around," I said hesitantly, eyes going to the many canvases lining the walls in different styles, colors, and genres.

"Oh sure." She blinked at us a couple of times. Then her face lit up with recognition. "Hey, you're David Allen, right? You show at Salavence?"

The smirk of pride on David's face was unmistakable as he answered. "In the flesh."

"Wow. Cool." She nodded her head as if star struck into muteness. "Well, uh, totally look around, and let me know if I can help you with anything. There are prices next to each canvas. And, uh, if you want to know more about a piece, just ask. Several of the artists are here right now." She gestured to the back.

"Thanks. Will do," David assured her.

As the purple-haired woman went back to her splattering, Ava leaned in close to David. "Wow, you're kind of a celebrity," she said quietly.

"Drop the 'kind of,' babe." David grinned at her.

I wasn't sure why David calling Ava "babe" should cause my stomach to clench around my pizza indulgence, but it did. I tried to ignore the sensation as I approached the man painting in the back.

"Justin Hall?" I asked.

"Just a sec." He barely looked up, too absorbed in his work.

"No rush," I replied, trying to sound nonchalant. "I'm just browsing." While he was preoccupied with his art, I took the opportunity to subtly look him over.

Justin appeared a few inches taller than Freddie Campbell had been, with a lanky build that looked more born of genetics than a dedication to the gym. His eyes held an intensity as he stared at the canvas, and his hand was as steady as a surgeon's.

"Some of his work," Ava whispered to me, pointing to the wall at our right.

I took a step closer, seeing his name written on slips of paper stapled to the wall just below a couple of the canvases. While I could see technical skill in the realism of his work, the subject matter was distinctly dark and sad. One painting featured a tree on fire, blood dripping to the ground from its limbs. Another was of a river flowing through a forest of skyscrapers, small drowning figures caught in the rapids. A third was an amazingly detailed image of a child's playroom, where toy soldiers were missing limbs and grimacing in agony. While the social commentary was interesting, the creep factor was way too high for my taste.

"Nice stuff," David said, nodding his approval. Clearly David's creep meter went higher than mine.

"Thanks," Justin said, suddenly at my side. "You're an art lover?" he asked David.

"I am. Something of an artist myself, even," David replied, sticking a hand out to shake. "David Allen."

Justin wiped his palm on his jeans before taking David's hand. "Sorry, I guess I'm not familiar with your work."

If I expected David to be put out by that, I was wrong. He just smiled and shrugged. "I like your sense of irony." He nodded toward the burning tree.

"I appreciate that." Justin swiped the hair out of his eyes. As he did, I noticed a light purple bruise on his cheek, and I wondered if it had been courtesy of his parking lot brawl with Freddie Campbell. "Are you in the market for a piece?"

Before I could dispel him of that idea, Ava jumped in. "Yes, we are!"

I shot her a look.

"Uh, Emmy here owns a winery, and she's always looking for local art to spruce up the place. Right, Emmy?" She sent me a wide smile with teeth and everything.

"Riiight," I said slowly.

"What sort of piece were you looking for?" Justin asked.

"About love," Ava again jumped in before I could answer. "You know, like lost love, unrequited love, fighting to win back a love…"

I could see Justin's jaw tensing. "Sorry. I don't paint about love," he said stiffly.

"Oh, all art is about love, isn't it?" Ava went on, unfazed. "I'm sure you've loved and lost, right, Justin?"

I narrowed my eyes at her. I should have known that Charlie's Angel Ava could get in trouble with "just talk."

"Uh, why don't you show me what you *do* paint," I suggested, taking a step between the increasingly agitated painter and my hapless friend. "And Ava and David can go look around. Over there." I pointed to the far side of the room, where Purple Hair was now using her fingers to smear the splatters.

I could see Ava about to protest, but before she could, David slung an arm around her shoulders. "Come on. Let's browse, babe," he told her.

"O-okay," she said, eyes still on Justin. "But if you need anything—" she started.

"We're fine," I assured her, giving her a wide, innocent smile of my own.

If Justin found our interaction strange, he didn't say anything, his intense gaze bouncing silently from me to Ava as David led her away.

"Sorry. She gets carried away," I said, trying to smooth things over.

Justin grunted but didn't say anything.

"Soooo…these are yours," I said, gesturing back to the macabre collection.

He nodded. "I have a few more over here," he said, leading the way to the opposite wall, where another cluster of canvases were labeled as Justin Hall originals.

"This one might work for you?" he offered, gesturing to a piece about eye level that featured two shadows entwined in what looked like a struggle to the death. A river of red paint bled down from one of them, dripping into a wineglass. "I call it *Dance with a Demon*," he went on. "It's my interpretation on the difficulties of battling addiction—in this case, alcoholism."

"It's…very intense," I said slowly, looking away so he couldn't read my expression. The last thing I wanted my patrons to think about while enjoying our varietals was the evils of overindulgence. Plus the blood was just kinda gross.

As I looked away, my eyes landed on a canvas propped up against the wall, not yet hung. "Is this one of yours too?" I asked, taking a step toward it.

"Uh, yes. But it's not for sale," he informed me.

"No?" I crouched down, taking a close look at it. To my surprise, it was a bright, sunny landscape in pastel hues. The tone and subject matter seemed a complete contrast to the other works hanging on the walls, depicting a field of flowers beside a bubbling stream. "This is beautiful," I said, meaning it. There was something about it that felt familiar, and while I hadn't actually come here looking for art, I could easily picture it hanging above the tasting room bar.

"I told you, it's not for sale," Justin repeated, more firmly this time.

"That's a shame," I said. I studied the picture again. "It's such a lovely piece. Do you have more like it?" I asked, straightening up.

But Justin just shook his head. "No." I had the distinct feeling I was losing him.

"Uh, maybe I could see what you were working on when we came in?" I suggested, hoping to get him talking.

He shrugged but led the way to his easel. "It's not done. And I don't know how it will turn out. I never do until the canvas finishes speaking to me."

I nodded, pretending to understand the artist's process, as I looked down at the half finished painting on his easel. Unlike the one I'd been admiring, the colors were all shades of black and gray, and while I could tell it was still taking shape, I could make out the face of a woman, partially obscured by some figure in black. Maybe it was my imagination, but she looked an awful lot like Juliet.

"This is…interesting," I said.

"It's not done," he reminded me. "But I could set it aside for you?"

"I, uh, I'm not exactly sure it sets the right mood for our winery," I hedged. "It's maybe a little dark?"

He glanced at the canvas, his eyes lost in thought. "Yeah. I get that." Then something I must have previously said seemed to click with him, as his expression changed, his head swiveling to face me. "Which winery was it that you said you owned?"

I swallowed. "Uh, Oak Valley Vineyards."

Recognition set in immediately at the name, and his jaw clenched, eyes going flat. "What's going on here?" he asked, his fists clenching at his sides.

"G-going on?" I asked, glancing over my shoulder to where Ava and David were now deep in conversation with Purple Hair over her splattering masterpiece.

"Yeah, going on. You didn't just randomly walk in here, did you?"

"Uh, no?" I said, though I had a bad feeling that wasn't the right answer.

"Juliet told you about me, didn't she? I know she was supposed to have her wedding at your winery."

I glanced over my shoulder again, reasoning that help was just a couple of steps away if need be. And, surely, Justin Hall wouldn't start throwing punches in his own studio, right?

"Yes, she was supposed to be married at my winery yesterday." I sucked in a breath of courage. "And you were there too, weren't you?"

The fire in his eyes kicked up a notch, and I could feel him getting ready to deny it.

"I saw you," I told him. "You bumped into me just before the ceremony was about to start."

If he had any recollection of the incident, it didn't show on his face. Though, he'd seemed distracted enough at the time that I wouldn't be surprised if he didn't remember me.

"So what?" he finally spat out. "So what if I was at Juliet's wedding?"

"What were you doing there?"

"Waiting to wish the bride and groom well," he said, though the sarcastic undertones led me to believe that was the last thing he'd intended to do.

"Did Juliet invite you?"

He narrowed his eyes at me. "Yeah," he said. But I could tell by the challenge in his voice that he was more than likely lying.

"Really? You two broke up on such good terms that she wanted you there to see her marry someone else?"

His jaw worked back and forth some more. "Sure. Why not?"

"Maybe because the *groom* didn't want you there," I said, watching his reaction carefully, gauging just how far I could push before he resorted to actual physical violence like he had with Freddie.

But Justin surprised me by laughing out loud. "'Maybe'? Heck, there was no maybe about it. That guy didn't want me within ten miles of Juliet."

"And why is that?" I asked.

But his eyes narrowed again. "That's none of your business. That's between me and Freddie."

"Only Freddie's dead now."

Justin took a step toward me. "Are you implying something, Ms. Oak?"

"Not at all," I said, instinctively taking a step backward to match his slow advance. "I just find it interesting timing. You and him getting into a fistfight the night before he shows up dead."

"It was hardly a fight," Justin protested.

"That's not what I heard."

"Well then, you heard wrong, get it?" he asked, his fist clenching at his sides again, as if physically reliving the moment. "I threw one punch, okay? And let me tell you, the guy deserved it."

"Oh? What did he do?"

"He—" But he caught himself and shook his head, as if trying to shake the memory of it away as well. "Never mind. It doesn't matter now."

"It might matter to Juliet," I said softly. "She's heartbroken."

At her name, his entire expression changed, softness suddenly lighting his eyes. "She okay?" he asked, displaying genuine concern that took me off guard.

"I haven't talked to her since the day of the wedding," I admitted. "She was pretty shaken up then. But her parents are with her."

He sucked in a breath and nodded. "Yeah, she and her mom are close. Mere will know how to comfort her."

Mere? This was the first time I'd heard anyone refer to Meredith Somersby that way. The nickname spoke to a closeness. "You know Juliet's mother well?" I asked.

Justin sucked in more air, as if he suddenly couldn't get enough of the stuff to sustain the onslaught of memories. "Yeah. I mean, I did. Juliet and I dated all through high school, you know."

No, I hadn't known that. "How long ago did you break up?"

He shrugged. "Maybe a year ago."

Just before she'd started dating Freddie, I noted.

"I mean, we were sort of off and on for awhile," he continued. "She—well, Juliet's dad wasn't my biggest fan."

It seemed Edward Somersby wasn't a fan of anyone his daughter dated. Then again, wasn't that the way it was supposed to be with daughters and fathers?

"So she broke it off because of her father?" I asked.

His eyes hit the floor. "Something like that."

"But you remained friends?" I pushed, still skeptical.

He was silent a beat then seemed to make a decision, raising his eyes to meet mine. "Look, the wedding was the first time I'd seen any of the Somersbys for months. Freddie and I...didn't see eye to eye. We argued. But Mere will tell you, I apologized for that at the wedding. I just—I'd had a couple of drinks the night before and got carried away."

Which really told me nothing about what he'd been doing at the rehearsal dinner, let alone the wedding, or what he and the dead man had fought about. Only that Justin had a tendency to lose control after "a couple" drinks.

"Meredith will tell you," he continued, as if pleading his case. "I found her as soon as I arrived at the winery. She said she was happy I was there, and she probably would have even invited me to sit with them for the ceremony if her husband hadn't walked up just then. That's when I took off and ran into you. I thought it best to make myself scarce around dear ol' dad."

I wasn't sure how much of what he was saying was the truth, but one thing he mentioned had my mind backtracking a bit. "Wait—you said her husband walked up while you were talking to Meredith Somersby?"

Justin frowned at me but nodded.

"Where had he been?"

The frown deepened in confusion, and he shrugged. "How should I know?"

"How long were you talking to Juliet's mom?"

He blinked at me, as if trying to recall. "I don't know. Maybe twenty minutes?"

Twenty minutes. Edward Somersby had told me he hadn't left his wife's side at all from the moment he'd arrived at the winery to when I'd come to fetch him. But clearly he'd been absent for some time. For all the half truths I felt I was getting from Justin Hall, he had no reason to lie about that.

Which meant that Edward Somersby *had* lied to me. The question was, why?

CHAPTER SEVEN

———

After taking Ava home, David graciously gave me and the rest of the ham and pineapple pizza a ride back to Oak Valley Vineyards. With the best of intentions to put the pizza away in the commercial kitchen's fridge, somehow it ended up on the marble counter, being devoured by one tired blonde as she indulged in comfort food. Since I was already indulging, I grabbed a glass from the cupboard and filled it with Pinot Grigio too. Let's face it, it had been that sort of day. Week. Maybe month?

Planning for our first wedding in a decade had been stressful enough that I'd had in my mind I'd take a couple of days off after the Somersby-Campbell nuptials were over to decompress and relax, even before tragedy had stuck. Now relaxing didn't seem to be in the cards, but at least I could take a moment to try at decompressing.

As I sipped from my wineglass, I pulled out my phone, shooting off a text to Juliet. I paused, trying to come up with the appropriate wording to convey my sympathy. I knew nothing I could say right now would ease her grief, but I just wanted her to know I was there for her. In the end, I went with a simple: *Thinking of you. Don't hesitate to reach out. My shoulders are awesome for crying on.*

While my official wedding planner duties hadn't included grief counselor, I figured it was the least I could do.

A couple of minutes later, her reply dinged in. *Thanks :)*

I itched to say more, but I held off. I took the smiley face as a good sign she was at least coping, but I knew unless she initiated it, she probably wasn't in the mood to chat with me. At least not yet.

"Anyone home?" I heard a male voice call from the winery's main entrance.

I immediately recognized it as that of Detective Grant, and put my phone down as a mix of emotions ran through me. As nice as the deep, familiar timbre was, the most likely reason he was visiting at this hour was related to the crime scene tape still fluttering around my courtyard terrace.

"In here," I called, dabbing at my mouth with a napkin. "Kitchen."

A moment later, he appeared in the doorway, and my first impression was that he looked about as tired as I felt. The shadow on his chin was well past five o'clock, his tie was loose, and the top button on his shirt was undone. "Hey," he said, stepping into the room.

"Hey, yourself," I responded, trying not to get too giddy at the scent of his musky aftershave as he came up beside me.

"What's for dinner?" Grant asked, leaning over to peek at my plate.

"Leftover pizza?" I said around a mouthful.

Grant raised one dark eyebrow at me. "I expect better of you, Emmy."

As Grant knew, before Mom had become sick and I'd made the decision to come home and take over the day to day operations of Oak Valley, I'd been working as a chef in the competitive Los Angeles scene. While I couldn't necessarily say I'd been top dog, I'd been well on my way to making a name for myself with private chef gigs to the who's-who of Hollywood and the occasional pop-up restaurant around a seasonal theme. I'd tried to keep my skills sharp hosting dinners and events at Oak Valley, but the truth was sometimes I missed the cathartic hands-on creating in the kitchen that had largely been replaced with paperwork and marketing since I'd returned home.

But that wasn't to say I was above takeout pizza.

"Sorry, kitchen's closed. Long day," I told him.

"Ditto." He nodded his head toward the box. "Got a slice to spare?"

I grinned, pushing the box toward him as he reached for one and dug in. I grabbed a second wineglass from the cupboard and filled it, placing it in front of Grant.

"I assume you're off duty?" I asked.

He shrugged. "Close enough." He grinned at me over the rim of his glass before taking a sip.

"I didn't see the CSI van when I pulled up," I said, hoping I sounded like I was just making casual conversation. "Are they done?"

Grant nodded, setting his glass down on the counter. "Almost. They should be finished processing the scene tomorrow and then release it."

"Meaning my terrace will be mine again?"

"Yes. You'll be free to enjoy it."

"I doubt I'll be doing that again," I mumbled, suppressing a shudder.

Grant paused midbite, a look of concern on his features. "We have no reason to believe the perpetrator would return."

While his words were meant to be comforting, the official jargon only served to drive home the fact that a murder had taken place there, making my pizza suddenly churn in my stomach.

"Thanks," I said, "but by perpetrator, I'm assuming you still mean Juliet?"

Grant sighed. "I mean *whoever* the guilty party is."

"Very diplomatic," I said. "Points for that."

The concern was replaced by the smile returning to his face. "I try," he said before taking another bite.

"Though I'm guessing that means you haven't gotten any other hot leads today?"

He shook his head, but when he opened his mouth to speak, his answer felt purposefully vague. "We're following up on several lines of inquiry."

"What about the bridesmaid's boyfriend?" I asked, picking a piece of ham off my slice and popping it into my mouth. "The one who saw Freddie going to the terrace. You talk to him yet?"

"I did," Grant said, swallowing before he elaborated. "His name is Brady Willows. He said he was chatting with the band when he noticed two people heading toward the terrace. About half an hour before the ceremony was to start."

"And one of them was Freddie?"

"Possibly, but he said he was far away enough that he couldn't be sure. The man he saw was wearing a tux, so presumably he was at least one of the wedding party."

"So we can make a healthy guess it was Freddie."

Grant shrugged. I had a feeling he didn't often guess. He was more a *just the facts, ma'am* kind of guy.

"Was Brady Willows able to tell you who the other person was?" I asked.

I watch Grant's face go from enjoying a slice of ham and pineapple to Cop Mode in seconds flat. "We have yet to ID the second individual."

I resisted the urge to roll my eyes. "Geez, I'm not with the *Times*. No need to go all official on me."

Cop Face cracked a little, the corner of his mouth hitching up. "We don't know who was with Fred—the man in the tux," he quickly corrected himself.

"Well, was the person with him in a wedding dress?" I asked pointedly.

Grant took a beat before answering. "No," he admitted.

I couldn't help the triumphant smile I felt spreading across my face. "Ha! Then it wasn't Juliet!"

"I'll admit, Brady Willows didn't see Juliet enter the terrace."

"I feel a 'but' coming on."

"*But*," he said, the corner of his mouth hitching upward again, "that doesn't mean she didn't enter the terrace from another direction later."

Dang. He was right. It didn't.

"Could Brady at least tell you if Freddie went to the terrace with a man or woman?" I asked.

"Woman. Brady said she was in a dress." He paused before adding, "In a short red dress." I could see the hazel flecks in his eyes infusing all sorts of meaning into that description.

"It was a wedding. Lots of women were in dresses," I pointed out.

He nodded. "Can you think of any reason Freddie would slip off to a secluded area alone with one of them just before the ceremony?"

I bit my lip. I had to admit, the first reason that sprang to mind was not a pleasant one.

Grant must have seen me coming to the same conclusion he had. "Yeah, me too."

"Okay, so it is possible Freddie was…chatting…with another woman before the ceremony," I said.

"It would appear that way."

"So maybe *she* killed him?" I offered.

"Or Juliet spotted them and killed Freddie in a jealous rage," Grant said, stabbing a slice of pizza in the air for emphasis.

"Or," I countered, "Juliet's dad spotted them, and *he* killed Freddie in a fit of anger."

"Juliet's dad?" Grant's eyebrows drew down.

I licked my lips, not wanting to cast the elder Somersby in a bad light—especially before I was paid in full—but the truth was I could see him in the role much more easily than Juliet.

"Is there something about Mr. Somersby I should know?" Grant asked, eyebrows still hunkering.

I did more lip licking, making a mental note to ChapStick before bed tonight. "Maybe. He didn't like Freddie. Like, really didn't like him. And he…he lied to me about his alibi."

The frown deepened. "*Alibi*?" he asked.

I cleared my throat. "Uh, yeah."

"Since when are you interrogating suspects for their *alibis*?" The line of his jaw was hard, the look in his eyes akin to the one my mom used to use when I'd gotten sent to the principal's office. For that matter, he was doing a spot-on impression of the angry principal too.

I straightened my shoulders, trying to shake off the feeling of being a kid in trouble. "I was *talking* with Mr. Somersby this morning about a financial matter, and the subject came up."

"Where he was when his future son-in-law was killed just happened to come up?"

I nodded emphatically. "Yep."

His eyes narrowed, never leaving mine, the hazel flecks flashing now with a challenge. "And what makes you think he lied about where he was?" he probed.

"Well...I was chatting with someone else later in the day who mentioned that Mr. Somersby was not where he said he was."

"Chatting." His look was unreadable.

I nodded. "Just chatting."

"Been doing a lot of chatting lately."

I shrugged. "I'm a chatty gal."

Grant sucked in a deep breath, letting it out slowly through his nostrils. He closed his eyes for a two count. Only when he opened them again, the hazel flecks didn't look any calmer. "Okay, tell me—where did Edward Somersby tell you he was when Freddie was killed?"

"Well, I guess it wasn't specifically when Freddie was killed, but he said he was with his wife *all* day. The entire time from the moment he got to the winery to when I retrieved him for the ceremony."

Grant nodded, as if he'd probably gotten much the same story. "And this other person you 'chatted' with?"

"Justin Hall."

His eyes narrowed. "You *happened* to run into Justin Hall this afternoon?"

I picked up my wineglass to avoid his hard stare. "Small world, right?" I mumbled.

"Emmy..."

How he could infuse one word with such a threat was a skill.

"Okay, fine!" I cracked, setting my wineglass down on the counter with a clink. "Baker said Justin hit Freddie, so we went to talk to him."

"*We*? Oh this just gets better and better, doesn't it?" He crossed his arms over his chest. "Let me guess—you and Ava playing Charlie's Angels again?"

I wasn't sure whether I loved or hated that he knew me so well. "You can't tell me you don't find it suspicious that Justin attacked Freddie the day before he died?"

"No, I can't," he admitted.

"*And* Justin was at the wedding. Uninvited." I paused. "I think."

Grant shook his head. "Okay, what did Justin tell you about Somersby?"

"Justin said he was talking with Meredith Somersby for a full twenty minutes when Edward wasn't with her. Plenty time enough to sneak onto the terrace and kill Freddie."

"When was this?" Grant asked, though I couldn't tell if he was taking my theory seriously or just humoring me.

"Just before I went to ask Mr. Somersby to line up with the wedding party. Justin actually ran into me as I was approaching Somersby."

I could see Grant mentally logging that bit of information.

"I assume Edward Somersby didn't mention this to you?" I asked.

Grant shook his head. "No. He didn't." He paused again. "But, that doesn't mean he killed Freddie."

"Innocent people don't usually lie."

"Innocent people lie all the time," Grant corrected me.

"But why lie about *this* unless Edward was doing something he didn't want the police to know about?"

"That is a great question."

I felt that triumphant beam hit my cheeks again.

"But," Grant went on, "it's one *I'll* ask him. I'd prefer it if you refrained from *chatting* with him about it."

I did a *zipping the mouth closed and throwing away the key* thing.

Grant chuckled, taking a step toward me. "You know, you're kind of adorable when you do that."

I swallowed, the sudden change of subject catching me off guard. Though I didn't totally mind my adorableness being Grant's focus. "Do what?" I asked.

"That." He took another step forward. "Act all innocent when I know you're cooking up some scheme to interfere in my investigation again."

"I'm not cooking up anything," I protested as he took another step closer. So close that he was well within my personal space and we were practically touching. He leaned in toward me, and all I could think about was how good he smelled and how close his lips were moving to mine. Close enough that I could almost taste them…

"See what I mean?" he whispered, his breath tickling my cheek.

"Huh?" I'll admit, my brain was a little foggy at the moment, having been taken over by surging hormones.

"Innocent people lie all the time," he whispered. Then his lips curled into a wicked smile as he chuckled softly.

My hormones froze, suddenly feeling like maybe we'd been played.

Only they didn't have a chance to find out for sure, as the sound of a small gasp came from the kitchen doorway.

I instinctively took a step back and cut my eyes to the sound to find my winery manager, Eddie Bliss, standing in the doorway.

"I, uh, I'm not interrupting anything, am I?" Eddie asked, clasping his pudgy hands in front of him as his eyes went from me to the deceitful detective.

"No," I said, my voice just a little higher than I would have liked. I tried clearing my throat. "Uh, no, not at all."

If Grant disagreed, he didn't say anything, his eyes still twinkling at me with amusement as the grin played on his luscious lips.

"I left my jacket in the tasting room, and I wouldn't have worried about it, but Curtis wanted to go out for drinks, and nothing else really goes with these pants," Eddie explained, gesturing down to the pink and green checked slacks he'd paired with a magenta button down shirt. "I mean, I guess I *could* have changed pants, but then I'd need a whole new shirt, and why get an entirely new outfit dirty when I could just pop over here and get my jacket…but I can come back later, I guess…"

"Actually, I was just leaving," Grant said. "Thanks for the pizza." He nodded to the open box on the counter before stepping around me toward the door. "I'll be in touch," he promised.

I'd be lying if I said I didn't watch him leave with a little sigh of reluctance.

One I heard mirrored from Eddie as Grant disappeared from view. "Oh, my, he's a cool drink of water, isn't he?" Eddie said, fanning himself. Then he frowned. "Goodness, don't tell Curtis I said that!"

I grinned. Eddie Bliss had to come to work for me after spending the last twenty-plus years as a house husband to his partner Curtis. When Curtis had been forced to take early retirement after a heart attack, Eddie had bravely stepped up as the breadwinner—even though he had zero skills at anything. And he was not exactly what you'd call a fast learner. More like he caught on at the pace of a snail on Valium. But, he was cheerful, friendly, and always optimistic, and customers seemed to like him even if he did often pour them the wrong wines. Plus, I couldn't afford anyone with actual skills, so I considered myself lucky to at least have a cheerful person bumbling through the winery.

"My lips are sealed," I promised him. They were also feeling a little lonely at Grant's departure, but I kept that to myself.

"Anyhoo, I'll just pop into the tasting room and grab my jacket," he said, going that direction. "Want me to lock up behind myself?"

"Please," I asked him. "I'm calling it a night."

"Will do!" he promised cheerfully. He stopped in the doorway, turning back toward me for a second. "You sure I didn't interrupt anything?" he asked again.

I shook my head. "No. I don't think you did."

He shook his head. "Shame."

My hormones wholeheartedly agreed with him.

CHAPTER EIGHT

———

The next morning came much too quickly, and I had a mental war with myself as sunlight filtered tauntingly through my bedroom curtains. I had a brief vision of sleeping in, lingering in my pajamas over a cup of coffee, and binge watching reruns of *Sex and the City* as I generally ignored the rest of the outside world. Then reality set in, reminding me that our tasting room *was* open (if anyone dared venture in while CSIs were still meandering around the grounds), I still had a stack of vendor bills sitting in my office to deal with, and winter being the low season for tourists, I knew I had some fancy juggling to do with our accounts to keep us out of the red this month.

That last thought finally burst my binge-watching fantasy bubble and propelled me out of bed and into a hot shower. I did a quick blow dry and minimal makeup thing and dressed in a pair of skinny jeans, which fit just *that* much more snugly after all the pizza the night before, a cute asymmetrical sweater with a cowl neck I'd picked up last time I'd been shopping in The City, and a pair of black leather boots with low heels that hit just below the knee. In fact the boots looked cute enough in my full length mirror that they prompted me to add a pair of hoop earrings and do another swipe of lipstick before I made my way down the stone pathway from my cottage to the main winery buildings.

After a quick pop-in to the kitchen to grab a cup of coffee and reluctantly refuse the cinnamon rolls Conchita was making—in deference to my too-tight jeans—I slipped into my office, determined to hit the ground running.

Unfortunately, after a couple of hours, I realized I was just running in circles.

No matter how much money I juggled around, there just wasn't enough in our accounts to make payroll for all the field workers who'd been diligently pruning our dormant vines *and* cover the Somersby-Campbell wedding without that check from Mr. Somersby. And while some of the vendors I called were very sympathetic and let us stall for a few days, others sounded like they'd heard every excuse in the book already and expected to start charging interests on our late payments. After ending a conversation with one particularly unsympathetic florist, I slammed my phone down on the desk maybe a little more harshly than it deserved and let out a string of curse words that would have made my grandmother Emmeline wag a finger at me in shame.

"Whoa. You kiss your mother with that mouth?"

I looked up to find Ava in my doorway and felt a blush hit my cheeks that she'd witnessed my tirade.

"Sorry. But, trust me, she deserved it."

"Rough day at the office?" she asked, clicking her tongue.

"Rough week." I sighed, trying to shove those thoughts aside. "What's up?" I asked, focusing on Ava instead as she came into the room, a light, flowy caftan in floral silks trailing behind her. She'd paired the retro look with a slimming black bodysuit underneath that gave the ensemble a modern chic feel. Especially with the silver jewelry accents she had at her ears and wrists.

"After the pizza last night, I was in the mood for something light for brunch." She held up a shopping bag. "I brought stuff for Brie and Baby Spinach Omelets."

"Brie? That's your idea of light?" I asked with a grin.

She shrugged, answering my smile with one of her own. "Okay, really I was just in the mood for brunch and was hoping you'd cook."

"You had me at Brie," I agreed. Hey, there was no shame in buying a larger size of jeans, right?

I shut down my computer and followed Ava into the kitchen, where she snagged one of the cinnamon rolls Conchita had left out and nibbled at the bar while I unpacked her grocery bag.

"So, I heard you had a visitor last night?" Ava said, popping a bite into her mouth. "Grant stopped by?"

I shot her a look as I pulled a carton of eggs from the bag. "You heard?"

"Ran into Eddie on my way in," she confessed.

"Figures," I mumbled, extracting a large wedge of cheese and a bunch of fresh baby spinach.

"So, what did Grant want?" Ava waggled her eyebrow up and down as if she was hoping the answer was *me*.

I shook my head to dispel her of that. "Nothing, really. He just stopped by to let me know the CSIs were almost done." Though, even as I said it out loud, I wasn't sure he'd ever really clarified why he'd stopped by.

"I don't suppose they've found anything interesting?" Ava asked.

"Not that Grant shared. Though, he did talk to the guy who saw Freddie heading to the terrace." I relayed the gist of the conversation I'd had with Grant to Ava about the woman seen with Freddie as I began cracking eggs into a bowl and separating them. I whisked the yolks with milk and a liberal amount of salt and pepper before pulling out my hand mixer to beat the whites before folding them all together.

When I was done, she was nodding her head up and down furiously. "I knew it. I knew Freddie was seeing someone on the side."

"We don't know that for sure," I said, trying to halt her runaway theorizing as I poured the egg mixture into a hot pan. "He was walking to the terrace with a woman. That's all we really know."

"Yeah, walking to a *secluded* area with a woman in a *short* dress. A red one. Isn't that the color hookers wear?"

I shot her a look.

"What?" Ava shrugged, popping another bite of cinnamon roll into her mouth. "She *could* have been a hooker."

"Or she could have been any one of our wedding guests. One of Juliet's aunts. A friend of the family."

"Yeah, a very *good* friend." Ava waggled her eyebrows up and down again.

"You're incorrigible," I told her, turning my attention back to the omelet, taking care not to brown the eggs.

I melted some Brie and added baby spinach to the mix before toasting some ciabatta bread in the oven to go along with it. As we ate, I shared with Ava my financial woes in the wake of the wedding that wasn't. "I fear I have the unpleasant task of tracking Edward Somersby down for that check. Again," I finished.

"He didn't bring it by yesterday?" Ava asked around a bite of omelet.

I shook my head. "I hate to bug him, but I'm not sure how long I can hold off the vendors. Some are threatening to charge interest." Which, if they did, could very well eat up our tiny profit margin on the entire thing—possibly even put us in the red.

"Want me to be your backup again? I've got Mandy watching the shop today."

Mandy was a girl we'd both recently met while she'd been working as a hostess at a nearby restaurant. She was in her early twenties and in that phase of still trying to "figure out what she wanted to be when she grew up." She also went to the local community college part time, so she was always looking for a little extra work to help pay for books and classes.

"You sure you wouldn't mind?" I asked, actually grateful for the company.

She shook her head and sent me a wide smile. "Call it repayment for brunch."

"Sold!"

*   *   *

We decided to take my Jeep into town, and twenty minutes later we pulled up to the Belle Inn Bed & Breakfast once again. Luckily there was a spot on the street just in front of the building, and as I beeped my car locked and we walked up the front pathway, I noticed a familiar figure sitting on the big wraparound porch.

Natalie Weisman was perched on a wooden swing that hung from chain links just to the right of the front door. She was dressed in leggings and a crimson sweater dress, and her legs dangled as she swayed back and forth. In one hand she held a mimosa and in the other her ever-present phone.

Recognition lit her eyes as she saw us approach, and she waved her drink by way of greeting. "Hey, Wedding Coordinator, right?"

"Emmy," I supplied, climbing up the steps to meet her. "And my friend, Ava Barnett."

Natalie nodded in Ava's direction. "Right. I remember."

"We're so sorry for your loss," Ava told her.

For a second she gave us a blank look, like she couldn't remember what loss we might be talking about. Then her eyes quickly hit the ground. "Right. Yeah. Everyone's real sorry."

It might have been my imagination, but I could swear that last part was mumbled with a hint of sarcasm.

"You and Freddie must have been close," I said, trying to keep my voice sympathetic, even though Natalie didn't strike me as looking like she was overcome with grief.

A feeling that was compounded as Natalie let out a bark of laughter, bordering on a smirk. "Sure, you could say that. We were real close."

Ava's eyes cut to mine, the look in them saying she thought the same thing of Natalie's brand of mourning.

"Uh, how is Juliet?" I asked, switching gears.

Natalie shook her head. "How should I know? The Somersbys have holed themselves up in their rooms, as if they have some monopoly on grief."

"Juliet was about to be Freddie's wife," I pointed out softly.

"Well, she wasn't yet, was she?" Natalie shot back. "His wife. I mean, how do we know he even would have gone through with it, huh?"

I shot Ava a look again before I asked Natalie, "You think Freddie might not have gone through with the ceremony?"

Natalie shrugged. "I dunno. Maybe. Maybe not."

"Did he say anything to you like that?" Ava cut in. "Like maybe he was having second thoughts?"

"No," she admitted. "But, I mean, Jules is cute and all, but she's kind of boring. I doubt she would have held Freddie's attention for long."

Ouch. Harsh words from the bridesmaid.

"So, you're saying Freddie might have put his attention elsewhere?" Ava asked, and I could feel her thinking of the lady in red Freddie had been seen with.

"What?" Natalie looked up, and something flittered behind her eyes. As if maybe she'd just realized she wasn't painting her cousin in the best of lights.

"I remember you mentioned a couple times at the rehearsal, your surprise at Freddie settling down," I jumped in. "Why is that?"

"Well, I mean, come on. This is Freddie we're talking about."

"Meaning?" Ava asked.

"Women loved Freddie."

"Any women in particular?" Ava pressed.

But Natalie shook her head. "No. I mean…that's not what I meant. He was just…charming."

I'd heard that adjective applied to him a few times in the last couple of days.

"I'm curious," I said, switching gears, "how come you were the only family member Freddie invited to his wedding?"

"Was I?" Natalie's eyes went to the silent phone in her hands. "I guess we're not a close family."

"What about you and Freddie?" I asked again. "I heard you fought."

Her eyes snapped up again. "Who told you that?"

I licked my lips, not sure I wanted to divulge my sources. There was something hard and slightly menacing about Natalie Weisman. Honestly? I could easily see her bashing someone over the head with a champagne bottle if they crossed her.

"I, uh, can't remember," I said lamely.

She narrowed her eyes at me, accentuating the dark eye makeup surrounding them. "I bet it was that Somersby," she spat out.

Oops. Had I given it away?

"Wh-what makes you say that?" I asked, trying not to look guilty as I snuck a glance at Ava again.

"That guy had it out for Freddie. Did you know he hired a private investigator to follow Freddie?"

No, I hadn't, and the shock must have shown on my face as she nodded emphatically. "It's true," she continued. "Crazy, right? I mean, who does that?"

"What do you think he was looking for?" Ava asked.

"Beats me." Natalie put her cocktail to her lips, sipping noisily.

"How did you find out about this PI?" I asked.

Natalie snorted as she swallowed. "Well, let's just say he wasn't a very good PI. I caught his clunker following us around Atherton just before we left for the wedding. He couldn't have been more obvious."

"And you confronted him?"

"Freddie did," Natalie said. "Was pretty upset about it too."

"And the PI told him that Edward Somersby hired him?" Ava asked.

Before answering, Natalie drained her cocktail and then stooped down to set the empty glass on the ground at her feet. "Not in so many words. Claimed some sort of client confidentiality or something. But it didn't take a genius to figure it out. I mean, Somersby pretended to be all civil when his daughter was around, but we all know how he really felt about Freddie."

"And how is that?" I asked, even though I already had a pretty good idea.

"He couldn't stand him. Didn't think he was good enough for Juliet. Please!" She blew out a puff of air. "As if anyone could ever be good enough for Saint Juliet."

"You don't sound like you and Juliet were that close either," Ava pointed out.

Natalie's gaze went to my friend. "Look, I've got nothing against the girl. I just don't think the world revolves around her, you know?"

I was pretty sure Juliet didn't think that either. Narcissists usually weren't known for philanthropy. And in

Juliet's defense, it *had* been her wedding day. Wasn't that the one time the world was *supposed* to revolve around the bride?

But I kept those thoughts to myself, instead nodding my understanding as Natalie continued.

"Anyway, I'll just be glad when I can be done with the lot of them. Juliet, that lapdog Andrew, and her better-than-thou parents." She paused. "I've been cooped up here for two days with them, and the police won't let us leave yet."

I bit my lip. "Did they say why they wanted you to stay?"

She smirked again. "Sure, they're looking at us all as potential suspects—taking our fingerprints, probing for motives, checking out alibis." It was said as a joke, but I had a feeling it was actually pretty close to the truth.

"What did you tell them?" Ava asked. "I mean, when they asked for your alibi?"

If Natalie was insulted, she didn't show it, instead just shrugging as she glanced at her silent phone. "Same thing we all did, I imagine. I mean, everyone was all over the place that morning. It was kind of chaos." She glanced up at me and gave me a sarcastic grin. "No offense, Wedding *Organizer*."

I gave her a pleasant if slightly forced smile back. "None taken. We're actually here to discuss some wedding business with Mr. Somersby. Do you know if he's inside?"

"Do I look like his keeper?" she asked, swiping her phone on and turning her attention to it as a clear signal she was done talking to us.

"Well, please pass along our condolences to your aunt and uncle," I told her.

She glanced up at me. "Huh?"

"Freddie's parents?" I said.

"Oh, sure. Yeah," she said vaguely, going back to her phone.

CHAPTER NINE

———

"A private eye?" Ava mumbled beside me as we pushed through the B&B's front door. "Wow. Mr. Somersby *really* didn't trust Freddie, huh?"

"Apparently not," I agreed, keeping my voice soft until the doors closed behind us. Even though Natalie seemed to be paying us no attention whatsoever now.

"What do you think he was after?" Ava asked.

"I don't know." I paused. "But I think I can guess."

"Freddie was cheating, and Daddy wanted proof?"

"It's possible," I said, even though I still hoped for Juliet's sake it wasn't true.

"Do you think the PI found that proof?"

"I don't know," I replied. "If he had, I can't imagine Edward not telling his daughter. She was minutes from marrying Freddie."

"Yeah, if Freddie hadn't turned up dead." Ava shot me a meaningful look.

"You think Edward killed Freddie because he was cheating on Juliet?" I asked, feeling it kind of farfetched, especially if he was in possession of proof of Freddie's infidelities that he could easily show his daughter.

"Maybe," Ava said, though I could hear hesitation in her voice telling me she was thinking along the same lines I was. "But what if it wasn't proof of cheating that the PI found? What if it was something worse?"

"Worse?" I asked. "Like what?"

Ava shrugged. "Something so bad that Edward killed Freddie to spare his daughter the knowledge."

"That would have to be pretty bad."

"Parents have done crazier things to protect their children."

I contemplated that idea as we approached the reception desk, where the same young brunette with a face full of freckles greeted us. I noticed her wearing a name tag today that read *Sam*.

"Welcome to the Belle Inn. May I help you?" the woman asked.

"Could you let Edward Somersby know we're here to speak with him again?" Ava asked, giving the woman our names.

"Of course. One moment please," Sam said. I watched her open a ledger book, scrolling her finger down the page until she found the right room number. Then she picked up an old-style cordless phone and rang the room. A moment later, we listened to her leave a short voicemail message with our names and the time and hung up.

"I'm sorry, but no one appears to be picking up."

I had a brief thought that maybe Somersby was avoiding us before Sam continued. "But, I believe I saw his wife go out to the back garden just a few moments ago," she said, pointing down a narrow hallway to our left. "Perhaps you could inquire with her?"

We thanked her and followed the hallway she'd indicated to a pair of French doors that led to a garden fenced in on all sides. Dormant rose bushes, fruit trees, and a few irises just starting to peek their heads out for spring flanked a small stone patio, creating a little oasis in the heart of downtown. While the sun was shining, there was still a nip in the late winter air, causing me to wish I'd brought a jacket.

We found Meredith Somersby seated at a pewter table in the center of the stone patio. Steam rose from a paper cup in her hands, and she was wearing an ivory blouse paired with a sunny yellow cardigan whose cheery color was a stark contrast to the defeated look on her face. She glanced up at us from beneath limp blonde hair as we approached. While her makeup looked just as put together as the last time I'd seen her, the cool complacency had vanished, and in its place were puffy half circles under her watery eyes.

"Good morning, Mrs. Somersby," I said softly as we reached her table.

Meredith set her cup down and straightened her posture, as if to compose herself. "Hello, Miss Oak," she replied. She forced a smile, even though her voice sounded tired.

"I was hoping to speak with your husband," I told her, feeling like a complete heel for bringing up money matters at a time like this.

"Oh?" she said vaguely.

"Uh, there is a small accounting matter I wanted to discuss with him," I said. I pursed my lips, internally cringing at how sexist the words sounded coming from my mouth. Clearly Mr. Somersby wasn't the only member of the couple with access to their bank accounts. However, seeing how fragile Meredith looked, I didn't have the heart to beg her to write a check.

But if it hit her the wrong way, she didn't indicate it. "Oh, I see," she said in the same vague voice that showed no interest in what I was saying. "Well, I'm afraid he's not here."

I almost felt relief at being forced to put off the unpleasant task a bit longer. "Do you know when he'll be back?" I asked, hugging my arms around myself to keep warm.

She shook her head, and her eyes seemed to water more. "No, he…" Her voice caught, and she had to pause a moment to compose herself again. "He went with Juliet to the police station."

"Police station?" Ava let out beside me, the surprise in her voice mirroring my thoughts.

She nodded, sniffing loudly. "That homicide detective requested that Juliet come in to answer some more questions."

I thought a dirty word. If Grant had brought her in for more questioning, that wasn't a good sign.

Ava walked around the pewter table and sat in the empty chair beside Meredith, putting a comforting hand on her back. "I'm sure it's just routine," she said. "Right, Emmy?"

I nodded as I sank into another empty chair opposite the two. "Right. Detective Grant is very…thorough." Which I felt was a generous adjective, given the several other choices that were running through my head as I wondered just what he might be asking of poor Juliet at that moment.

"I'm sure he'll get to the bottom of what happened to your daughter's fiancé, and then she can finally have some peace," Ava added.

Meredith nodded. "I hope you're right." She took a deep breath. "Poor Juliet is so broken up about Freddie's death. This morning she even took off her engagement ring because she couldn't even look at the thing without bursting into tears."

My heart ached for the girl. "I'm so sorry you are all going through this," I told her honestly.

Meredith nodded again, putting her tea to her lips and taking a fortifying sip. "Thank you. And I appreciate the comforting words." She nodded toward Ava. "But I fear that detective has the wrong idea about Juliet."

I feared that too, but the last thing I wanted to do was add to Mrs. Somersby's emotional state. "Oh?" was the best I could come up with in the reply department.

She nodded, her eyes coming up to meet mine. "Before they went to the station, he was asking her about other women in Freddie's life."

I pursed my lips, itching to ask much the same question. "I'm assuming there weren't any. I mean, any who stood out as close to Freddie?" I watched her reaction carefully.

But if Meredith had any qualms about Freddie's fidelity, she didn't show it. Instead, she shook her head, her hair skimming the top of her shoulders. "No. Of course not. I mean, he was devoted to Juliet. Absolutely devoted."

Ava and I shared a look. It appeared that being blind to Freddie's wandering eye ran in the family. At least among the female members.

"I know Juliet was devoted to *him,*" I said, choosing my words carefully. "Are you sure it was a two way street?"

Something in Meredith's face changed, her jaw working back and forth as she swallowed hard. "You've been talking to my husband, haven't you?"

While I had, it wasn't solely his opinion I was going on. But I nodded, hoping to entice her to go on.

"Edward is overprotective," Meredith stated. "He's always been like that. He didn't approve of Juliet's last boyfriend either."

"Oh?" A tidbit of info I already knew, but I just continued nodding.

"No, he didn't think he was good enough for Juliet. So it was no surprise he didn't like Freddie either. I doubt any man would live up to Edward's expectations when it comes to his daughter."

"But Freddie was falling especially short, wasn't he?" Ava asked.

Meredith shifted her gaze to my friend. "I suppose," she conceded. "But Freddie loved Juliet. I could tell. This was just Edward being overly skeptical."

"Was there something in particular Edward was skeptical about when it came to Freddie?" I asked, feeling the chill start to travel from my skin to somewhere deeper in my bones the longer I sat on the cool metal chair.

A frown formed between Meredith's well plucked brows. "What do you mean?"

"Well…" I looked to Ava, wondering how much I should say about our conversation with Natalie. "I heard Edward hired a private investigator to follow Freddie."

Meredith's cheeks flushed. She dropped her gaze to the table and took a slow sip of her tea. "He did," she admitted finally, setting the cup back down with an unsteady hand. "Some investigator in The City."

"Do you know why?" I asked.

She sucked in a long breath before meeting my gaze. "I told you. Edward was overprotective."

"Does that mean the private investigator didn't find anything?" Ava pressed.

Meredith looked down into her teacup again. "No. Of course he didn't. That man didn't find even so much as a parking ticket."

"You met with the PI?" I clarified.

"W-well no. Edward told me about it. After the fact. And he assured me the man found nothing."

While I had no doubt Meredith was telling the truth about what her husband had conveyed, I wasn't totally convinced that Edward was 100% forthcoming. With me or his wife. If Edward had found something worth killing Freddie over, chances are he'd want to protect his wife from it just as much as his daughter. Considering he'd fibbed about his whereabouts leading up to the discovery of Freddie's body, I took anything from his mouth with a grain of salt.

"Do you happen to have the contact information for that investigator?" Ava asked, her mind clearly going where mine was.

Meredith blinked at her in surprise. Then her eyes narrowed. "What for?" she asked, her gaze pinging from Ava to me. "I already told you that he didn't find anything on Freddie. Don't you believe me?"

"Of course we do," I said quickly, giving her what I hoped was a trusting look.

"Uh, it's for me," Ava said. "I mean, I might want to hire him."

Both Meredith and I sent her questioning looks.

"Oh?" Mrs. Somersby said, a note of disbelief still in her voice.

"Yes. I, uh, I think my boyfriend might be cheating on me," Ava answered. I watched her glance at the Earl Grey tea bag sticking out from the top of the woman's cup. "His name is Earl," she said quickly.

I bit my lip to keep from laughing.

"Emmy's been helping me keep tabs on him, but maybe it's time that I hired a professional," Ava said, letting out a sigh.

"That's right," I agreed, forcing a neutral expression. I slid an arm around Ava's shoulders as if trying to comfort her. "Men," I muttered, trying to sound disgusted.

Meredith looked from my friend back to me. After a moment, the older woman nodded. "I understand," she said softly, giving Ava a look of pity. She stooped to retrieve her purse from the ground beside her chair. Then she dug around in the bag, finally producing a business card. "This is the man my husband hired," she said. "I hope you're wrong about your boyfriend, but if not, maybe he can help."

"Thank you," Ava said, giving the woman a sad smile. She took the card and stuffed it into her purse.

Mrs. Somersby picked up her purse and empty teacup and stood. "Now, if you'll excuse me, ladies, I think I need to go lie down." Her eyes met mine. "When Edward returns, I'll ask him to call you about settling the accounts."

Then she turned and walked out of the garden more briskly than I would have thought, given the downtrodden state we'd first found her in.

* * *

"And the Oscar for Best Actress goes to Ava Barnett," I said as we walked back to my Jeep.

She winked and gave me a mock bow on the sidewalk. "I'd like to thank the Academy and my best friend, Emmy Oak," she said with a grin.

"I almost feel bad for lying to Mrs. Somersby," I said, beeping my car open and jumping inside to escape the chilly breeze.

"*Almost*," Ava said, emphasizing the word as she slipped into the passenger seat beside me. She pulled the card from her purse. "It did get us this."

"You really think the PI found something about Freddie that Edward didn't share with his wife?" I asked, turning the car on and cranking up the heater.

Ava shrugged. "Look, he openly hated Freddie, and he lied about his alibi. I'm thinking chances are 50/50 he lied about the investigator's findings."

"*I'm* thinking chances are 100% we should leave this to the police," I told her.

But it was useless, as Ava already had her phone out, dialing the number on the card.

"What are you doing?"

"Getting some answers," she said, putting her phone up to her ear.

"Wait—what are you going to say?" I asked, feeling a little anxiety start to form as Ava waited while it rang on the other end.

She shrugged. "I'm an Academy Award winning actress. I'll wing it," she said with a wink.

I resisted the urge to roll my eyes.

"Did you just roll your eyes at me?"

Okay, I didn't resist *that* hard.

"Emmy Oak, I'll have you know—hi, this is Ava Barnett," she said, switching gears midthought as someone picked up on the other end.

Though, as she continued, I realized that someone was actually voicemail.

"I was hoping to speak to a"—Ava looked down at the card again— "Sean Carter about a private matter. Very sensitive. Uh, if he could please call me back as soon as possible, that would be great." I listened to her rattle off her number before hanging up and sending me a shrug. "I guess now we wait?"

"Now," I told her as I pulled away from the curb, "we go grab a hot cup of coffee and mind our own business."

"Geez, you're no fun."

I could tell Ava didn't even try to resist the eye roll she sent me.

* * *

Fifteen minutes later we were settled at our favorite table at the Half Calf, a cute little coffee shop next to Ava's jewelry store that featured a cow jumping over the moon on their signage and made the very best caramel lattes on the planet. I sipped at my cup, which had just cooled off enough to drink without burning the top layer of my tongue as Ava set a plate of their new Crustless Vegetable Quiche in front of me. I was really going for broke with this comfort food thing today. Then again, it was crustless, so low-carb, right?

At least, that's what I told myself as I dug in with gusto. I think I made little moaning noises in the back of my throat as the first tangy, creamy bite hit my tongue.

"I told you it was good, right?" Ava said around an equally large bite that muffled her speech.

I nodded. "Ava for the win."

I watched as she checked her phone for the second time since we'd entered the restaurant.

"No call back from the PI?" I surmised.

She shook her head, chewing thoughtfully. "I wonder…"

"That's never good," I mumbled, going in for another bite.

If she heard me, she ignored it. "You know, what if we're overcomplicating things?"

I shifted in my seat to face her. "How so?"

"Well, a witness saw Freddie walking toward the terrace with a woman in a red dress, right?"

"Right."

"And just a short time later, he's found dead on the terrace. So, wouldn't the most logical assumption be that the woman in red killed him?"

I raised an eyebrow her way. "I'd say that doesn't sound like a bad place to start." I paused. "Not that *I'm* starting anything."

There went Ava's eyes again, rolling around in her head so far I swear she could see her brain. "Come on, Emmy. You don't really mean that."

"I do. Grant is investigating the death. I trust him."

"That's all very lovey-dovey and cute," Ava said.

I opened my mouth to protest that Grant and I were nether lovey nor dovey, but she didn't give me a chance, running right over me.

"But what about Juliet?" she said.

I bit my lip. "What about her?"

"How hard do you think this is on her in the meantime? I mean, Grant has her down at the police station right now. After she's just lost the love of her life. On her wedding day."

"I know," I conceded. "I feel terrible for her."

"Wouldn't you feel even more terrible if we just let Grant lock her up for a crime she didn't commit?"

I shook my head, wrapping my hands around my cup for suddenly needed warmth. "Grant wouldn't do that. He's good at his job."

"But he's been wrong before," Ava pointed out.

She was right. Grant did have a habit of following the evidence, regardless of the direction it took him in. He was by-the-book, treating everyone as a suspect, and it didn't leave a lot of room for compassion. But I'd never known him to actually send an innocent person to jail.

My warring emotions must have shown on my face, as Ava charged on. "You and I both know Grant has good intentions. But he's not the entire sheriff's office either. If they're set on Juliet, she could end up in a lot of trouble before the truth comes out. And experience a lot of unnecessary heartache."

"I'm not sure there's anything we can do about that," I said.

"Well, for starters, we can find the Lady in Red."

"But we don't know who she is. Or even who she was to Freddie, really."

Ava pursed her lips. "The bridesmaid's boyfriend wasn't able to give any more description of her?"

I shook my head. "Not that Grant shared with me."

"You know, if she was someone Freddie was seeing, there's got to be some record of her in his life. Texts or private messages or something."

"Which would all be on his phone. Which is probably in the possession of the police right now." I gave Ava a pointed look, trying to reiterate my idea to leave this to the authorities.

Which, predictably, she ignored. "Yeah, but the records still have to be somewhere. I mean, everything is in the cloud these days anyway, right?" She picked up her phone. "What was Freddie's cell number?"

"Why?" I asked, even as I pulled my own phone out of my purse and scrolled through my recent calls. I'd dialed his number enough times the day of the wedding that it was easy to spot.

"Because," she said as she punched it into her own phone, "with that we can find out who his cell carrier was."

"I doubt they'd just give you access to his call records," I reasoned, even as I watched her plug his number into the search bar on an internet browser.

"Ah, here it is," she said, turning the screen around so I could see. "And you're right. I'm sure they won't tell me anything. But," she added, clicking a couple of links and putting the phone up to her ear, "they might tell *Juliet* something."

"Juliet?" I asked, feeling a frown form between my eyebrows as I listened to the faint sound of ringing on the other end of Ava's phone.

Only she didn't have time to explain, as whoever she was calling picked up.

"Yes, hi," she said, her voice taking on a higher pitch than usual. "My name is Juliet Somersby. I'm calling in regards to my fiancé's account."

I stifled a groan. "Really taking this acting thing to heart, huh?" I mumbled.

Again, my best friend ignored me, plowing ahead with her phone conversation.

"His name is Alfred Campbell." She was silent for a moment while someone spoke on the other end of the line. "That's right," she said. "Alfred Campbell. C-A-M-P-B-E-L-L." She sucked in a breath and pushed it out slowly. "I'm afraid I have some horrible news. He tragically passed away recently," she continued, making her voice quake as if she were on the verge of tears.

I had to hand it to her. Maybe she'd missed her calling.

She paused as someone spoke on the other end again, then added, "Thank you for your condolences. Yes, it was very sudden." She heaved an exaggerated sigh. "Anyway, I'm trying to settle Freddie's affairs, but I don't have access to the login information for this account. As I said, it was sudden, and Freddie didn't leave any mention of his passwords lying around."

She held up a pair of crossed fingers in front of her as she listened to the person on the other end.

"A death certificate," she said, looking doubtful for a moment. "Uh, I'm sure I can get one eventually, but, you see the medical examiner still has the body—er, my poor Freddie. I don't know who to contact, and well…I'd hate to tie up payment waiting on all of that?" The last part was said with a lift of a question as she shrugged at me, giving it her best shot.

I shrugged back. It was as good a story as any. I mean, who didn't like to be paid on time?

"Uh-huh?" she said back into the phone, nodding, fingers still crossed. "Right, I understand." Pause. "Yes, if you could reset the password, that would really help me out. I'm just so overwhelmed right now." She choked out a rather convincing sob.

After another brief silence, Ava's face lit up. "Oh, could you?" she gushed into the phone. "That would be wonderful. Thank you so much." She motioned for me to grab something for her to write with.

I pulled a pen and scrap of paper from my purse, handing it to her as she did more nodding into the phone. Then I watched her scrawl down a series of numbers and letters, reading each one back to the operator to double check her information.

"Got it! Thank you again," she said when she'd finished. "You've been so helpful." She hung up and sent me a look of triumph.

"You never cease to amaze me," I told her.

"Thank you. Now, let's find out who Freddie was reaching out and touching."

I shook my head. "Just when I'm in awe of you, you have to pull out the terrible puns."

She stuck her tongue out playfully at me as she pulled up the website of Freddie's carrier again and typed in his number and password. A moment later, she was into his account and had pulled up Freddie's call history, listing the dates and times of any calls he had made or received recently.

I immediately recognized the most frequently listed number. "That's Juliet," I said, tapping the screen. "And that one looks familiar as well," I added, noting another series of digits that showed up often in the log.

I pulled up the list of wedding party numbers I had saved in my phone and cross referenced it with the statement, identifying the frequent number as belonging to Baker Evans.

"What about this one?" Ava asked, pointing to another number that showed up multiple times. "Is that one of the wedding party too?"

I quickly scrolled through. "No. It's not on my list."

"Freddie seems to get an awful lot of calls from this person." She lifted an eyebrow. "San Fran Peninsula area code."

I copied the number into a white pages search and hit *Enter*. After a couple of clicks through search results, I found it belonged to a woman from Palo Alto.

"Bridget McAllister," I read aloud, staring at the name on the screen. I glanced back at Freddie's call history. In the past month, he'd received at least twenty calls from the woman's number.

"Look, the two most recent calls lasted over ten minutes each. That's not a telemarketer," Ava remarked, skimming her finger down the records. "This one is even in the middle of the night." She sent me a meaningful look.

"You're right," I conceded. This looked an awful lot like Freddie and Bridget were more than just friends. "I think we may have found the other woman."

CHAPTER TEN

———

"She's originally from Orlando, graduated from Foothill Community College with an AA degree in communications, and she's got 300 friends," Ava said, reading aloud from her phone.

"Are you on her social media?" I asked.

Ava nodded. "It's the fastest way to find out anything about anybody."

"Okay, so please tell me Bridget has professed her undying love to Freddie Campbell on her page."

Ava shrugged. "Not exactly. But if he was seeing her behind Juliet's back, they'd want to keep it on the down low."

"*Anything* useful on there?" I asked, leaning closer as she perused the profile.

"Well, she likes posting recipes. Here's one for dump cakes." She scrunched up her nose. "Any cake with the word 'dump' in it doesn't sound appealing."

"What else?"

"A couple of cat memes. Some birthday wishes. Oh she's a Capricorn."

"Very suspicious," I joked.

"These are her most recent posts," Ava said, pointing them out.

One was a shared link to a blog about pole dancing for fitness. The second was a DIY article on how to create purses from old, cut up pairs of jeans. And the third was a picture of Bridget with two other women.

All three ladies were standing on a balcony in tight-fitting, low-cut dresses that made me chilly just looking at them. But only Bridget was wearing red.

"That's got to be her!" Ava decided, waving her arms so excitedly she almost knocked over her latte.

"When was this?" I asked, squinting at the small font to read the date.

Ava did the same. "Saturday."

I lifted my eyes to meet Ava's. The day of the wedding that wasn't to be and Freddie's death.

"And check out the caption on this photo," Ava said.

I glanced at the picture again, noticing each woman in it was holding up a glass of red wine as they posed in front of a railing that overlooked the rolling hills of a vineyard. The caption read, *"Wine tasting weekend with my best girls."*

"Looks like Bridget was in Wine Country this weekend," Ava noted. "*And* she was wearing red!"

"So you think she crashed the wedding, killed Freddie, and then went wine tasting with her gal pals?"

"It's possible," Ava said, nodding. "I mean, there are probably—what, six wineries that offer tastings within a five mile radius of Oak Valley? She could have easily killed Freddie and then met up with her friends at the next winery down the road."

I glanced back at the photo again. "I wonder if Grant knows about Bridget McAllister."

"Sounds like a great excuse to call him." Ava grinned at me over the top of her cup.

I shook my head, his warnings to stay away from the investigation last night ringing in the back of my mind. "I don't think he's going to appreciate any leads that come from me." I paused. "At least not without some evidence behind them."

Ava stabbed her finger at the photo of the red dress. "Evidence!"

"*Coincidence*," I corrected. "All this says is she went wine tasting in a red dress—not that she was at Oak Valley."

Ava frowned, grabbing her phone and swiping her fingers across the screen again. "Okay, well, how about this." She paused in her scrolling, flipping her phone around to show me the screen. "Look. She just checked in on her page at the Red Duck Winery."

I bit my lip. "That's only a few minutes away."

Ava nodded. "And if she's enjoying her wine like I do on girls' weekends, I bet she's in a chatty mood."

"I don't know…"

But Ava was already gathering our plates and napkins. "Look, we'll just talk. That's it. And if she confesses, well, then you have a *great* excuse to call Grant."

I'd like to say that last part made no difference in my decision to follow her out the door. Then again, I'd like to say I was a natural blonde who needed no help from Clairol too.

* * *

The Red Duck was originally a small, family run operation much like Oak Valley, though in recent years it had been bought by one of the corporate giants in the region. While the new owners had kept the charming labels with little wooden mallards on them, the winery itself was little more than a tasting room and vineyards—all the actual wine production being done at the corporate headquarters in large vats that mixed grapes from any number of the small vineyards that the company had acquired over the years.

The same wood paneling covered the walls of the tasting room—though now it was whitewashed to a rustic chic feel—the duck themed décor had been ditched in favor of large modern posters of the various varietals their parent company produced, and the old wooden bar had been replaced with a shiny chrome thing that looked like it belonged in a New York nightclub. Overall it had a stark feel that was in direct contrast to the homey atmosphere we tried to cultivate at Oak Valley. Though, as I took in the packed tasting room filled with weekend patrons, I was rethinking that strategy.

"Wow, this place is busy," Ava noted as we wove through the room. "Forgive me for saying it, but I don't hate what they've done with the place."

"Forgiven," I assured her as I surveyed the room. "Any sign of Bridget McAllister?"

Ava pursed her lips. "Hard to say. There are a lot of people here. Oh, thank you," she said, addressing a server who handed us a couple of glasses of red wine.

I sipped, thoroughly expecting to hate it. Unfortunately, it wasn't bad. Not quite like our Pinot Noir, but not altogether terrible. And if the crowd was any indication, Red Duck was doing a heck of a lot more business than Oak Valley. I sipped again, hoping that chrome bars and glossy advertisements weren't indicative of Oak Valley's future.

"There," Ava said, nodding toward a table at the back of the room. "She looks like the pictures we saw, right?"

I glanced in the direction she indicated and spotted three women at the table, all in outfits designed to maximize skin and minimize modesty. Two brunettes and a bleached blonde, who threw her head back to laugh at something one of the others had said, giving me a great view of her face—clearly the same Bridget McAllister we'd seen on social media.

Her natural black roots showed at the scalp of her straw-colored hair, and while her makeup was artfully done, it was applied with a heavy hand. She was dressed in a tight-fitting cheetah print dress that was so skimpy for the season that my skin goose-bumped just looking at it. Though, I supposed with enough alcohol in her system, she wouldn't mind.

And by the way she was throwing her head back and laughing again—loudly enough that the couple at the next table frowned and vacated their seats—it appeared she had a good amount of vino in her veins.

Ava pointed toward the empty table. "Shall we?"

I nodded my agreement, following her and taking a seat next to the trio of girls' weekenders.

"I'm so wine wasted," one of the brunettes, dressed in a low cut purple spandex dress, said.

"Cheers to that, beeeeeaches," Bridget agreed, mangling the word in a slur. Both she and the other brunette—dressed in a bodysuit that looked like it came from Catwoman's closet—raised their glasses.

Ava shot me a devilish look. "This should be easy," she mumbled.

"What do you mean eas—" I didn't get to finish my thought, as Ava turned in her chair and faced the three women.

"You ladies look like you're having fun," she said, a wide friendly smile on her face.

"Heaps of it," Catwoman answered.

"I'm on my fourth glass of fun," Purple Spandex replied, giggling as she held up her wine.

I noticed Bridget didn't say much, her eyes looking a little glassy.

"I'm Ava," my friend said. "And this is my bestie, Emmy. We're having a girls' weekend."

"Oh, us too!" Purple Spandex said. "Ohmigod, Sonoma is the best, right?" She leaned in toward me, mock whispering as if letting us in on a secret. "They give you free wine."

I bit my lower lip to stifle a laugh. "You don't say?"

Purple Spandex nodded vigorously.

"It's not free, you idiot. We paid a tasting fee," Bridget corrected her friend.

Spandex blinked, wide-eyed. "Well, it was practically free," she amended.

"You in town for anything particular?" Ava asked, directing her question to Bridget.

"Whadda ya mean?" Bridget answered, swaying slightly in her seat.

"Oh, just that a lot of events are held in Sonoma. You know, like conventions, parties, weddings…" She let that last one trail off, watching Bridget's face.

Bridget's eyes narrowed, eyelashes practically touching as they fluttered up and down. "No," she said quickly.

"We're just here to get away," Purple Spandex quickly added. "You know, let loose? Bridge is breaking up with her boyfriend."

"Oh?" I said, hoping to cover my clear curiosity with a sip of wine.

"We didn't break up," Bridget denied hotly.

Purple Spandex rolled her eyes. "Well, you should! Geez, I thought we decided he was a rat. Didn't we?" She turned to Catwoman.

"He really is bad news, Bridge," Catwoman agreed.

"I can relate," Ava said, jumping in. "I think my boyfriend, Earl, is cheating on me."

I choked on my sip of wine, coughing up Merlot.

But Ava ignored me, plowing ahead. "Is your guy a cheater, too?" she asked Bridget, all sympathy in her eyes.

Bridget didn't answer, her bright red lips forming a frown.

"Worse!" Purple Spandex answered for her again. "Her guy is married."

"He isn't married," Bridget denied again.

"Well, close enough. He's engaged. To this, like, wealthy chick," Purple Spandex said.

"Oooo...anyone I might have heard of?" Ava asked, leaning in.

But Purple Spandex shrugged. "Dunno. Bridge won't give us a name." She shot her friend an accusatory look, as if she were committing a BFF sin by withholding it.

Bridget scowled in response. "Why don't you mind your own business, Kaitlyn!"

Purple Spandex blinked innocently at her. "Ohmigod, I'm just trying to look out for you."

"Well, nobody asked you to," Bridget shot back.

"Uh, maybe we should go get a refill, huh?" Catwoman interjected, rising from her seat to guide Purple Spandex away from the table.

"What? What did I do?" Purple asked, even as she rose and let herself be led away.

"She's just touchy right now..." I heard Catwoman consoling her as she led her to the bar.

Leaving Bridget alone.

I felt a limited time opportunity calling.

"I'm sorry about your boyfriend," I said, going for Ava's brand of sympathy.

Bridget's watery eyes shot up to meet mine. "What?"

"Uh, I just meant, I'm sorry you're having issues. That...must be hard."

She blinked at me, and I saw the first hint of real emotion behind her eyes. "Yeah." She looked down into her glass.

"Look, I don't mean to pry"—I was such a liar—"but I feel like I've seen you before. Have you been to Oak Valley Vineyards by any chance?"

Her head shot up so fast I feared she'd have whiplash. "What?"

"Oak Valley Vineyards. It's a few miles north."

"I-I..." Her gaze pinged between Ava and me.

"You *were* there, weren't you," Ava jumped in. "Saturday, maybe?"

Bridget's face paled under her makeup, her mouth moving up and down without any sound coming out.

"For Freddie's wedding," I prompted softly.

At hearing his name, a sob escaped her before she quickly covered her mouth with one hand. I watched her eyes leak over as she nodded.

I reached out and covered her other hand with mine. "I'm so sorry for your loss," I told her, honestly feeling sympathy for the woman. While she might have been on the brash side, I could tell she was genuinely grieving.

"Thank you," she squeaked out when she'd finally composed herself enough to speak. She sniffled loudly, wiping her nose with the back of her hand. "How did you know?" she asked, eyes going from Ava to me again.

"Freddie told us," Ava said before I even had a chance to formulate a plausible answer.

"He did?" Bridget squeaked out. "He...he talked about me?"

I bit my lip, hating to lie to her. "Uh, sort of."

"Were you friends of his?" she asked, confusion plain on her face as she sized us both up anew.

"Uh, acquaintances," I said, leaving it at a half truth this time. "So, you *were* there at the wedding, then, weren't you?"

She took a deep breath in and let it out on a shaking sigh. "I was. I...well, when Freddie told me he was going through with it, I convinced Kaitlyn and Erin we needed a girls' trip to Wine Country." She gestured toward the bar, where her companions were trying to get the sommelier's attention.

"But you were really coming to see Freddie," Ava surmised.

Bridget nodded. "I-I know it's stupid. I mean, he broke it off. Said he was getting married. But I thought if I showed up here, he'd see how much *I* really loved him, and he'd…well, he'd reconsider. I didn't tell the girls."

"So you crashed the wedding?" Ava asked.

She looked down into her glass. "I guess." She let out a sad chuckle. "You should have seen Freddie. He was so frickin' surprised to see me. I thought his eyes were gonna bug out of his head."

"But he wasn't happy to see you," I guessed.

Bridget's face clouded. "No. Not happy."

"What did he say?" I prompted.

"He said I couldn't be there. That I was going to ruin everything."

"This was on the terrace?" I clarified.

Bridget nodded. "Yeah, I guess. Freddie led me to this patio thing. He didn't want anyone to hear us."

"Then what happened?" Ava asked, inching her chair closer to Bridget.

"Well, I-I told him I loved him. That, you know, we'd be alright without Juliet's money." She paused. "I mean, that had to be why he was with her. It's the only thing she had that I didn't, right? Money."

While it was clear the two women came from divergent financial backgrounds, I could see far more differences between the brash Bridget and Juliet the philanthropist. Bridget's taste in cheetah prints, for one. Granted, Bridget seemed like maybe she'd had a harder life than Juliet's own sheltered one, but I couldn't imagine Juliet ever lashing out at her bridesmaids the way Bridget just had at her friends.

But I kept those thoughts to myself, just nodding sympathetically as the other woman went on.

"It was useless, though. Freddie said it didn't matter. That he was marrying Juliet. That he loved her, and he wasn't going to let me ruin it. Then he…" She paused, more tears leaking down her cheeks. "He told me to leave. That he was done with me for good. He just wanted Juliet." She sniffed loudly and looked up at the ceiling, dabbing under her eye makeup.

"I bet that didn't feel good," Ava noted.

Bridget shot her a look of disdain through her tears. "Yeah, it was a friggin' picnic. What do you think?"

"I think I would have been devastated," I added. "Felt used. Angry, even…" I trailed off.

Bridget spun her scowl on me. I blame it on the wine that it took a second before the frown morphed into a look of fear and she caught on to what I was implying. "Wait—you don't mean…? Oh, no. No, no, no, no, NO!"

The last word was uttered so loudly, a few patrons turned our way to see what the commotion was.

"We don't mean anything," I said softly, trying to calm her down.

"Look, Freddie was *alive* when I left him on that patio. He told me to get out, so I got out."

"Did anyone see you leave?"

"I…I don't know. But I didn't kill Freddie! I didn't even know he was dead until I saw it on the news that night!"

A thought occurred to me. "Did anyone else know you and Freddie were seeing each other? His cousin? Or Baker maybe?"

"Baker?" She scrunched up her nose. "God, why would Freddie tell him? I mean, honestly, I don't even know why he hung around that guy. He was such a loser."

"What about Freddie's cousin? Natalie?" Ava asked.

But Bridget just blinked at her. "I didn't know Freddie had a cousin."

"Where did you go when you left Freddie?" I asked, switching tactics.

"I went back to the hotel to fix my makeup. I'd been cryin', okay? I was a wreck. I freshened up. Then I caught up with the girls at Buena Vista." She looked from Ava to me again, as if trying to gauge if we believed her story. "I would never hurt Freddie. I mean, why would I? I loved him."

"And he rejected you," Ava pointed out.

"No, y-you have it all wrong. It wasn't me. It was them!"

"Them?" I asked. I glanced over my shoulder, making sure her friends weren't coming back to the table yet. I didn't see them at the bar anymore, but they weren't hovering near us either, so I took it as good sign. "Who is 'them'?"

"Those…people," she spat out. "Those rich guys he was hanging out with. They did this to him, not me."

"Why do you think they killed Freddie?" Ava asked. I saw her eyes cut to mine, and I could tell she was thinking the same thing: which *they*?

Bridget snorted, and I resisted the urge to get her a tissue. "Because he knew all their dirty little secrets," she said, her words starting to slur together again as anger subsided.

"Like what?" I asked.

But Bridget just laughed at me. "Yeah, right. Like I'm gonna tell you." She looked me up and down again. "You're probably one of them."

"One of…the Somersbys?" I wasn't sure if I should be insulted at the way she said it with a sneer or flattered that she thought my net worth had several more zeros behind it than in reality.

"All of them! That whole friggin wedding party. Thinking they're better than me. They made Freddie think he was better than me. Well, how do they like things now, huh? Freddie told me everything. Yeah, that's right," she said, nodding her head up and down like a bobble doll. "Oh yeah, now I know all the dirty little secrets too. And guess what? I'm not going to forget what you people did to Freddie." She abruptly switched from nodding to wagging her head back and forth in a negative. "No sireee, all of you people are going to be sorry you ever—"

"Bridge?"

I startled at the sound of the two brunettes coming back to the table and looked up to find Catwoman frowning down at her friend, a look of concern in her eyes.

"Everything okay?" she asked.

"Oh, sure," Bridget slurred. "These two—"

"Were just leaving," I cut in, quickly pushing my chair away from the table.

"Nice to have met you," Ava mumbled quickly as we made a hasty exit.

I could feel all three pairs of eyes on my back until we'd pushed outside, the cool breeze hitting me in the face.

"Wow," Ava said, once we were out of earshot. "What do you think of that?"

"I think Bridget has had way too much to drink."

"You think she was telling the truth about the 'dirty little secrets'?" Ava asked, doing air quotes.

I shrugged. "Honestly? Hard to know. I think she might have been a little crazy with grief."

"Or maybe just crazy," Ava added with a grin.

I couldn't help a chuckle as we got back in the car. "That too," I agreed.

CHAPTER ELEVEN

———

By the time we arrived back at Oak Valley, the sun was setting, creating a pastel watercolor of the sky in brilliant pinks, purples, and dusky blues. As I got out of the car, I took a moment to appreciate its beauty, watching the sun sink behind the hillside dotted with our dormant vines just starting to hint at the promise of green, before I led the way through the winery doors. I immediately heard voices in the tasting room. Glad to hear we had paying customers, I peeked my head into the room and spotted two men at the bar.

And my dreams of *paying* customers vanished into thin air.

"What's David doing here?" Ava asked, a step behind me.

"That's what I'd like to know," I said.

David Allen was perched on a stool sipping a glass of my Pinot Noir (again) as he laughed at something a tall, redheaded man had just said. As David spotted us and glanced in our direction, the redhead turned around, and I recognized him as Juliet's bridesman, Andrew.

"Ems!" David said, hailing us over with a wave. "And Ava, my darling! I was just having a drink with Andrew Phillips. You remember him, of course?"

"Of course," I replied, approaching the pair and shaking hands with Andrew. "Nice to see you again," I told him.

"Hope I'm not taking advantage of your hospitality—" he began.

"Not at all," David cut him off, assuring him heartily, "Emmy loves visitors."

"Some more than others," I mumbled, giving him a pointed look.

"I, uh, just stopped by," Andrew continued, "because I promised Juliet I'd come pick up the rest of the wedding decorations." He paused. "Not that she has a use for them now, but she thought maybe I could donate them to the Y or something. You know, for events or parties."

"That's very generous of her," I said.

"Well, that's Jules." Andrew sent me a sad smile, and I could tell he genuinely cared about her.

"How is she?" Ava asked, perching on the stool beside David.

Andrew shrugged. "As well as can be expected, I suppose." He shook his head. "That police detective had her down at the station today."

I bit my lip. That, I knew. "She okay?" I asked, glad at least it didn't sound like she was in handcuffs.

Andrew nodded. "She will be. She was sleeping when I left her. But I have a bad feeling that guy thinks she had something to do with Freddie's death."

That made two of us. "Did Juliet tell you what the detective asked her?"

Andrew shook his head. "Not specifically." His focus was momentarily taken away as Jean Luc walked through the room, a case of wine in his arms to stock the bar.

"Andrew here was telling me he and Juliet go way back," David cut in. "In fact, he was even there when Juliet and Freddie met." David sent me a meaningful look.

I leaned against the bar beside Andrew. "Oh really? Where did they meet?"

Andrew tore his gaze way from Jean Luc's thin frame with difficulty. "Uh, yeah, it was at a cocktail reception. One of the fundraisers Jules had put together."

"Freddie was a donor?"

Andrew snorted. "I doubt it. But Freddie liked to mingle with those who had money."

"You weren't a big fan of Freddie's, were you?" Ava asked.

I watched his reaction carefully.

But Andrew just smiled widely. "Gee, what gave it away?" he asked, heavy on the sarcasm.

"Any particular reason?" I fished.

"I can think of several. All *female*," Andrew said, emphasizing the word, even as his eyes wandered to my sommelier leaning down to retrieve a glass from below a low cupboard. It took him a beat to tear his gaze away and finish his thought. "If you know what I mean."

I did. In fact, I'd just been talking to one of those *reasons*, but I kept that to myself for now. If Andrew and Juliet were as tight as they seemed, I didn't necessarily want word getting back to Juliet about the mistress. At least not now while she was grieving.

"Any women in particular?" Ava asked, catching my eyes in a way that let me know she was thinking the same thing I was.

Andrew shrugged. "I don't know. But I know Freddie was taking advantage of Jules. Freddie was with her for one thing only, and it wasn't love."

"What was it?" Ava asked.

"Money." Andrew's face clouded, and I could feel tightly restrained anger just below the surface.

"Didn't Freddie have money of his own?" David asked.

"So he said," Andrew spat out. "But he took advantage of Jules's generosity at every turn. In fact, the only thing I ever saw him give her was that engagement ring."

"It was a very nice ring," I pointed out, playing devil's advocate.

But Andrew wasn't having it. "Well as far as I'm concerned, that guy got what was coming to him. Juliet deserves better."

While I agreed with the last part of that statement, something about the first part felt distinctly personal.

I was about to ask more, when Andrew drained the last of his wine and set the glass down on the bar. "Think I could load up those decorations now?"

"Uh, sure, let me see if Conchita can gather them up for you," I offered.

"I can help," Ava said, leading Andrew away by the arm. While I didn't doubt her helpfulness, I had a feeling it was partly to keep him chatting.

"Now that is a loyal friend," David said as the pair disappeared down the hallway.

"Andrew?" I asked.

David nodded. "Did you know he even moved to LA after college just to be near Juliet?"

I hadn't. "They must be very close."

"If I had to guess, I'd say he'd do just about anything to protect Juliet." He gave me that meaningful look again.

"Wait—are you saying Andrew killed Freddie just because he thought he wasn't good enough for Juliet?"

David shrugged. "It's a thought."

"It feels like a pretty farfetched one."

"Who knows what drives people to kill?" David said.

I was about to refute that statement, but I remembered that someone in David's family *had* been driven to kill and was currently doing 50 to life for it. So I figured it might be a bit of a sore spot.

"You just here for the free wine again?" I asked, changing the subject as I gestured to his glass.

He shook his head. "Au contraire, my fine beverage purveyor. I'm actually here because I thought you might be interested in a chat I had today with a certain local artist."

I raised an eyebrow his way. "Let me guess—Justin Hall?"

David put his finger to his nose then pointed it at me to indicate I'd been right.

"Okay, I'll bite. What did you two talk about?"

David shrugged, swirling the last of his wine in his glass. "Life. Art. Paintings."

I rolled my eyes. "How long are you going to drag this out?"

David gave me a devilish grin that spoke to how much he loved teasing me. "Honestly, that's what we talked about. But there was one piece of art in particular that interested me."

"Go on…?"

"When we visited the studio yesterday, I noticed one of his paintings wasn't exactly like the others."

"The landscape?" I guessed, remembering the cheerfully colored canvas I'd seen propped against the wall.

David nodded. "You noticed it too, then."

"I did. In fact it was the only one of his paintings that I really liked. But Justin told me it wasn't for sale."

"He told me much the same thing today," David said.

"I mean, not that I could afford it anyway," I amended. "But it was pretty. Almost had a familiar feel to it, you know?"

"Funny you should say that, because I *do* know." He got that gleam in his eyes again, and he pulled out his phone. "I thought it felt familiar too, but I couldn't place it until today." He swiped a couple of times then turned the screen to face me.

On it was a photo of the same painting I'd seen in Justin's studio. The same sunny sky and cheerful field of flowers. Only the painting was now surrounded by an ornate gold frame and was hung on a wall.

"That's the same painting!" I said, feeling a frown of confusion wrinkle my forehead. "But it wasn't framed yesterday, and that doesn't look like Justin's studio."

"It isn't Justin's studio. I found this photo on an auction house website. This painting is *Sunlit Pasture* by Pablo Miscetti."

"Who is that?"

"He was a part of the Impressionist movement. His work is generally thought to be on par with his contemporaries, such as Claude Monet, Henri Matisse, and Edgar Degas. *Sunlit Pasture* is one of his later works." David paused. "Painted over a hundred years ago."

I shook my head. "Okay, so Justin was making a replica of this guy Miscetti's painting?"

"Appears that way," David agreed.

"Why?" I asked, almost more to myself than him. Justin hardly seemed the type to want to copy Impressionist masters. His paintings were abstract and dark. And he seemed rather proud of them. Why would he suddenly switch his style to something so different?

"That, I can't tell you." David turned his phone back around, scrolling. "There is a market for replicas, which may be what he is looking to tap into. However, I can tell you that the original *Sunlit Pasture* is set to be in an auction in San Francisco at the end of the month."

"What do you think something like that will sell for?" I asked, my mental gears turning.

He frowned at the phone. "Conservative estimate? Three, maybe four, hundred."

"Four hundred dollars?"

David gave me a crooked smile. "You're so cute. Four hundred thousand dollars."

"Whoa. That's a lot of money."

David kept his poker face on. I knew the circles the Allen-Price family ran in had a much different idea of "a lot" than I did. But to a starving artist like Justin...it could make a huge difference. Heck, to a starving winery like mine, it could make a *world* of difference.

"So what did Justin say about the painting when you visited him?" I asked.

David sighed and sipped his drink. "Unfortunately, not much. He tried to steer the subject away, quite untactfully, I might add."

I glanced at David's phone. "Very coincidental that he would paint it right when the original is set to be sold."

David shrugged. "Like I said, there is a market for replicas. Maybe Justin thought it was a timely endeavor, as interest is generated in that piece from the auction."

"Or possibly, Justin wasn't just replicating the painting. He was forging it."

David raised an eyebrow my way, a grin snaking across his features. "That's a pretty big accusation, Ms. Oak. What exactly do you think Justin plans to do with this forgery?"

"Sell it for four hundred thousand dollars." I pointed to his phone to illustrate my point.

"That would be a great theory," David agreed.

"Thank you."

"*If* the original wasn't already at the auction house." He pointed to the phone to illustrate *his* point.

Unfortunately, his point was a better one. "Oh. Right." I frowned.

"What did you say to her?" Ava said, coming back into the room and presumably seeing the disappointment on my face.

"Just that I don't see why Justin Hall would forge a painting," David answered.

Both of Ava's blonde eyebrows went up toward her hairline. "Someone needs to catch me up and fast," she said, grabbing an empty glass from behind the bar and helping herself to the open bottle of Pinot.

"David went to see Justin Hall today," I told her, grabbing a glass myself. Hey, everyone else was drinking my wine—if you can't stop 'em, join 'em.

I opened a new bottle as David filled Ava in on what he'd learned, finishing with showing her the auction house website.

"I'm with Emmy," Ava finally said. "This feels too coincidental to be innocent."

"But what is Justin hoping to do with the forgery?" I asked, voicing David's previous thoughts. "The real one is already at the auction house."

Ava frowned and sipped thoughtfully. "Well, what if maybe Justin was planning to swap out the fake for the original?"

"Would that be possible?" I asked, turning to David.

He sucked in a breath, inclining his head toward the framed painting displayed on his phone. "Maybe. But I'm not sure how Justin would get that close to the original. Security is pretty tight at these places."

"Maybe he planned to break in after hours?" Ava offered. "Maybe he had a partner on the inside? Or maybe he planned to attend the auction and make the switch somehow there?"

I thought back to the rough-around-the-edges vibe Justin had given off at his studio. He'd struck me as deceptive, short-tempered, and violent. Not necessarily the type to rub elbows with the kind of people who dropped four hundred big ones on an Impressionist painting.

However, I could think of one person who absolutely did seem the type to mingle in those circles *and* we knew was not above a little dishonesty when it benefited him.

"What about Freddie," I said, formulating my theory out loud.

Both Ava and David turned my way. "What about him?" Ava asked.

"Well, what if Freddie was the partner on the inside, so to speak? Maybe Justin painted the forgery, and Freddie was going to swap it out at the auction."

"I don't know," David hedged. "Didn't those two hate each other? Like, to the point of physical blows?"

"They did fight Friday night," Ava said, narrowing her eyes in thought. "That's true. But maybe it wasn't about Juliet."

"Maybe it was about the painting!" I said, picking up her train of thought. "Let's say Freddie knew this Miscetti painting was coming up for sale at the auction. He's heard Juliet mention this artist ex-boyfriend. He gets an idea to create a forgery and commissions Justin to paint it. Only something goes wrong."

"Maybe Justin wanted a bigger cut," Ava suggested.

"Or Freddie did," David added, nodding as he digested this new theory.

"They fight at the rehearsal dinner, Justin takes a swing at Freddie, but Baker steps in and breaks it up before he can do much more. So, Justin shows up at the wedding the next day and confronts Freddie."

"They argue again," Ava said, picking up my thread. "And Justin kills him in a fit of rage!" She slammed her fist down on the bar top.

"That," David said, stabbing his wineglass her way, "is a very dramatic theory."

"Thank you." Ava did a little curtsy.

David grinned. I wasn't entirely sure he'd just given her a compliment.

"The only problem is proving it," I said.

"Maybe we could check Freddie's phone records again for any calls to Justin's studio?" Ava suggested.

David's grin widened. "'Again'?"

"We might have finagled access to them," Ava said.

"I'm impressed," David said, and this time I think he actually meant it. "You girls are much more devious than you let on."

"Thank you. But we're women," Ava corrected. "Not 'girls.'"

"Oh, trust me," David said above the rim of his glass. "I'm well aware of your womanly attributes."

Ava giggled and playfully reached across the bar to slap his hand.

I narrowed my eyes. Was she flirting with him again?

"Even if we saw Justin's number come up in Freddie's phone records," I said, trying to get the conversation back on track, "that doesn't prove they were in cahoots."

David snorted his wine. "Cahoots? Who are you? Jessica Fletcher?"

I ignored him with no small effort.

"Well, what about the PI?" Ava asked.

David turned to her. "PI?"

She quickly filled him in on the private investigator that Mr. Somersby had hired to look into Freddie. "If he was following Freddie, maybe he saw him meet with Justin? Or followed him to the auction house? Or something that might link him to the forged painting?"

I had to admit, that was not a half bad thought. "I don't suppose he's gotten back to you?" I asked her.

She shook her head.

"Maybe tomorrow we should try visiting him in person—"

I barely had the words out before Charlie's Angel Ava pounced on them.

"I'll be here at nine!"

* * *

After David and Ava both left the winery—not together, I was happy to see—I locked up and realized I was famished. And just a little buzzed. All I'd ingested since noon was a slice of quiche and two glasses of wine.

I ducked into the kitchen and checked the fridge for inspiration. Luckily, it looked like Conchita had been shopping recently, and I had my choice of several ingredients. I did an eeny meeny minie mo, and since I'd already had a low carb, if rich and comforty, kind of food day, I decided to stick with the theme and make Roasted Eggplant Mozzarella with Homemade Basil Marinara Sauce.

As I assembled the ingredients for the sauce and set them sautéing and simmering in a large pot, my mind wandered over everything we'd learned that day and the myriad of people who might have wanted Freddie dead. While Edward Somersby had originally topped my list (and not just because he still owed me money), I had to admit the more I learned about Freddie, the more people who had line-jumped him in that list.

Bridget McAllister, for one. The fact that witnesses had seen her sneaking away with Freddie to the crime scene just before Freddie was found dead was a definite red flag. She'd been jealous enough of Juliet to drag her girlfriends to Wine Country and crash Freddie's wedding. And we only had her word that she'd left him alive on my terrace…and not grabbed a champagne bottle in a fit of if-I-can't-have-you-no-one-can passion.

Of course, I reasoned as I moved on to slice my eggplant, Bridget hadn't been the only one to crash the wedding. Justin Hall had been there too, presumably uninvited and coincidentally just hours after punching Freddie in the face. Possibly over a forged painting? I had to admit, I was dying to know if that PI had inadvertently uncovered a link between the philandering groom and the violent artist.

Then again, the PI brought me squarely back to Edward Somersby, who had not only lied about his alibi but had also gone so far as to pay someone to investigate Freddie. Meredith Somersby had said Edward told her that the PI hadn't found anything. But I knew Edward wasn't above lying—he'd also told me he was with her the entire morning of the ceremony, which we knew to be false. If the PI had uncovered one of Freddie's secrets—like possibly being involved in art forgery or sleeping with Bridget McAllister—it could well have been the thing to push the protective father right over the edge. And of all my suspects, it was most likely that Edward could have transferred some of the feathers from Juliet's gown to the crime scene. I knew for a fact that he and his wife had visited her in the bride's suite to see her in her dress.

"Anyone home?"

I jumped, almost slicing my thumb along with the eggplant on my cutting board, at the sound of a voice accompanied by a knock at the back door. I sucked in a deep breath and exhaled the adrenalin as I crossed the kitchen to find Detective Grant's face on the other side of the glass insert.

I unlocked the door and swung it open. "You scared the bejeezus out of me," I told him.

He raised one eyebrow at me. "Bejeezus?"

"Trust me, it's better than the dirty words I was thinking."

He grinned and nodded. "Okay, let's go with bejeezus then," he said, stepping into the room. "It smells great in here."

"I'm making roasted eggplant mozzarella," I told him, closing the door behind him and returning to my slicing. "With homemade basil marinara."

"Don't suppose you made enough for two?"

I had to admit, the sheepish grin that accompanied that self-invitation was too cute to resist.

"Only if you grate the cheese," I agreed, nodding toward the mozzarella on the island.

"That, I can do," he said, quickly washing his hands at the kitchen sink before digging in.

"So, I heard you had a long chat with Juliet Somersby today?" I said, trying to infuse my voice with a casual conversational tone as we prepped together.

"You heard that, did you?" Grant asked, his eyes twinkling at me as he started grating cheese.

"I was looking for Edward Somersby, and his wife told me. Official wedding planner business," I said, defending myself.

"I see." Grant didn't say anything further, but the hazel flecks in his eyes were dancing with a frenzy of amusement.

"So?" I prompted.

"So what?"

"So, are you going to tell me what you asked her?"

Grant pretended to think about it for a beat. "No."

I rolled my eyes. "That is totally unfair. I'm sharing my homemade sauce with you. Which, by the way, was rated 4 stars by Bradley Wu in his food column last month. The least you can do is share about your day with me."

Grant chuckled softly, the sound so rich and warm that for a moment I forgot what we were talking about. "Okay," he finally said. "You want to hear about my day? I had coffee on my commute to work, had a meeting with my captain, then interviewed a person of interest in a murder investigation. I had a ham sandwich for lunch, visited my brother for a couple of hours this afternoon, and spent the rest of the day on paperwork."

"I didn't know you had a brother," I blurted out. I'd never heard Grant speak of any family before. Somehow he'd always felt like the kind of hard guy who didn't have any—a lone wolf.

Grant nodded. "I do. Six years older."

"And he lives in Sonoma?"

Again he nodded, though the way his eyes stayed on his pile of cheese gratings instead of meeting mine told me he was possibly regretting not skimming over that part of his day.

"What's his name?" I asked.

"Jake." One word answer. Eyes still on his task.

"Are you two close?" I pressed, feeling a rare opportunity to peek at what made Grant tick before this small crack in his impersonal wall closed up again.

"Used to be. When we were younger."

"Did something happen to change that?"

Grant sucked in a deep breath, and finally raised his eyes to meet mine. "I grew up, and he stayed the same."

My confusion at that statement must have shown on my face, as he elaborated.

"Jake is autistic."

"Oh," I said lamely, not really sure how to formulate an appropriate response to that. Part of me wanted to say I was sorry—the difficulty he was having talking about this made it clear that having a brother with special needs hadn't been easy. But the last thing I wanted to do was offend by making it seem like his brother was something to be sorry about. So, I settled for a neutral, *"Oh,"* followed by, "I see."

Grant cleared his throat. "It's fine," he said, as if reading my mind. "Most people don't really know how to react when I talk about my brother."

I smiled, feeling suddenly sheepish. "When you put it like that, it sounds stupid to worry about the right word." I paused. "Tell me about Jake."

He hesitated a moment, but I could see him meeting my gaze now, so maybe the awkwardness of the subject had passed. "Well, he lives in a group home near the library. Lots of great staff who kind of make it like a family atmosphere for them. He's in his own world a lot, but if I had to describe him, I'd say he's a seven-year-old who's just really tall and shaves."

I couldn't help a laugh. "Sounds fun."

He nodded. "He can be."

"I'd love to meet him someday," I blurted without thinking.

Which, if I had been thinking, I'd have realized was maybe pushing personal a little too far. The laughter on Grant's face faded, and his eyes went back to the cheese. "Maybe," was all I got.

I tried to ignore the heat creeping up my collarbone at being shut down. I cleared my throat, changing the subject. "Anyway, the recap of your day was great, but you *did* gloss over the most interesting part."

"Did I?" Grant asked. He finished with the grating and set his neat little shredded pile aside then leaned against the counter.

I shot him a pointed look. "You know you did. The 'person of interest.' Juliet Somersby."

He kept a perfect poker face. "What about her?"

"Come *on*!" I whined. "You're killing me."

The poker face cracked with a half smile. "I know. And it's way too entertaining."

I narrowed my eyes at him. "You know, angry chefs have been known to burn marinara before."

He laughed out loud. "You would never stoop that low."

"No," I agreed. "But just tell me this—is Juliet still a suspect?"

Grant paused a moment before answering. "We're looking into several different leads right now."

"That tells me nothing."

"I know." He waggled his eyebrow up and down at me.

I rolled my eyes. "Fine. But by the end of this meal, I plan to drag at least something out of you."

"This should be fun," he mumbled, the flecks in his eyes dancing again with the challenge.

* * *

An hour later, we'd polished off the warm, gooey eggplant, stopping just short of licking our plates, and somehow a bottle of Pinot Noir had disappeared along with it. And I'd failed miserably at getting anything out of Grant, other than the standard lines he'd been giving the press. He didn't outright say Juliet was a suspect, but he didn't say she wasn't. And considering I hadn't heard of anyone else being taken down to the station for a three-hour interrogation, I had to assume she was still at the top of his list.

"So…any plans to interview any other persons of interest tomorrow?" I asked as I cleared our plates from the counter and set them in the sink to soak.

"You don't quit, do you?" he asked, coming to stand beside me.

"Never." I lifted my chin and grinned at him.

"I like that about you."

The compliment surprised me, which must have shown on my face, as his lips curled ever so slowly upward and he took a step closer. "I can think of a couple of other things I like about you too, if you want a list."

"A list would be great," I squeaked out.

He took another step toward me, our bodies almost touching.

"Let's start with this," he said softly.

And before I could react, his lips moved down to whisper over mine.

All time stood still. And I might have even floated a little. His mouth nibbled over mine, and my hands instinctively moved their way up his chest with a mind of their own. A chest, I might add, that was broad and all hard muscle beneath my fingertips. Heat surged through my body, lighting up all sorts of places a good girl did not talk about.

His body pressed against mine, and my legs went weak. I was just about to suggest we take this somewhere my weak limbs could have a break—like maybe my bedroom—when the door to the kitchen flew open.

"Oh! Oh my!"

It was like being awakened from the very best dream, and my body screamed in protest as Grant suddenly detached his lip from mine and put a foot of distance between us. I was groggy with lust as I turned toward the source of the intrusion.

Conchita stood in the doorway, a paper bag in one arm as her wide brown eyes went from Grant to me.

"Oh, I'm so sorry. I didn't know you were with your detective."

"He's not *my* detective," I mumbled automatically.

Grant raised an eyebrow my way.

"I mean, he's not…we're not… What did you need, Conchita?" I asked, turning away from Grant's amused stare, before my face actually caught on fire, and toward my house manager with the worst timing in the world.

"Oh, I just was going to put away these persimmons we picked up on the way back from town…but I can do it later."

"It's okay," Grant piped up. His voice was gravelly, as if maybe hormones had gotten the better of him too.

Or maybe he was just trying not to laugh at my embarrassment.

"I was just leaving," he added.

"Oh?" Conchita asked.

"Oh?" I whined.

Grant sent me an apologetic smile. "Early morning tomorrow. Lots of persons, lots of interest." He shot me a wink.

I tried to tamp down the surge of disappointment as I held up one hand in a wave. "Bye."

He gave me one last amused grin before leaving the way Conchita had just come in.

I heard a sigh, and it took a moment to realize it wasn't mine. Conchita stared after Grant wistfully.

"Ay, *mija*, if you have a brain in your head, you better make him *your* detective soon." She fanned herself with one hand. "He is too *caliente* to resist."

She was right. If she hadn't walked in just then, I didn't think I'd have had any resistance in me. There was no telling where the night might have taken us.

Instead, I told her good night and retired to my cottage alone.

Again.

CHAPTER TWELVE

———

My phone rang bright and early the next morning, jarring me out of a fitful sleep. I fumbled on my nightstand in the semidarkness, knocking over a book and a bottle of water before I found the offending object.

"Hello?" I croaked out, the several glasses of wine I'd drunk the previous day making themselves evident in my voice.

"Good morning, sweetheart," my mother sang cheerily in my ear.

"What's wrong?" I asked automatically as I glanced at my bedside clock. Five forty-five. Way too early for nonemergency calls.

"Wh-why would you think anything is wrong?" my mom asked, her voice suddenly wary.

"It's really early, Mom."

"Is it? I've been up for hours." She paused. "At least, I thought I had."

I rubbed the sleep from my eyes and sat up in bed, propping my back against the pillows as I looked out the window and saw the first pink hues of the sunrise peeking over the hills. "It's fine," I reassured her quickly. "I'm up."

"Oh good," she responded, the cheeriness back.

"How are you feeling?" I asked, guilt creeping in as I tried to remember when the last time I'd been to visit her was. Two weeks ago? Maybe three? With the wedding prep, I'd been so busy that the days had seemed to fill even before they'd begun. Which, I knew, was no excuse.

Last year when Hector and Conchita had finally broken down and told me how bad my mom's memory was getting, I'd come home with the intention of helping her run the winery. But a stubborn streak ran through the women in our family, and she'd insisted she didn't want to be a burden on my life—that she would be perfectly well cared for in an assisted living facility. At first, I'd staunchly shot down that idea—images of elder neglect and thieving orderlies immediately springing to my mind. But when we'd visited Sonoma Acres, I'd realized it was actually a beautiful facility just south of town that was more like a resort than a hospital. Mom had friends there, she had lots of activities to keep her busy, and there were always staff on hand to make sure that on the bad days—days when she couldn't recall what decade it was, let alone the day—she was made comfortable and watched over in a way that would have been hard to duplicate here at Oak Valley.

But even as comfortable and cared for as I knew she was, I still felt guilty I'd let so much time pass since last seeing her.

"I'm feeling fine, Emmy," she answered to my relief. "Just fine. You worry too much."

I smiled into the phone. "I worry an appropriate amount for a daughter who loves her mother."

"Psht," she said, blowing air into the phone. "Don't get all mushy on me, now."

I laughed, feeling my spirits bolstered by her teasing.

"Did I tell you I got a new roommate?" she asked.

I shook my head, even though she couldn't see me. "No."

"Frances. She's from Indiana. She keeps saying she needs to 'warsh' things. Isn't that cute?"

"It is," I agreed.

"Anyway, I'm trying to teach her how to use Facebook so she can keep up with her grandkids." I knew Mom was probably a good decade younger than most of the residents at Sonoma Acres, the "early onset" dementia having unfairly started to take her away too young. But I was glad she was having some good moments lately.

"That's awesome," I told her.

"Enough about me, though," she said. Her voice was suddenly tight, causing my shoulders to tense up. "I'm calling because I saw something troubling on the news. They said a man died at the winery. Is that true?"

I grimaced. I'd been hoping she wouldn't find out about the murder, but that had clearly been a pipe dream. "Yes, but we're fine," I told her, trying to sound reassuring. "The police are looking into what happened, and I'm confident that they'll get to the bottom of it." At least eventually.

"The police or your detective?"

I narrowed my eyes at the phone. "What do you mean *my detective*?"

Mom laughed softly. "Just because you haven't been to visit in a few weeks, that doesn't mean Conchita hasn't."

I closed my eyes. "Conchita has a very active imagination," I said. I did not mention the scene she'd witnessed last night that I'm sure was only going to be fuel for that imagination.

"Oh. That's too bad," Mom said. "He sounded nice."

"He is nice," I said automatically. "I mean…he's a nice guy. He's just not *my* guy. We're…" Dating? Occasionally sharing a meal and making out? Constantly running into each other at crime scenes? "…friends," I finally finished. Though I wasn't sure that title was totally accurate either.

"Oh. Okay, well, I guess a friend is good," Mom agreed.

I sighed in relief, glad to have dodged that bullet at least.

"Well, come visit soon," Mom added. "I miss you, sweetheart."

I felt a pang of sadness. "I miss you, too," I said softly. Then I promised I'd come see her that weekend before hanging up and falling back into my pillows again, a mix of nostalgia, sadness, and love sloshing around my insides as I watched the sun rise over Oak Valley.

Once the sky was a warm purple, I reluctantly pulled myself out of bed and into a hot shower, where I indulged under the spray a bit longer than normal in order to properly wake myself up. Then I dressed in a pair of black skinny jeans, a pretty maroon sweater that Eddie had given me for Christmas, and gray suede ankle boots with a slim heel. I did a quick makeup routine before heading down to the kitchen and losing myself in several cups of coffee as I browsed the morning news on my phone. None of it was good, so I switched to celebrity blogs, reading all about the latest Kardashian escapades.

Promptly at nine o'clock Ava pulled up to the winery in her vintage green GTO convertible. She'd gone full retro chic today, with a white silk scarf tied over her hair and big sunglasses that made her look like a blonde Jackie O. The only unexpected element was David Allen sitting in the passenger seat next to her.

"David," I said, shooting a questioning look toward Ava as she pulled to a stop.

"He showed up at my door with coffee this morning," she explained.

"Did you really think I'd let you two gir"—David paused, eyes cutting to Ava as he stopped himself just in time— "extremely capable *women* go shake down a private eye without me?"

I rolled my eyes. "We're not *shaking down* anything. Now who's living an 80s crime show?" I teased.

David grinned. "I always thought I'd make a great Columbo."

"Oh no," Ava said, shaking her head. "You have to be Charlie."

David frowned, shoving his too long hair out of his eyes. "Charlie?"

"Yeah. And we're your angels." She gave him a flirty grin.

One that David returned in spades. "Oh, I like the sound of that." He cut his eyes to me. "Come on Angel Number Two. Let's get going or we'll be stuck in traffic forever."

I took a deep breath and assessed my life choices. Unfortunately, most of them were too late to change, so I slid into the tiny back seat of Ava's car and settled myself in for a very long ride into The City.

* * *

The office of Sean Carter, PI, was located in an old building in the Bayview, where the streets were narrow, parking was at a premium, and the sky was perpetually foggy at this time of year, adding a gray layer to the already grimy feel of the street as we searched for a spot at the curb. A block and a half up, Ava finally found one, putting her top up for security. As I stepped from the car, a mixture of salty sea air and rotting garbage hit me, mingling with the cloyingly sweet scent of someone having recently used the alley beside us as a restroom.

"Charming area," David Allen commented, wrinkling his nose as he caught a whiff too.

"Let's get this over with," I mumbled.

"Hang on," Ava said, fumbling with her key. "I just want to double check all the locks."

I didn't blame her. I gave it 50/50 odds we'd still have all four tires by the time we came back.

David graciously fed the parking meter for us, and then we all traversed the sun-bleached stretch of cracked sidewalk leading up to the entrance to Carter's building. Several of the tan bricks that comprised the exterior were crumbling at the corners, and two of the front windows were shattered and boarded over. As we pushed open the glass door, the inside of the building wasn't much more promising, with drab beige walls and threadbare blue carpet that reeked of stale cigarette smoke.

I scanned the business listings on a black felt board near the front door and saw that Sean Carter's office was located on the third floor. The elevator appeared to be out of order, so we hoofed it up the two flights of stairs. At the end of the third-floor hallway, we found a door with a frosted glass window and a copper plaque that read *Carter Investigations*. I rapped my knuckles on the door and then stepped back, waiting to see if anyone answered.

The sound of shuffling papers could be heard from the other side, and a man cleared his throat. "Be right there," he called in a gravelly voice that sounded as if he'd been a devout smoker all his life. After a few moments, footsteps clomped toward us, and the door swung open.

The man looming in the doorway was short and husky, with thick gray stubble and beady dark eyes. He wore scuffed brown loafers and a wrinkled brown suit that was at least one size too small for his round frame, which I supposed was why the coat was unbuttoned. "Yeah?" the man asked, unsmiling.

"Hi," Ava said, undeterred by the less-than-welcoming greeting, giving him a sunny smile and offering him her hand. "My name is Ava Barnett, and I—"

"You're the chick that keeps calling me," he said, cutting her off. His expression changed from a look of irritation to one of suspicion, eyes narrowing.

"So you did get my messages," Ava said breezily. "That's great because I'd like to hire you."

"Let me guess—you think your boyfriend is running around on you?" His gaze slid down to her chest—encased in a white shirt open at least two buttons at the top—and a small smile curled his lips.

"I would never!" David Allen took a step forward, slinging a protective arm around Ava's shoulders and dropping a kiss on the top of her head.

The smile died on Carter's face. "Huh."

"Uh, actually, we were hoping to hire you to look into a man my friend is marrying," I said, giving him the cover story the three of us had concocted in the car on the way over. "We, uh, we're not sure he's right for her."

"Oh yeah?" He shifted his stance, tearing his eyes from Ava's cleavage to assess the three of us. Finally he must have seen something in our trio that convinced him we could be paying customers, as he stepped back to allow us entry. "Come on into my office."

I gingerly stepped over the threshold into a room that had more beige walls and more threadbare carpet—this time in an unappealing gray that I wasn't totally sure was by the manufacturer's design. I sat on the edge of a shabby brown chair that faced the desk, and Ava did the same on a matching, equally shabby chair. David stood behind us in the small office as Carter waddled around his desk and sank into a ripped leather seat with a creak.

"So, tell me about this guy you want me to look into for ya." He leaned his elbows on the smattering of manila files covering the top of his faux wood desk.

"Well," I started, glancing to Ava for reassurance, "one of my friends from school is getting married. And we…we have our doubts about the groom."

"Lots of doubts," Ava added.

"Right. We think he may be cheating on her. And maybe even into some criminal activities."

Carter's bushy eyebrows rose. "You don't say?"

Ava nodded. "We were hoping maybe you could find some information about him that we could use to persuade our friend not to go through with the wedding."

"Alright," Carter said, pulling a piece of paper from the ancient printer behind him. He grabbed a pen and turned back to the desk. "Let's start with the basics. What's the guy's name?"

I licked my lips. "Alfred Campbell."

Carter's pen froze, hovering above the paper. His eyes slowly rose to meet mine. "Excuse me?"

I cleared my throat. "Uh, Alfred Campbell?" I hated the way my voice rose on a question at the end.

Carter's eyes narrowed again, bouncing from Ava to me to David, standing behind us like a silent bodyguard.

"Freddie Campbell?" Carter repeated.

I nodded.

He straightened up in his seat and dropped the pen onto the desk with a click. "Alright, what's the gag?"

"G-gag?" I asked, trying to channel innocence with my voice.

"You heard me." He pinned me with a look. "Freddie Campbell ain't marryin' anybody. He died two days ago."

Dang. Apparently my mother wasn't the only person who'd watched the news recently.

"Uh…he did?" I said unconvincingly. I glanced to Ava, Award Winning Actress Extraordinaire, to help me out.

"Okay, here's the truth," Ava said, lying through her teeth. "Juliet Somersby is a friend of ours. We all went to college with her."

"You all went to college," he repeated, eyes going up to David in disbelief. Granted, David's ripped jeans, black T-shirt sporting some rock band's logo, and hair falling into his eyes didn't exactly scream academia.

"We did," Ava went on, nodding her pretty blonde head. "And Juliet is heartbroken over Freddie's death."

"*That* is very true," I chimed in.

"But we think maybe he wasn't such a nice guy after all. We think it would help Juliet's grieving process if she knew the real truth about who he was."

Carter made a noncommittal sort of grunt in the back of his throat and did some more assessing of the three of us. "You know, you ain't the first one who's come to me wanting the goods on Campbell."

"We aren't?" I asked, trying my hand at innocent again.

He shook his head, and I saw dandruff flakes falling to his shoulders like snow.

I stifled a gag reflex and averted my eyes.

"No, you ain't. Your friend Juliet's dad wanted me to look into the guy too."

"What a coincidence!" Ava chirped.

"Is it?" Carter's eyes went from me to Ava again.

"Uh…so what did you find out when Mr. Somersby engaged your services?" I asked.

Those eyes narrowed until they were just two dark slits staring at me from beneath bushy eyebrows. "Nothing."

I felt my stomach sink. "Nothing?" Maybe Edward had been truthful when he'd told his wife the PI hadn't come up with anything.

Carter shook his head. "Nothing on *Freddie* Campbell," he amended, his eyes taking on a mischievous gleam as he put emphasis on the name.

"What do you mean?" Ava cocked her head to the side.

A slow smile snaked across Carter's face. "*Freddie* Campbell is squeaky clean. But I can't say the same for *Frank* Campbell."

"Wait—Freddie used another name?" I asked.

Carter nodded at me. "Oh yeah."

I felt a frown forming between my brows. "Why would he do that?"

Carter's grin widened. "I'd be happy to tell you." He paused. "For a fee."

My turn to narrow my eyes.

"Hey, you did say you wanted to hire me, right?" Carter spread his hands wide, palms up.

I sighed and dug around in my purse, searching for my wallet. I finally found it and pulled out a twenty.

Carter laughed. "What, do you think I charge babysitter rates? I got hours invested in this guy, and if you want the fruits of my labor, you gonna have to pay real money."

"Didn't Edward Somersby already pay you for your labor?" Ava pointed out.

Carter's laughter died, his beady eyes sharp again. "Somersby's late on his bill."

"I know the feeling," I mumbled.

I looked from Ava to David. The twenty was all I had.

Ava pursed her lips and swiveled in her seat to give David the full benefit of her wide, pleading smile.

David sighed. "Right, of course it always falls to *Charlie* to bail the angels out."

Carter frowned, clearly not getting the reference, but as David stepped forward and extracted a few twenties from his wallet, I could tell the reference didn't matter in the least to the PI. He only had eyes for the cash.

"What kind of bill are we talking?" David asked, counting out a small pile of twenties.

"Add a couple more," Carter instructed.

David paused, shooting me a look before adding the last of his money to the pile. "This is all the cash I have on me. Better be worth it, Oak," he mumbled in my direction.

One could only hope.

"Okay, spill it," I directed Carter as David put his significantly slimmer wallet back into his pants pocket.

Carter scooped up the pile, and by the look in his eyes, I'd guess he was just barely containing himself from making out with the stack of cash. "Sure. Whadda you want to know about our boy Freddie?"

"Let's start with this alias," Ava said.

"Aliases," Carter corrected. "More than one."

"More than one?" I choked out.

Carter nodded. "Our Freddie Campbell was also Frank Campbell, and prior to that, Alfred Camptown."

"Whoa." Ava blinked, mirroring my surprise. "I'm guessing Freddie wasn't just changing his name for fun?"

"Most people don't, doll," Carter said.

"So, why was Freddie?" I asked.

"If I had to guess, it had to do with outrunning his wives."

"Wait—wives?" My mental hamster was slow to jump on his wheel. "What do you mean, wives? Freddie was marrying Juliet."

Carter laughed, a hacking sort of cackle. "Well, let's just say she wasn't his first. I found marriage certificates in both those other names. Took a little digging, but they both traced back to Freddie Campbell. As far as I could see, he had a pattern. He'd marry some chick—usually well off—stick with her long enough to put a healthy dent in her bank accounts, then take off. He changes his name and then pulls the same thing with a new girl."

While I'd been expecting to hear all sorts of awful things about Freddie from the PI, this was not one of them. "Freddie Campbell was a con man," I mused out loud. "Juliet's dad was right all along."

Carter snorted. "Oh, even dear old Dad hadn't guessed this one."

"But you did tell him about it," Ava pressed, shooting me a meaningful glance.

"Sure. I mean the guy hired me, right?"

So Edward *had* been lying to his wife.

Then again, so had Freddie it seemed. Multiple times.

"You followed Freddie around, correct?" David asked.

Carter nodded. "I always start with surveillance."

"Did he happen to visit an art studio? The Art Initiative off Broadway?"

Carter frowned. "Not that I saw. Why?"

"Just curious if Freddie had dealings with one of the artists there. Justin Hall?"

But Carter shook his head. "Sorry, name don't ring a bell. Mostly that Freddie character just hung around with his best friend. Some guy named Baker Evans."

"He visit anyone else?" I asked, thinking of Bridget.

Carter looked up to the ceiling, as if trying to recall. "I know I seen him a couple a times with some chick he referred to as his cousin. The two of them even spotted me one time, but I lost 'em. I always do." He winked at me, clearly proud of himself.

Little did he know that small blunder had led us to him.

"Other than that," he went on, "the guy was just with the new fiancée. He did a real good job charming that one."

"Poor Juliet," Ava mused. "He was just playing her all along."

"Guy was kind of an expert at that," Carter said, leaning back in his chair again, causing it to moan in protest. "The most recent ex-wife was smart enough to get a prenup, but Freddie cleaned her out anyway. Got access to her accounts online, transferred everything to some offshore bank, then—boom. Guy vanishes. Hits her with divorce papers via messenger. He was a smooth operator."

"I don't suppose you have a name for this recent ex-wife?" David jumped in.

Carter thought about that for a beat. "Sure. For a fee."

"He just gave you all the cash he had!" I protested.

"That's okay." Carter flashed a row of yellow teeth. "I take plastic, too."

I glared at him. There was no way any one of us was going to hand a credit card to this sleazeball.

"I've got some cash," Ava piped up from beside me.

I turned in my chair to face her. "You sure?" I glanced at Carter. "I mean, how do we even know he isn't just making all of this up?"

Carter shrugged. "You want proof? I'll make you a copy of the last marriage certificate *Frank Campbell* signed."

Ava leaned toward me. "Hey, that could be info worth killing over."

I was about to protest that Freddie Campbell—or Frank Campbell or whoever he was—seemed to be a walking billboard of reasons someone might be killed, but I didn't get the chance as she pulled a couple of twenties from her purse and turned to address Carter.

"Make the copy."

Carter's twitchy fingers reached for the cash.

But I beat him to it, snatching the bills out of Ava's hand.

"Not so fast," I said, holding them out of his reach. "Marriage certificate first. Then you get the rest of the cash." I wasn't about to let him string us along any further.

The stocky man scowled at me but swiveled in his chair and grabbed the pile of manila folders off the corner of his desk. He riffled through the stack until he found the one he was looking for. Flipping it open, he skimmed a sheet of paper and then nodded to himself and placed it in his printer. A moment later the machine roared to life and spit out a copy of the paper, which he slid across the desk to me.

"There. That's his most recent ex," he said. "From what I could tell, he pulled a disappearing act on her just before he met the Somersby girl." He held out his hand.

I laid the twenty-dollar bills in his palm.

"Pleasure doing business with you," he said, pocketing the cash. "Now, if there's nothing else..." He trailed off, rising from his seat and crossing the small room to open the door as a signal for us to leave.

I could think of nothing I wanted more than to be out of that office.

I grabbed the copy from the desk, only glancing at it long enough to ascertain that it was, in fact, a marriage certificate, before exiting the office. David and Ava were quick on my heels, and as soon as we were clear, Carter shut the door decisively behind us.

"I feel like I need a shower," Ava said, making a face at the frosted glass bearing his name.

"Ditto," I agreed, suppressing a shudder that had nothing to do with the lack of heating in the building.

"So, who was the unlucky bride?" David asked, nodding toward the paper in my hands.

I held the copy out, scanning the document until I got to the name of the poor woman who had fallen prey to Freddie's con.

I sucked in a breath and heard Ava let out a soft, "No way," beside me, surprise hitting her at the same time.

The name of Freddie's previous wife was Natalie Weisman.

CHAPTER THIRTEEN

——————

"This can't be right," I breathed, staring down at Natalie's name on the printout.

"Wait—does this mean that Freddie married his *cousin*?" Ava's nose crinkled in disgust. "Eww."

"I think it more likely means Natalie's been lying to us all along," I said, reading the rest of the document. There wasn't a whole lot to it except the marriage date (just over a year ago) and the place (Las Vegas).

"I still don't get it." Ava shook her head. "Why would Freddie's ex-wife want to pretend to be his cousin?"

I felt that frown forming between my brows again as we made our way back down the stairs. "Great question."

"Maybe Natalie traced her *Frank* Campbell back to Juliet's *Freddie* Campbell," David suggested as he held the building's door open for us.

Damp, cool air immediately hit me in the face, and I ducked my head and wrapped my arms around myself as we walked back to the car. "Carter did say Freddie cleaned Natalie out," I said, thinking out loud. "Maybe she was tracking him down in order to get her money back?"

Ava nodded. "If I'd been duped by some guy, I could totally see myself doing that."

"So, she finds Freddie and demands her money. I still don't get the cousin angle though," I admitted.

Ava unlocked her car (still sporting four tires. Hurray!), and we all got in as David picked up the thread. "Well, what if Freddie didn't have her money anymore?"

"You mean, like, he spent it?" Ava asked, turning the car on and cranking up the heater.

David nodded in the back seat. "It was several months ago. Maybe Freddie used it all up and was setting his sights on Juliet's bank accounts to fund his future lifestyle."

"I could see that," I said, feeling the theory solidify in my mind. "A future lifestyle that could all be in jeopardy if Natalie tips Juliet off about who Freddie really is. So, Freddie has to keep Natalie quiet. Maybe he promises her a cut of the haul he's expecting to get from Juliet if Natalie can just be patient and keep quiet until he marries Juliet."

"So, Freddie agrees to let Natalie pose as his cousin," Ava said, pulling away from the curb, "in order to keep tabs on him until she gets her money back."

"Which is all very plausible," David said. "But I don't see what motive Natalie would have to kill Freddie. Especially if she wanted her money back."

"You're right," I admitted. "Killjoy."

David chuckled.

But Ava wasn't as easily deterred. "Well, what if Freddie decided at the last minute he wouldn't pay Natalie back? Or maybe he never meant to—maybe he was just stringing her along until he married Juliet and got access to her money. Maybe he was planning to disappear again on both of them."

"That would fit with his MO," I agreed. "So, Natalie finds out she's being duped—again—and she follows Freddie to the terrace."

"Where she grabs the most convenient weapon," Ava said, raising her hand up above her head. "And kills him with it!" She brought her fist down hard on the steering wheel.

I rolled my eyes. "You really like that part of every theory, don't you?"

She shrugged. "Just going for dramatic emphasis."

"You know, Natalie was with Juliet in the bridal suite most of the morning. I could easily see her accidentally transferring some feathers from Juliet's dress to the crime scene," I said.

"I wonder what Natalie would have to say about all this," David piped up.

"You think Grant is still keeping the wedding party in Wine Country?" Ava asked.

"I don't know." I shrugged. "But I think we should find out."

* * *

An hour and a half later, the three of us were standing at the reception desk of the Belle Inn, facing Sam the freckled-faced clerk again. She'd informed us that Natalie had not, in fact, checked out yet, and then agreed to call up to her room. Unfortunately, several rings in, it appeared no one was answering.

"I'm sorry," Sam told us. "Ms. Wiseman isn't picking up. Would you like to leave a message for her?"

I bit my lip, not really sure all of our accusations would fit on a pink memo pad or thirty second sound bite. "Oh, no. Thank you," I told her. "We'll just try back later."

"So now what?" Ava asked, once we'd stepped back outside into the chilly air.

David glanced at his watch. "Sorry, my lovelies. Now I have a date."

I detected the slightest hint of disappointment on Ava's face.

But before I could warn her against whatever emotion had produced it, David added, "With Dr. Julius Barnaby." He grinned. "Poker game at the club."

The club was the local golf club, the Links, and Dr. Julius was about to be fleeced by Wine Country's best card shark. I felt a pang of sympathy for the good doctor as I watched Ava grin in relief.

"I could drop you off?" she offered. "It's on the way to Silver Girl."

"I'd be much obliged," David said with a mock bow her way. Then he turned to me. "But it's a bit out of the way from Oak Valley."

I waved him off. "I'm fine. I'll call Conchita or Hector to come pick me up." Which was actually preferred to spending more time with Flirty and Flirtier. I hoped Ava knew what she was doing. The brooding bad boy thing David had going on was only halfway an act. Issues ran deep in the Price-Allen family, and while David had fared better than some of his family—who were now deceased, depressed, or in jail—he hadn't been totally immune to their dysfunction.

I made a mental note to have a long chat with her later about David—preferably over a bottle of wine and a chick flick—when we had a few spare moments. Until then, I waved to Ava from the B&B's porch as she tied her scarf over her hair and roared off in her GTO with David in the passenger seat, grinning like a wolf who'd just been invited into the sheep's convertible.

I pulled out my phone and was about to dial the winery to beg a ride from one of my employees, when I spotted a familiar face coming up the walk to the B&B. Thick glasses, crooked nose, acne scars.

Baker Evans.

He paused when he got to the steps, recognition taking a moment to light his face. "Oh. Hey. Emma from the winery, right?"

"Emmy," I corrected automatically.

"Right." He paused again. "Were you looking for Juliet?" He nodded back toward the building.

"Uh, actually, I was hoping to talk to Natalie," I told him truthfully. "You don't happen to know where she is, do you?"

He shook his head. "She took off about an hour ago. She said she was going to do some window shopping downtown."

I tried to hide my disappointment. "Did she happen to mention when she'd be back?"

He shrugged. "Sorry. She didn't say." He paused again and cocked his head to the side. "Why? Everything okay?"

I hesitated, not sure how much to share about what the PI had told us. But Baker had been Freddie's childhood friend, and it was quite possible he'd been at Freddie's previous wedding…maybe even both.

"Actually, I was wondering if I could ask you a couple of questions about Freddie," I told him.

His eyebrows drew down. "Why?"

"Uh, some things have come up," I answered vaguely. "You said you've known him a long time, right?"

He leaned his back against the porch railing and crossed his arms over his chest. "We were best friends," he said, an almost defensive tone entering his voice.

"So, you knew pretty much everything about him," I said, studying his reaction.

"Sure."

"Like, say, the fact that he'd been married before under the name Frank Campbell?"

Baker froze, his features unreadable. "How'd you find out about that?" he asked, his voice flat and monotone, giving nothing away.

I waved off the question. "It doesn't matter. But you did know Freddie had been married before?"

He shrugged. "Well, yeah. Of course. That's not something he'd keep from me." There was the defensive tone again.

"Did you know *who* he was married to?" I asked, scrutinizing his expression for any little tell.

But he just blinked. "Wh-who? No. I mean, look, it was a brief marriage. A mistake. Freddie didn't like to talk about it."

"So you never met his ex-wife?" I asked, finding this hard to believe. "Even though you were his *best* friend."

Baker cleared his throat, averting his eyes. "No, I never met her. It was—it was an impulse thing, you know? Freddie met some woman in Vegas, they got married on a whim, and it didn't last. Big surprise, right?"

"He told you that?"

Baker nodded. "Yeah. He gave me the gist. Like I said, he didn't like to talk about it much. I got the impression that his ex-wife was a total nutcase."

"So, why did he use the alias?"

"Alias?" Baker laughed. "Wow, you make it sound so nefarious."

Being a con man kind of was, but I didn't tip that hand quite yet. "Freddie did change his name," I pointed out.

"Yeah, he did," Baker admitted. "He had to. Said his ex was stalking him. Like I said, she was a nutcase. Freddie just wanted a clean start in LA, you know?"

"So Freddie never mentioned his ex-wife's name to you?" I asked pointedly. "Or how much she was worth?"

"Worth?" Baker did more blinking. "What do you mean?"

"His ex-wife was wealthy," I told him.

"Well, good for her, I guess," Baker mumbled.

"*Was,*" I clarified. "Before Freddie cleaned her out."

"Wh-what are you talking about?" If Baker knew any of this, he was doing a good job of covering it up. The stocky man actually looked bewildered. "No, look, I think you've got some bad information from someone here. Freddie would never take some woman's money."

"So he wasn't about to take Juliet's?" I asked.

"No!" Baker shook his head vehemently. "No, Freddie *loved* Juliet," he said with conviction that made me believe him. Or at least believe that was what Freddie had told him.

"What does this even have to do with the wedding, anyway?" Baker asked, the defensive tone back in his voice. "I mean, you are the wedding planner, right?"

I cleared my throat. "Right." I paused, hoping a brilliant cover would come to me. I'd been so gung-ho about confronting Natalie, and then Baker, that I hadn't really thought about it until now why a winery owner would be so interested in Freddie's personal life.

"Uh…if Freddie has an ex-wife, she may be his next of kin now. We, uh, have some accounts to settle with someone." Which was at least half true.

Baker blinked at me, but the flimsy explanation must have been enough, as he just shook his head. "Sorry. Like I said, Freddie never mentioned a name. Your guess is as good as mine." He shrugged and walked inside the B&B, leaving me alone on the porch again.

While I had more than a guess at who Freddie's previous wife had been, it appeared that Baker had been left in the dark. It occurred to me that maybe the women in Freddie's life weren't the only ones who'd fallen for his charm.

I pulled out my phone and dialed Conchita, who said she and Hector were heading into town to catch a movie anyway, and they would be happy to drop my car off at the B&B on their way. With twenty minutes to kill before they arrived, I realized I hadn't eaten in hours and wandered across the street to the café. I ordered their January special—French Onion Soup with Sherry, which was pure heaven in a bowl. It warmed me from the inside, and I may have even elicited some funny looks from the other patrons when I moaned a la *When Harry Met Sally* over the sweet caramelized onions and tangy Gruyère.

By the time I finished and made my way back to the B&B, Hector was just pulling up into the small back lot in my Jeep, with Conchita following behind in the couple's red pickup truck.

I waved as he cut the engine and stepped out. "Thank you so much," I told him. "I hope this wasn't a bother."

"Not at all," he reassured me, his weathered face breaking into a smile. After my father had passed away, Hector had almost stepped into that paternal role—which was a perfect complement to the mother hen complex Conchita had developed, first while looking after my mother and then seamlessly transferring to me when I'd come back home.

Not that I minded. They were a wonderful and welcomed set of second parents.

"Come on, we're going to be late," Conchita called from the window of the pickup, hailing her husband. "You know I hate missing the previews."

Hector chuckled. "And you need your popcorn. And Milk Duds." He winked knowingly at me.

Conchita blinked at him. "Of course. Why else go to the movies?"

I couldn't help but smile at their cute banter. While they'd been married for almost twenty years, instead of fizzling out, the initial passionate fire of first love had heated and grown into a deep warmth that I could see still brought a twinkle to Hector's eyes as he walked around to the passenger side of the truck. He slipped in and gave Conchita a quick peck on the cheek that had her giggling like a girl as she waved good-bye to me.

I hoped to one day have the kind of affection that still brought twinkles to a man's eye after twenty years. Grant's face briefly flitted across my mind, but I shut that thought down quickly. Grant was the opposite of the settling-down type. He was more the rev-you-up-and-leave-you type. I wondered briefly if he'd had someone back in San Francisco before he'd abruptly been transferred to Wine Country. He'd never mentioned anyone, but then again, we hadn't had the type of deep, meaningful conversations that drew those moments out. Mostly we'd just had brief dinners followed by even briefer make-out sessions.

"...not what I meant!"

My thoughts were interrupted as raised voices filtered toward me from across the parking lot.

"It's exactly what you meant," the other person shouted back.

I paused, my hand on the door to my Jeep, as I recognized one of the voices.

Edward Somersby.

I peeked around the hood of my car and saw that the second voice belonged to Mrs. Somersby. The pair were standing several yards away, engaged in what appeared to be a heated conversation. Meredith was speaking in a low tone that I could only make out as a murmur, but her eyes were blazing.

"...don't know why you're upset," I heard Edward say as the couple walked closer to me.

Instinctively, I ducked down below my car's windows to avoid being seen.

"Why I'm upset?" Meredith shot back, louder now.

"Keep your voice down," her husband hissed.

Dang it. I wished she wouldn't.

The next line was lost on me as she complied, and I risked ducking my head up again to catch a glimpse of her body language. She was leaning in close to Edward, eyes narrowed, hands gesturing wildly. And the more she talked, the angrier she appeared, and the louder her voice rose until I could make out the tail end of her tirade.

"...money is missing!"

My pulse quickened. Missing money? My thoughts immediately went to Freddie. Had he possibly had his hand in Juliet's finances already? Juliet had appeared blindly in love with Freddie—maybe so blind she'd trusted him with her accounts?

"...don't know that!" Edward snapped back. The next part was mumbled quietly to his wife, his eyes darting around as if worried someone might overhear the argument. Good instincts.

I crouched down below the window again to avoid being caught eavesdropping, but I could still hear him finish his thought.

"...and I'll handle it."

"How?" Meredith asked.

"That's not your concern," he said, his voice growing louder as he walked closer to my position. "Just know that I'm taking care of it right now."

He was so close I could hear his footsteps. My heart was hammering in my ears as I ducked low and waited for him to pass my hiding spot.

Unfortunately, I hadn't taken a good look at the car next to me in the lot. Heavy footfalls stalked closer, and my breath caught in my throat as I realized I was parked right next to the Somersbys' black Mercedes.

In a panic, I hurled myself into the bushes that lined the little lot. I wedged my way between two shrubs just as I heard a car door open and shut and an engine turn over. My gaze snapped to the windshield. Edward didn't seem to have noticed me. He was too preoccupied with glaring at his wife through the rearview mirror as he reversed the Mercedes. Behind the car, I caught a glimpse of Meredith Somersby, her own expression dark as she stormed back toward the Victorian.

Edward pulled the car out of the parking lot and took a right onto the road that ran beside the bed and breakfast. With the coast clear, I quickly emerged from the bushes, not even bothering to pick the stems and leaves out of my hair. Instead I jumped into my Jeep and whipped it into reverse, quickly backing out of my own parking space.

If Edward was about to "handle" some missing money that Freddie had taken, I was dying to see exactly where he was going.

Luckily, traffic was sparse this time of day, and I caught up to the Mercedes about a mile down the road. I was careful to keep a respectable distance, not wanting Juliet's father to realize that he was being tailed. He took a right on Andrieux and then a left on 2nd, winding the luxury car past the fire station and up toward Napa St., where he took a sharp right. I felt my spidey senses tingling as he turned down a familiar side street and pulled his car to a stop at the curb in front of a converted warehouse space.

The Art Initiative. Justin Hall's studio.

I crept my car slowly past, slumping low in my driver's seat as I peered through the passenger window and saw Mr. Somersby get out of his car and stride purposefully toward the glass door of the studio. A thousand questions whirled through my mind. What did Justin Hall have to do with money that Freddie stole from Juliet? Were Justin and Freddie in on it together? And, more importantly, what was Edward Somersby about to do?

I turned down the next street and circled back around the block, stopping short of Justin's building. Not wanting to be recognized, I pulled into a parking spot a half a block away and climbed out of my car, sticking close to the other shop fronts as I approached the space. I tried to see in the front window, but with Justin's space at the back, all I could make out were the figures of the two men. Edward had definitely come here to see Justin, as they stood deep in conversation about something. What, I had no idea.

I bit my lip, looking around. An alley ran alongside the warehouse. On instinct, I ducked down it, quickly walking its length until I was about where I thought Justin's space might be. A small window was above me, just out of reach of my 5'7" self, and I quickly glanced around for anything to stand on to reach it. Luckily, several wooden pallets were stacked along the side of the building, and I grabbed a couple, using them to hoist myself up to see over the windowsill.

The first thing I saw was that the artists in the initiative sorely needed to clean their windows. My view was partially obstructed by a layer of grime that was possibly as old as the original Miscetti. The second thing I noticed was that the studio was empty.

The two men I'd seen talking together were both gone. I stood on my tiptoes as the pallets beneath me wobbled precariously, trying to see farther into the building. But there was no sign of Edward Somersby or Justin Hall. Where had they gone? It had only taken me a couple of minutes to sneak over to the window.

Instinctively, I swept my gaze to the far corner of the studio, squinting at the floor beside Justin's easel where the replica of the Pablo Miscetti had been. Empty.

The painting was gone, too.

I blinked, my mind trying to piece together how the painting, Edward, Justin, and missing money were all tied to Freddie. My brain was trying so hard to make sense of it that even though my ears vaguely picked up the sound of footsteps nearby, my mind didn't think to register it as significant.

Until it was too late.

I spun around toward the source of the sound, my foot slipping on the stack beneath me.

Just in time to see a large pallet come careening toward my head.

Wood collided with bone and flesh, and pain exploded behind my eyes, blurring my vision. I felt myself falling for a split second before my head crashed into the asphalt below me.

Then everything went black.

CHAPTER FOURTEEN

———

"Emmy? Emmy, can you hear me?"

Sounds mixed together in a mumbled jumble that felt like it was coming to me from underwater. Cars on a city street, the far off sound of a police siren, muffled conversations.

"Emmy? Open your eyes, Emmy!"

And someone calling my name. Over and over. Getting louder. As my mind focused on that one sound, I realized not only was it getting louder, but the note of concern it held was heightening. The fear ratcheting up little by little as it repeated my name.

"Emmy! Wake up, Emmy!"

I pulled in air through my nostrils, trying to suck in the energy to respond to the voice. My body felt heavy and weak, and I wasn't sure I could even move my eyelids, let alone make enough sound to stop the voice from yelling at me. I exhaled, feeling my lips part as a small moan escaped me.

"Emmy?" the voice called again. Male. I could tell it was male now. "Open your eyes."

I was trying. Trying with every ounce of energy I had. Finally I managed to pry one open, then the other, blinking against the sudden onslaught of images that were as foggy as the mumbled noises had been at first.

"There you are," the voice said. "God, you scared me."

I blinked some more, feeling my muscles get the hang of it as the source of the voice came into focus. Dark hair, square jaw dusted with a day's worth of stubble, dark eyes staring down at me with concern.

"Grant?" I managed to croak out.

A small smile pulled at his features in response, though it was as weak as I felt. "Hey. You're back."

I grunted again, trying to turn my head to figure out where I was. Bad idea. Pain exploded on the left side.

"Careful. It looks like you fell pretty hard."

Fell. I tried to think back to the last thing I remembered. I *had* fallen…off the stack of pallets. But it hadn't been just clumsiness on my part.

"Someone hit me," I said, feeling the fog start to lift from my brain.

The concern etched on his brow deepened, his jaw clenching. "Hit you?"

I nodded, feeling the back of my head scrape on hard ground. More ouch.

"What happened?" he asked.

I motioned for him to help me sit up, and once I'd achieved that feat, I took a moment for the world to stop spinning before answering him.

"I was standing on those pallets," I told him, gesturing to the now toppled pile against the building, "looking in the window, and someone hit me with another one and I fell." I reached up to touch the side of my head, wincing at the pain as I encountered the sore spot. When I pulled my fingers away, there was fresh blood on them.

"Did you get a look at him?" Grant asked.

I closed my eyes. But all I remembered was the split second of hard wood rushing up to meet my face. I shook my head. "Sorry. It all happened so fast."

Grant gently tilted my head forward so he could get a better look at the injury. When he pulled back again, his expression was tight with worry. "I should get you to the hospital. You've got a nasty gash back there."

"I'm fine," I protested, knowing health insurance was so far out of my financial reach, it might as well have been a golden egg. I was currently hovering somewhere above the poverty line where health care was free and somewhere below the line where it was actually as "affordable" as the government thought it should be. But I figured Grant didn't need to know the details.

"It's just a bump," I told him, wiping the blood on my pants so he wouldn't see it.

"Your bump is bleeding," he said, glancing at my head again.

"Just a little."

He shot me a look that told me he didn't buy that for a second.

I cleared my throat, trying to change the subject. "What are you doing here anyway?" I asked.

"I was hoping to chat with Justin Hall," he said.

"Oh? About?"

"Nice try, Oak." He grinned at me, though it was still just short of actually humorous. "It's an ongoing investigation. I can't share any details with you."

"Right," I said, though the fact that he was even here did share something with me. Justin Hall was on his radar. Now whether that was due to me telling him Justin punched Freddie before he'd died or that he'd found out Justin had something to do with forged artwork and possibly missing money, was another question.

One I feared I would not be getting an answer to today.

I let Grant gently pull me to my feet and didn't even try to reject his offer of support as the world did another spinning act on me.

We stopped there a beat before Grant asked, "Can you walk?"

"Maybe. Where are we going?"

"My car," he said, already propelling me slowly forward. "We're going to the emergency room."

I groaned. "Do you know how expensive that's going to be?" Though as my steps swayed a little like I'd had too much Chardonnay, my protests were becoming weaker. Truth was, a visit to the doctor didn't sound like a terrible idea right then.

"I'll bill the department," Grant said.

"You can do that?"

He shrugged. "I can try."

"Hmmm." Try wasn't exactly a promise of reimbursement. "What about my car?" I asked, gesturing to my Jeep parked up the street.

He gave it a quick glance. "Give me your keys, and I'll have an officer drive it home for you."

I hesitated. But, in all honesty, I wasn't sure I could have driven myself home if I'd wanted to in my current state. I reluctantly handed my keys over to him as I let him lead me to his black SUV, parked just to the right of the alleyway, and hold the passenger door open for me. I shivered as a gust of cold air blew past us, and my teeth involuntarily chattered.

Grant paused to shrug out of his brown leather coat and handed it to me. "Here. You must be freezing."

I smiled at him, grateful. I took the jacket and slipped it around my shoulders, instantly shrouded in warmth as I climbed into his SUV.

As Grant walked around to the other side of the car, I glanced down the street and couldn't help but notice the empty spot by the curb where Edward Somersby's Mercedes had been. The shop front to the Art Initiative studio was dark, the lights turned off inside the space, and it appeared to be deserted. Justin and Edward Somersby were long gone by now. I found myself wondering if either of the men could have been my attacker. Maybe Edward had noticed me following him after all. Or perhaps Justin had seen me snooping around and had decided to try to scare me off. I suddenly felt very vulnerable and fortunate that I'd only been knocked unconscious. I shuddered, realizing how much worse my fate could have been.

Grant slid in behind the steering wheel, turning the engine on so that the heater started blowing out lukewarm air. "So, are you going to tell me what you were doing in the alleyway behind Justin's art studio?" he asked.

"Do I have to?" I answered.

If I was expecting amusement, I didn't get it. Instead he turned his Cop Face on me and gave me a slow nod. "Yeah. I think you better."

I sighed. "I was trying to find out what Edward Somersby was saying to Justin Hall about the missing money."

Grant's expression didn't change except for one dark eyebrow arching upward ever so slowly. "Missing money?"

I bit my lip. "Yeah. Probably Freddie took it."

Grant shook his head. "Okay, Emmy. Start from the beginning," he instructed as he pulled the car away from the curb.

I did, reluctantly coming clean about everything I'd learned that day, from the fact that Freddie had multiple names and multiple wives to go with them, to the argument I'd overheard between the Somersbys. I stopped just short of accusing Justin of forgery, as to be honest, I really didn't know what, if anything, that had to do with Freddie. And the look I was getting from Grant about how much involvement I'd had so far prompted me to minimize wherever possible. In fact, he appeared about ready to burst a blood vessel by the time we pulled up to the emergency room entrance.

"I want you to promise me something," he said, his voice tight as his hands gripped the steering wheel.

"What?" I hesitated to ask.

He turned to me, and I could see his eyes were dark, the hazel flecks flashing angrily. "Stay out of this Freddie Campbell mess."

I bit my lip. "I'm kinda already in it."

He shook his head. "No, you keep inserting yourself in it."

A small bristle of anger pricked at the back of my neck. "Are you saying this is my fault? That I asked to be attacked today?"

His jaw worked back and forth, his eyes narrowing. "No. I'm saying that if you were at home, watching some stupid Meg Ryan movie, this would not have happened."

"Meg Ryan movies are *not* stupid."

He pulled in a deep breath, and I could almost mentally hear him counting to ten. "Emmy, this is a murder investigation, and you need to stop getting involved."

"It happened at my winery! To one of my clients. Who, by the way, has still not paid me. So, yeah, I'd say I'm pretty involved whether I want to be or not."

"The *want to be* is what worries me," he shot back.

"You know want?" I said, anger suddenly giving me the energy I'd lacked earlier. "I can take it from here, *Detective*. Thanks for the ride." I unbuckled my seat belt and jumped out of the car before Grant could stop me, stalking toward the ER entrance on my own. I vaguely heard him protest behind me, but I ignored it, marching up to the intake desk, where the sight of me must have been worse than I felt, as I was quickly whisked away to a curtained off exam area.

Adrenaline ebbed as I was examined by the on-call doctor and it was determined that I would need three stitches to close the wound and should probably not be alone that night in order to watch for signs of a concussion. I promised the doctor I would call my best friend to come stay the night in my guest room. I didn't add that this wasn't the first time we'd had the same arrangement—sadly, Ava knew the protocol for concussions well.

Which was maybe why Grant had been a little overly protective.

I tried not to mentally replay the events of the evening, the images making my head pound, and guilt crept in at how harsh I'd been with him. Instead, I tried to zone out as I was treated, given a prescription for painkillers, and finally discharged nearly two hours later. I paused in the ER waiting room before leaving, wondering if I should bother Conchita and Hector again or try to get an Uber back to the winery. A decision that I never actually had to make, as I spotted Grant sitting at the far end of the room, looking bored behind a six month old copy of *People* magazine.

He must have felt my eyes on him as he looked up and set the magazine down. He crossed the small space in three quick strides. "Hey. Ready to go?"

While I'd walked away from his car full of gumption, I felt like I'd had the gumption kind of whacked, stitched, and drugged out of me at that point. So I just nodded and let him lead me out the door and across the lot to where he'd parked his car.

"You waited for me?" I asked, hearing my voice sound small.

He gave me half smile. "I had to. You're wearing my jacket," he joked.

I glanced down. He was right. I was still encased in his protective layer that smelled like old leather and his woodsy aftershave. I made a motion to shrug out of it, but he stopped me.

"Hang on to it. It's a long drive back to the winery." He shot me another smile—this time the full thing—before holding the passenger door open for me.

I climbed in and spent the rest of the drive in silence, feeling exhaustion seep into my bones. The sky was dark and dotted with a thousand brilliant stars as Grant parked in the vineyard's gravel lot and came around to help me out of the car. His hand was warm at the small of my back as he walked with me down the stone pathway that led to my small cottage. I had to fish around in my purse for my keys, and I noticed my hands were shaky as I fumbled with the lock and finally got the door open.

"Thanks," I said, turning to Grant.

"Anytime. Rescuing damsels in distress is kind of part of my job description," he responded.

I shot him a look. "Do I look like a damsel in distress?"

His eyes went up to the bandage at the side of my head, then back down to meet mine before a knowing grin hit his lips.

I rolled my eyes. "Okay, fine. I might look a little in distress right now."

"Just a little." He paused, lifting a hand to touch my hair. It came away with a small leaf. He looked from me to it and shook his head. "What have you been up to today, Emmy?"

I bit my lip. Had I left out the part about hiding in the bushes to avoid Edward Somersby in the parking lot?

"Can we skim over the details?" I asked.

He dropped the leaf onto my carpet, eyes meeting mine. "Yeah, I think we should."

Relief washed over me.

"Did the doctor mention a concussion?" he asked softly.

I licked my lips. "He said it was a possibility. That I shouldn't be alone. I was going to call Ava..." I trailed off at the intensity of his eyes on mine.

"But I'm already here," he said, his voice husky and deep.

I nodded dumbly. "Right. You are."

He took a step closer, his hand going to my hair again. Only this time he gently tucked a lock of it behind my ear, making my pulse quicken. His hand slid down to the nape of my neck, careful to avoid my stitches as he gently guided me toward him.

My pain temporarily forgotten, I leaned forward and closed my eyes, melting into him as his lips met mine. They were soft, and his stubble tickled my chin. He let his hand glide to my shoulder and trail lightly down my arm before circling my waist. His touch made me tingle all over, and a soft moan escaped my throat as he pulled me firmly against his body. The tingling turned into a vibrating sensation, radiating between our hips. As the rhythmic pulsing continued, I realized it was actually coming from his pants pocket.

"I think your phone is ringing," I murmured against his lips.

"I'll let it go to voicemail," he said breathlessly, pulling me closer and covering my mouth with his as the vibrating stopped.

A few moments later, however, the persistent buzzing started up again.

Grant broke away from the kiss, letting out a frustrated groan as he retrieved the phone from his pocket and pressed it to his ear. "Grant," he said gruffly into the receiver.

I took the moment to catch my breath, my head spinning for a whole new reason that night. Though as I watched Grant's posture go rigid and his expression turn from that of mild annoyance at the intrusion to one of alert interest, my hormones instantly tamped down.

"When?" he asked the caller, his tone clipped and direct. He nodded to himself as the person on the other end of the line responded. "All right. I'm leaving now. Be there in fifteen." He ended the call and abruptly turned toward the door. "I have to go."

"What's wrong?" I asked, a feeling of dread pooling in my belly as I followed him.

He met my gaze, and I could see emotions warring there about how much to tell me.

"What is it?" I pleaded, feeling that dread grow the longer he didn't answer.

Finally he must have realized I'd find out sooner or later anyway, as he responded, "There's been an incident at the Belle Inn Bed & Breakfast."

"Incident?" I asked, hearing the panic in my own voice. "What kind of incident?"

Grant sucked in a deep breath. "They found a body."

CHAPTER FIFTEEN

———

I felt my skin go cold, my heart racing. "Wh-who?" I asked. "Who is it?"

Grant shook his head. "It was just called in. I don't have a positive ID yet."

I closed my eyes, imagining the worst. The entire wedding party was staying there. The Somersbys, Juliet, Baker, Andrew, Natalie. As well as the other bridesmaids and several of the groomsmen.

And now one of them was dead.

I opened my eyes, realizing Grant already had the front open and was saying his good-byes.

"...sorry, Emmy, but I have to go."

"I'm coming with you," I said quickly.

"No." He gave me a stern look. "You're hurt, and you need rest. A crime scene is the last place you need to be right now."

I pursed my lips. "The doctor said I shouldn't be alone."

Grant opened his mouth to protest, but I didn't give him the chance.

"Conchita and Hector are in town tonight, and even if call Ava now, she won't be here for another twenty minutes. What if I *am* concussed and slip into a coma before then?"

While it sounded like a feeble argument to my own ears, I gambled on the fact that Grant was not one to take chances where safety was concerned. A gamble that paid off as he spat out the word, "Fine," before stepping out my door.

I quickly grabbed my purse and followed him, pausing only to throw the lock before I caught up to him in the parking lot.

Fear gnawed at me as we sped down the tree lined driveway, my mind turning the members of the wedding party over in my mind as I wondered just which one of them was dead. Grant waited until we were at the main road before putting his sirens on, and I clutched the armrest of his car to steady myself as he hit speeds well in excess of the posted limit the entire way into town. In half the time it usually took me, we were pulling up to the Belle Inn, the large Victorian building taking on an ominous look in the dark, now bathed in red and blue lights as they flashed against its turrets and ornate moldings.

Three squad cars and an ambulance already littered the street directly in front of the B&B. Grant pulled to a hasty stop behind the ambulance. He got out on the street side and came around to open my door, pausing to give me a warning look.

"You're here as silent observer," he told me. "Hang back."

I nodded. "Duly noted. I will be hanging."

As promised, I kept my distance as I followed him up the steps and into the building, where the first thing I saw was the reception clerk, Sam, her voice raised to near hysteria as she spoke to one of the uniformed officers.

"I just don't know how something like this could happen," she told the policeman between sobs.

The officer gave her a sympathetic look. "Excuse me just a moment, ma'am," he said before turning to address Grant. "The body is out back." He hiked his thumb over his shoulder. "Victim is a female in her midtwenties..."

My pulse roared in my ears, and I suddenly felt sick. *A woman in her midtwenties...*

Juliet.

I stepped around the trio and quickly made my way down the hall that led to the back garden.

"Emmy, wait," Grant called after me, but I ignored him.

Please don't be Juliet, I thought, trying to shove down the horror building in my chest. What if we'd been right that afternoon, and Natalie had killed her con man husband? Had Natalie decided she needed not only revenge on Freddie but his new bride-to-be too?

With my heart in my throat, I pushed the back door open and stepped out into the cool night air. A line of yellow tape had been posted to set up a barrier around the crime scene, which was contained to the far corner of the garden. Nearly a dozen people were crowded together at the edge, watching the proceedings with concerned looks and downcast eyes. I recognized the bridesmaid with the bob and her boyfriend, both staring at the scene with somber expressions. Baker was at the edge of the crowd, hands shoved into his pockets, eyebrows drawn down in a frown.

I practically wilted with relief as I spotted Juliet among the group. She was leaning against her bridesman, Andrew, her tear-filled eyes staring at the subject of the police's attention—a sheet covered mound just behind a pair of rose bushes. Near them stood the elder Somersbys—Meredith clung to her husband, who had apparently returned from his mysterious meeting with Justin Hall.

Grant caught up to me just as I was descending the back steps to join the crowd. His hand clamped down on my shoulder, and he spun me around so quickly that it made me dizzy. "I thought I told you to hang back," he hissed, his eye blazing.

"I-I was just joining the rest of the onlookers," I said lamely, gesturing to where the B&B patrons and passersby alike appeared to have gathered to watch the gruesome scene unfold.

Grant's eyes cut to the group, some of the fight leaving them. "Right," he said shortly. "That's a good idea."

"The officer said the dead woman was in her midtwenties?" I repeated, glancing at the assembled crowd again, trying to ascertain who was not there. Natalie seemed missing. So was the other bridesmaid.

Grant nodded. "I'm going to go talk to the ME now," he said, gesturing to a guy in a blue hazmat looking suit who was bent down beside the sheet covered mound.

Presumably the unlucky woman.

I swallowed down a lump in my throat and nodded, following him to the edge of the crime scene tape, where I watched him flash a badge and cross the barricade. He bent down and spoke to the ME. While I was a couple of feet away, I was still close enough to hear most of the exchange.

"Any idea how long she's been here?" Grant asked.

"Liver temp is 93, so I'd guess no more than three to five hours. One of the guests"—the ME pointed in the direction of Meredith Somersby—"found her when she came out for some air earlier."

"When was that?" Grant asked, pulling out his small notepad.

"Just after eight."

Grant nodded then gestured to the sheet. "Let's have a look."

The ME lifted the corner just enough so that Grant could look under it.

It was also just enough so that at my angle, I got a glimpse of the body beneath it too.

The dead woman's legs were twisted at an unnatural angle, a large purple bruise graced her slim neck, and she was staring up at the sky with sightless eyes.

I felt the blood drain from my face as I stared at the corpse. I knew that woman.

"I'm guessing those were made premortem?" Grant asked, pointing to the bruising on her neck.

The ME nodded. "My guess would be strangulation, but I'll have to get her on my table to be sure."

"Do we have an ID?" Grant asked, jotting info down on his notepad.

"There was a driver license in her wallet, which we found in her purse," the ME said, holding up a clear plastic evidence bag containing a sparkly black clutch. Her name is—"

"Bridget McAllister," I finished for him, the shock finally having worn off.

Both Grant and the ME turned to stare at me, and I felt some of the blood rush back into my cheeks.

"I, uh, met her yesterday," I told them. "Wine tasting."

Which seemed a good enough explanation for the ME, who dropped the sheet back into place and continued taking the small samples of evidence needed before he moved the woman.

Grant, on the other hand, didn't look quite as satisfied, returning his notebook to his pocket as he made his way back over to my side of the crime scene tape.

"What do you mean you met her yesterday?" he asked, suspicion making the flecks in his eyes move at a frenzied rate.

I licked my lips. "She was in town with a couple of friends. Girls' weekend."

He narrowed his eyes. "Why do I have the feeling that's not the whole story?"

Because he was a good cop.

I took a deep breath, glancing toward Juliet. While I'd initially wanted to spare her the pain of having found out Freddie'd cheated on her, with the death of the other woman, it was bound to come out now anyway.

"Bridget was also in town for another reason. Freddie's wedding."

The flecks in his eyes went nuts with that one, but his face stayed the same hard, unreadable stone that I would guess had made less innocent people than myself crack. "Tell me," he demanded.

Considering the circumstances, I did. I spilled everything. Well, okay, maybe not *everything*—I wasn't sure that getting Freddie's phone records under false pretenses was actually illegal, but it would most certainly be frowned upon. Especially by Cop Mode Grant. But I told him everything that Bridget had spilled to us at the Red Duck and how she'd confessed to being the lady in red that the witness has seen going to the terrace with Freddie just before his death.

"She told you she was there?" he confirmed.

I nodded. "She said she left Freddie alive, but I didn't totally believe her then." I glanced back to the sad lump under the sheet, wondering if the outcome would have been different if I had.

"I'm going to need the names of these friends she was with."

I bit my lip. "I don't know last names. But Purple Spandex's name was Kaitlyn. And Catwoman was maybe Ellen…or Erin?"

"Catwoman?" Grant frowned at me.

"She was dressed in a black bodysuit that reminded me of Michelle Pfeiffer…" I trailed off. "Anyway, I didn't really get their names, but I know they were at the Red Duck yesterday. Maybe there are credit card receipts there or something."

Grant nodded. "I'll look into it."

I paused, remembering the tail end of my conversation with Bridget. "There was something else Bridget said."

"Oh?"

I licked my lips. "Well, she was pretty drunk at the time, and upset about Freddie, so I didn't put a lot of stock into it."

"Go on," he prompted.

"She said she knew all their secrets."

"Whose secrets?"

I glanced over at the wedding party, still standing in awkward somberness around the yellow crime scene tape. "Them. Freddie's friends and family."

Grant frowned. "What sort of secrets?"

I shook my head. "She wouldn't say. Just that Freddie had told her everything. Only, at the time I didn't really take her that seriously." I paused. "I wish I had."

"It's not your fault," Grant said.

I glanced up at him and, despite the chill in the air, felt warmth at the concerned look in his eyes. "Thanks." I glanced at the body under the sheet again. "But that doesn't help her."

Grant let out a deep sigh. "It looks like I'm going to be tied up here for awhile."

"I'll call Ava," I offered. "She's not far." And I knew she'd want to know what was going on anyway.

Grant nodded and surprised me by stepping forward and catching me in a hug before backtracking to the scene.

I sent Ava a quick text, telling her what had happened and asking her to meet me at the B&B. She shot back the appropriately freaked out response, promising she'd be there ASAP.

I glanced over at the wedding party as I waited, Bridget's gloating about secrets ringing in the back of my mind. Had she seen something at the wedding? Had Bridget come to the B&B to confront one of them about these secrets? Maybe even to cash in on her knowledge of them? She hadn't struck me as the type to be above a little blackmail. And she certainly hadn't seemed fond of any of them. The question was, whose secret was worth killing over?

I watched Edward Somersby, standing staunchly beside his wife. Any sign of their previous argument over "missing money" had vanished, his arm wrapped firmly around his wife's shoulders in a show of support. Meredith's face was pale and stoic, though I could well imagine the state of shock she was in if she'd been the one to find the body. I knew only too well how jarring that could be.

Andrew was murmuring comforting words to Juliet, and if one didn't know better, the two almost looked like a couple themselves. I wondered again at David's thought that Andrew might have been even more protective of Juliet than her father. Could their friendship run so deep that Andrew would have killed to protect Juliet—not just from marrying a con man but also from a mistress coming to the B&B to make trouble for the grieving bride?

My gaze shot to the edge of the crowd, where someone else had just arrived on the scene. Natalie's short black hair shone in the moonlight, her eyes riveted to what was happening behind the fluttering yellow tape. I wondered if Bridget had known about Freddie's past wives...was that one of the secrets?

I darted a glance toward Grant. He was bent over the corpse, speaking in low tones to one of the uniformed officers.

I took the opportunity to skirt the edge of the growing crowd toward Natalie. Her back was to me as I approached, her arms wrapped tightly around her middle, and as I got closer, I noticed she was trembling.

"Natalie," I said, reaching out to place a hand on her shoulder.

She jumped at my touch and whirled to face me, her eyes wide. Her pale face was a shade lighter than usual, and she let out a sharp exhale when she saw me. "You startled me."

"Sorry," I told her. "Did you just get here?"

Natalie licked her lips and nodded. "I spent the afternoon downtown. What happened?" she asked, gesturing to the body.

"Someone strangled a woman to death."

Natalie winced at my words, though I couldn't tell if she was acting or actually properly horrified. "Who is it?"

"A friend of Freddie's."

Natalie's skin paled further. "Wh-what do you mean, a friend?"

"I mean a close friend. Bridget McAllister."

"Ohmigod…" Natalie swayed on her feet and might have collapsed on the spot had I not reached a hand out to steady her.

"So you knew her?" I surmised.

Natalie licked her lips, eyes darting to the side, almost as if instinctually looking for an escape route. "Sort of. I mean, I knew of her. I found out about her when Freddie and I—" She stopped herself abruptly, seemingly realizing what she was saying.

"It's okay," I told her softly. "I know the truth about you and Freddie."

She gave me a dubious look.

"I know you're not his cousin."

That did it. Any resolve she had crumbled, and she stumbled backward until her legs came up against a stone ledge, where she sat with an unceremonious thud. She leaned her elbows on her knees and covered her face with her hands. "It wasn't supposed to end like this," she said on a sob.

I sat beside her, not sure if I should comfort her or interrogate a confession out of her. I glanced back toward the crime scene, where Grant was chatting with another detective in plainclothes now. "How was it supposed to go?" I asked her.

Natalie sniffed, lifting her head. "I was supposed to get revenge," she shot out, the venom in her voice clear even through her tears.

"Freddie's dead. I'd say that's pretty good revenge."

But she shook her head. "No, you don't understand. He took everything I had. Everything. And the whole time he was sleeping with her!" She pointed toward the corpse. "It wasn't enough that he took all my money. He had to take my dignity too?" She sobbed, anger and grief mixing together.

"Did you know about Bridget before Freddie left you?" I asked softly.

She shook her head. "No. Not really. I mean, there were signs, but it wasn't until he left and I started looking for him that

I found out about *her*." She sneered in the direction of the dead woman.

"When did you finally find Freddie?"

"A couple months ago," Natalie admitted. "I saw his picture in a society column with his new fiancée." She shot her eyes toward Juliet. "Different name, but it was close enough. And it was definitely him."

"And you confronted him?" I guessed.

She nodded. "He didn't even try to deny it. That he'd used me." She shook her head, eyes still on Juliet. "I don't know what was worse—thinking about him with that trashy McAllister or seeing him with Princess Juliet."

"So why subject yourself to that?" I asked. "Why play his cousin and come to the wedding?"

Her eyes went to the Somersbys, narrowing. "I was going to get what I was owed." She turned to face me. "At first I just wanted to tell Juliet everything, you know? Just out that lying, cheating, sonofa—"

"But you didn't?" I interrupted before her language got more colorful.

She shook her head. "No. You have to understand, Freddie was charming when he wanted to be. He told me he was sorry. That he still loved me."

"And you believed him?" I asked, trying to keep the sarcasm out of my voice.

She sighed. "Part of me wanted to. Freddie said if I kept my mouth shut, he'd pay back everything he took from me. And then some."

"When he married Juliet," I finished for her.

She nodded. "He said that family was loaded. That as soon as he married her, he'd have access to everything. So, I made him a deal—I got to be 'cousin' Natalie so I could stick close until I got my money, and he got to marry his pampered princess. We'd both win."

"At least until he disappeared again," I said.

Natalie's eyes shot to mine. "He wouldn't have dared."

"He'd done it once," I said, watching her reaction. "What made you think he'd really stick around to pay you back?"

"H-he said he was sorry. That he loved me," she repeated, though it held less conviction this time. I saw warring emotions behind her eyes and wondered if this was the first time she'd considered that possibility, or if it was one that Freddie had already confirmed—and she'd killed him for it.

Finally she just sniffled loudly again and stood. "It doesn't matter now though, does it?" Her eyes went to the mound under the sheet. "Freddie's dead, and so is his trashy sidepiece. And Princess Juliet gets to mourn him as the perfect little fiancée left behind." She paused, her eyes going dark, her features hard. "And I'm left with nothing again."

Before I could ask more, she turned and practically ran back into the B&B, her shoulders hunched as she brushed past the uniformed officers.

I was tempted to follow, but I spotted Ava pushing through the crowd, eyes darting around until she spotted me. I waved, rising from the stone wall and meeting her near the entrance to the building.

"Wow, looks like I missed out on quite an eventful evening," she said, glancing to the fluttering yellow tape.

"You don't even know the half of it," I told her.

She frowned, eyes going to the left side of my head. "What happened to you? Are you okay?"

I nodded. "I'll explain in the car."

CHAPTER SIXTEEN

———

It actually ended up taking me the entire car ride back to Oak Valley plus two more hours and two pints of ice cream to retell all that had happened since Ava and David had left me at the B&B earlier that day. By the time I had Ava all caught up, we were both exhausted and fell asleep on the sofa.

I awoke the next morning with a crick in my neck, sugar breath, and a pounding headache. Though after ingesting a painkiller and a cup of coffee, I was almost starting to feel human again.

Ava and I took turns in the shower, and I let her borrow a long-sleeve, emerald green wrap dress that I had to admit looked even better on her than it did me. I went for a simple pair of jeans, a black sweater with a trendy asymmetrical hem, and my favorite pair of knee-length black boots that made me feel like a superhero when I wore them. With the way my headache had only subsided to a dull roar with the pain pill, I needed to channel all the superhero I could get that day.

Once Ava and I had done the hair and makeup thing, we followed the scents of maple and bacon to the kitchen, where Eddie was going over the day's itinerary with Conchita.

"...we have the tourist bus pulling up at four, and I was thinking you could whip up one of your famous charcuterie boards for the—" Eddie stopped midsentence, eyes cutting to me as I entered the room. "Oh my word, what happened to you, girlfriend?" he said, rushing toward me and staring at the fresh bandage on the side of my head.

Conchita dropped the sheet pan of bacon onto the counter with a clang and was a step behind him. "Ay, *mija*, what have you done now?"

"I didn't *do* anything," I protested, trying to wave off their clucking. "I...fell."

"She was attacked," Ava jumped in.

I shot her a look. Apparently she had never been the object of Mother Hen and her little Cluckette.

"Attacked!" Conchita gasped and made the sign of the cross.

"Girl, I hope the other guy looks worse," Eddie said, making a *tsk*ing sound between his teeth.

"I don't know," I said honestly. "I didn't get a good look at him."

"Or *her,*" Ava amended.

"Was it a mugging?" Conchita asked. "I tell you, this area is getting too dangerous."

"This was no random mugging. It was Freddie's killer!" Ava said.

I shot her a much more strongly worded look as Conchita gasped again and Eddie's eyes went wide with the promise of dramatic gossip. "A killer! And you got away? You are amazing!"

Actually I'd been out cold, but I took the compliment where I could.

"We don't know for sure it was Freddie's killer," I said, quickly filling them in with the CliffsNotes version of the evening before Ava could add any more dramatic flair. Conchita served us all Maple Bacon Pancakes as I told them everything, and the mixture of salty, sweet, syrupy goodness actually had me feeling a little more fortified to face the day.

However, when I finished my narrative, Conchita didn't look any more calm, and Eddie was practically dancing on his toes, the bright pink flowers on his dress shirt making me dizzy.

"What if the same person who hit you on the head went from the studio to the B&B and killed this Bridget?" Eddie asked.

"I-I hadn't thought about it." And now that I did, the pancakes suddenly weren't sitting so well in my stomach.

"It would be too coincidental not to be the same person," Conchita said, nodding sagely at me.

"From what you said, it sounds like Natalie could easily have wanted Bridget dead," Ava said, licking some syrup from her finger. "But what would she have been doing at Justin Hall's studio to catch you there?"

"Good point," I told her.

"Unless she just happened to see you there," Eddie piped up. "She was supposedly window shopping, right? Maybe she happened to be in the area."

"It's possible," I hedged. "But why attack me? Unless she has some connection to Justin Hall, why would she care if I was looking in his windows?"

Eddie frowned. "I guess she wouldn't."

"What I want to know," Ava jumped in, "is why *Edward Somersby* was there. Didn't both his wife and Justin say Edward hated him?"

I nodded. "I know. I thought that was weird too. And Edward went there to 'handle' some missing money."

Ava pursed her lips together, pushing her fork around in the last of the maple syrup on her plate. "Okay, going with the theory that Freddie had Justin paint the Miscetti in an effort to defraud someone at the upcoming auction, maybe Freddie had to steal some money from Juliet to commission it?"

I nodded. "I could see that."

"Then Edward somehow finds out the money is missing and confronts Justin to get the money back?" Conchita asked.

Ava shrugged and turned to me. "You said the painting was gone when you looked in the windows yesterday?"

"I didn't see it anywhere," I told her.

"I wonder if Justin has swapped it out already."

"You mean, the reason it's not in his studio could be that it's hanging on the wall of the auction house in a gilded frame right now?" Eddie asked.

"*If* he was forging the painting to be auctioned at all," I said. "This is all just a theory. We don't even know for sure that Justin was doing anything other than branching out into a new style of painting."

Three faces turned to look at me, the exact same expression on all of them—that I was possibly the most naive person they'd ever met.

I rolled my eyes. "Okay, fine. Let's assume forgery."

"Well, I think if we're going to *prove* forgery, we need to know if the painting at the auction house right now is the real deal or the one from Justin's studio," Ava reasoned.

"And how are we going to do that" I asked, almost afraid of the answer.

Ava grinned at me. "Feel like a drive into The City?"

* * *

San Francisco Bay Auctions was located in the financial district, which was over an hour's drive away on a good day. On a morning where commuters were jamming the freeways, you could easily double that. On a morning like the current one, where the freeways were jammed with traffic *and* there was a three car pileup, it was over two and half hours later that we finally parked in the lot beside the large, glass fronted building on Montgomery.

I curled my cramped legs out from behind the passenger side of Ava's GTO, and we both took a moment to shake feeling back into our limbs before walking through the entrance.

A woman with short gray hair and small, tasteful diamond earrings greeted us from behind the front counter. "Are you here for today's furniture auction?" she asked, peering up at us from a pair of bifocals. "If so, you can pick up your bidder number here. The auction will begin in an hour in room 3A."

I shook my head and gave her a smile. "I was actually hoping to have a closer look at a piece that is being offered in next week's artwork auction."

The woman nodded. "All of the larger items are on display in the canary room." She lifted one hand to gesture behind her. "Straight down there and to the right. Gladys should be out on the floor if you have any questions."

We thanked her and stepped around the front counter. Though the outside of the building was clean and sophisticated, I was surprised to find the interior a bit cramped and cluttered. Nearly every square inch of the walls was lined with old framed photos and paintings, and a large showroom featured a sprawl of furnishings and tables covered in knickknacks and various items that were up for bid. It reminded me of an antique flea market.

I slowly made my way through the large room, scanning the walls for any sight of the Pablo Miscetti landscape.

"There," Ava whispered beside me.

I followed her pointed finger and spotted it near the back-left corner, hanging between a painting of a bouquet of white lilies and a portrait of a young, rosy-cheeked girl with brown curls. I quickened my pace, sidestepping around a plush red velvet sofa with ornate, carved wooden arms, Ava a beat behind me.

I came to a stop in front of the painting and stared up at the work.

"So how do we tell if it's the original or the fake?" I whispered to Ava.

My friend bit her lip, squinting her eyes at the canvas. Finally she shrugged. "Beats me."

"We should have brought David Allen." Words I never thought I'd utter, but in hindsight his expertise could have come in handy right about then.

"I don't know," Ava whispered back. "If Justin is really this good, you think even David could tell the two canvases apart?"

I had no idea. I just knew that I felt like this trip was starting to veer into wild-goose-chase territory.

"May I help you ladies?" A voice pulled my attention to the right. I looked up to find a middle-aged woman in a black pantsuit standing a few feet away. A silver-plated nametag reading *Gladys Brown* was pinned just below her collar.

"We were just admiring this piece," Ava said, giving her a wide smile.

"It's called *Sunlit Pasture*, and it was painted in 1863 by—"

"Pablo Miscetti," I finished for her.

"I see you know your art history," she said, her tone indicating her surprise.

"We're big fans of Miscetti's work," Ava explained.

"Well, this is a lovely example, isn't it?" Gladys asked, turning to the piece. "The way he captures the sunlight through the trees feels almost magical."

"Uh, how long has it been in your possession?" I asked.

She frowned at the odd question. "Oh, I'm not sure. I'd say at least three weeks. Maybe four? This painting is coming up at the end of the month, and we usually like to have items available for display well ahead of the scheduled auctions."

"Has it been out on the floor this whole time?" I asked, glancing around me for any visible sign of security cameras or guards. I was having a hard time seeing how Justin could surreptitiously swap out the large canvas without anyone noticing.

"Most of the time," she said, nodding. "Why do you ask?"

"Uh, we were just wondering how much interest it's generated." Ava shot her that sunny smile again.

"Oh. Yes, well, I'm sure there will be plenty of interest. Miscettis don't come up for sale very often."

"Can I ask if you've had this authenticated?" I said, feeling myself grasping.

She frowned. "I'm sure it has been. We collect paperwork on all items. We would never take on items that have a dubious provenance." She leaned in confidentially. "You never can be too careful with forgeries out here, you know?"

How careful was exactly what I wanted to know.

"Any chance we can get a look at that paperwork?" Ava asked. "You know, just to reassure ourselves it's authentic before we bid on it next week."

Gladys frowned again before nodding slowly. "I don't suppose there's any harm in that. I'll, uh, have to see if Mr. Keller is in his office. You don't mind waiting a moment?"

"Not at all!" Ava showed off two rows of white teeth.

Gladys turned and walked back the way she'd come.

Anticipation mounted in my chest as we waited for her to return, staring at the painting until my eyes started to blur for any indication it had recently been in the Art Initiative. If it was really over a hundred years old, there was no sign of wear or dust. Then again, if the owner was trying to get top dollar for a piece worth almost half a million, chances were he'd had it professionally cleaned first.

Beside me, Ava leaned in and sniffed at the painting.

"What are you doing?" I whispered.

She shrugged. "Just trying to see if it smelled like fresh paint."

That wasn't a half bad idea. I leaned in, too, getting my nose close enough to the canvas that it was almost touching and taking a big whiff.

"Excuse me!"

I spun around to find Gladys staring at the two of us with a perplexed look on her face. "What are you doing?"

"I like to employ all five senses when enjoying art," Ava said quickly.

"Uh-huh." Gladys didn't look convinced.

"So you do have proof the painting was authenticated?" I asked, trying to ignore the heat in my cheeks.

"Uh, yes." She opened the manila folder in her hand and moved to stand between us, showcasing the documentation inside. It was paperwork I was sure any art collector would be familiar with. Which would have been great if we were actual art collectors. As it was, I was staring at a bunch of grading numbers and insider jargon without a clue what they meant.

"I take it this means it is an original Miscetti?" I finally asked.

Gladys nodded. "Yes. It was authenticated by the Foxton Foundation. They're incredibly reputable."

"When was this done?" Ava asked, peering down at the documentation. "Recently? Like, after it arrived here at the auction house?"

"No." She shook her head. "No, I believe the owner had this done prior to bringing it to us." She scanned a finger down the page until she got to the section in question. "Yes, you can see here, the receipt is signed and dated from about six months ago."

She was right. I could see that plainly. But it wasn't the date that had my attention. It was the name of the painting's owner who had signed the paperwork.

Edward Somersby.

CHAPTER SEVENTEEN

———

"It all makes sense now," Ava said as we made the trek back up 101 to Sonoma. "Edward owns the Miscetti. *That's* why he was at Justin's studio."

"You think he knew that Justin was planning to forge the painting?" I asked.

Ava nodded, keeping her eyes on the road. "Yes. Because Edward is the one who told Justin to forge it!"

"Wait—you think Edward paid Justin to forge his own painting?"

"Who better to swap them out?" Ava said, turning in her seat to face me. "Let's say Edward brings the real painting to the auction house. It's all authenticated because it *is* authentic. But then he hires Justin to create a replica, and somewhere along the line he swaps the two paintings out."

I nodded. "I supposed it wouldn't be that odd for the painting's original owner to ask to see the item at the auction house. Maybe even as it's being packaged up to ship to the new owner?"

"Right. Then Edward pockets the proceeds from the auction, but he still has the original Miscetti."

"That's a lot of trouble to go through just to hang on to the painting," I mused.

"Maybe he didn't intend to hang on to it. Maybe he was going to sell it privately."

I glanced at her across the interior. "How would he do that?"

She shrugged. "I dunno. But there's got to be a black market for art, right? I mean, paintings get stolen all the time.

They resurface years later...you know money must have changed hands."

"In this case a lot of money," I noted.

"Four hundred grand," Ava reminded me. "People have killed for less."

"So, you think Freddie somehow found out about Edward's plans...and Edward killed him?" I asked, mental gears turning.

Ava nodded. "Or maybe Freddie found out and tried to blackmail Edward over it. Get his hand as deep in the family cookie jar as he could before he pulled his usual disappearing act."

"And maybe he told Bridget about it," I mused, puzzle pieces falling into place as I watched the passing fields out the window. "That could have been one of the secrets she said she knew about the Somersbys."

"She could have tried to pick up where Freddie left off with the blackmail. Told Edward she would keep quiet for a fee."

I bit my lip. "You know, it actually doesn't sound that farfetched."

Edward Somersby had been the first person on my radar as having possibly killed Freddie. And with all we knew now, he was right back up there at the top of the list again.

* * *

Ava dropped me back off at the winery before heading to Silver Girl to catch the bulk of the afternoon crowd. The first thing I did was try calling Grant, but unfortunately it went straight to voicemail. I left a message asking him to call me back before I wandered into the kitchen and made myself a quick lunch of a turkey and avocado sandwich.

While I did *not* plan to tell Grant about our trip into The City, I did think the fact that Edward owned the original Miscetti that Justin had been painting a copy of was info he should have. It was the one piece that tied it all together, and the more I thought about it, the more I could see Edward Somersby in the role of Freddie's killer.

Edward had been to see Juliet in her dress before the ceremony—he could have easily gotten some of the feathers from the dress on him that transferred to the crime scene. His whereabouts were unaccounted for, for at least twenty minutes in the time frame Freddie had died. He hadn't been a fan of Freddie's to begin with, and if his future son-in-law had turned to blackmail, that could well have been the thing that tipped Edward over the edge. Or, maybe it had been a culmination of things—the info Edward had gotten from the PI about Freddie's aliases, the blackmail over the painting, and possibly even finally seeing Freddie sneak off with Bridget McAllister to the terrace just moments before he was supposed to marry Edward's daughter.

I polished off the sandwich and checked for a return call from Grant (none) before I made myself sit at my desk to respond to some of the vendor messages that had been piling up. I'd managed to put off most of them—at least for a little while longer—by the time the bus of tourists from Okinawa pulled up that afternoon. The group was jovial and tipsy, having already hit two other wineries that day, which made for a lively tasting where several cases of wine were ordered to be delivered to their hotel.

As happy as I was with the outcome of the afternoon, my mind was elsewhere the entire time. After the bus finally departed, I checked my phone again for any call back from Grant.

Nothing.

I really should leave the entire thing to him. He was, after all, the professional.

But murder, forgery, and false alibis aside, if Edward really was guilty, I was one of his victims, too. While I'd lived to tell the tale, he'd knocked me out cold. I still had the headache to prove it. And, there was the not-so-small matter of our bill that he still had not paid. Really, it would be irresponsible of me as a business owner to not try one last time to collect.

Having talked myself into it—or at least prepared a reasonable defense if Grant caught me in the act of it—I grabbed my purse, told Jean Luc to lock up when he was done cleaning up the tasting room, and hopped into my Jeep back toward the Belle Inn B&B.

Twenty minutes later, I was relieved to see the Somersbys' Mercedes in the parking lot. I pulled into an empty slot a few spots down from it and quickly beeped my Jeep locked before traversing the small pathway beside the back garden to the Victorian.

It looked much less ominous now in the daylight, though it somehow looked tired and sad, as if the house itself had known the tragedy that had occurred there. Shutters were closed, curtains drawn, and lights muted against the late afternoon chill as crime scene tape fluttered in the breeze, the soft flapping of plastic audible over the muffled conversation of the still present crime scene techs and the uniformed officer standing guard over the scene.

I tried to ignore the hollow feeling in the pit of my stomach as I passed by the spot of Bridget's last breath on earth. I quickly made my way around to the front of the building and pushed inside. As soon as I did, I was greeted by the sound of raised voices coming from the parlor.

I paused, shooting a quick look in the direction of the reception counter.

Empty.

I took a step toward the conversation I could hear escalating quickly.

"...told you to leave me alone, Justin!" a woman's voice said.

Justin? Iiiinteresting. My heart sped up as I peeked around the door frame to the parlor.

Juliet Somersby was standing by the large picture window, arms crossed over her chest, her eyebrows drawn down and lips pursed in anger as she faced her ex-boyfriend. Justin's back was to me, but I recognized the shaggy blond hair and baggy jeans dotted with paint.

"Jules," Justin said, his voice lower. "You don't mean that."

"You bet I do!"

"Just give me a chance to explain—"

"No," she snapped, cutting him off. "There's nothing left to say."

"*I* have things to say to you," Justin said.

He shifted his stance, and I feared being spotted, so I quickly ducked back into the hallway. Though, with the way Juliet was shouting, I had no problem hearing the conversation as the pair continued.

"Go! Just go, Justin!"

"Jules, please—"

"Can't you understand I'm in mourning?"

The sound of heels clacking across the wooden floor was my only warning that Juliet was headed my way. Not wanting to be caught eavesdropping, I stepped to the side, pressing my body against the wall beneath the stairs as she stalked out of the parlor and down the hall. Though she didn't so much as glance in my direction, I caught a glimpse of her expression in the hallway mirror. Her complexion was ruddier than usual, and her features were tight with anger.

Justin appeared a moment later, and I froze, thinking very quiet thoughts. Though he, too, seemed singularly focused and didn't glance my way.

"Juliet, wait!" Justin called, taking off in the same direction she'd just disappeared.

I stayed where I was, hugging the wall in the shadows, until I heard his footfalls fade into the distance. I wondered what Justin had been doing there. Juliet had clearly been upset with him about something. Was she still angry with him about his altercation with Freddie? Or had she found out about his arrangement with her father to pawn off the counterfeit artwork?

I glanced up and down the hall to make sure I was alone and gingerly stepped from my hiding place and past the parlor door, noting that the room was now empty. Then I backtracked to the reception counter again, though that was still empty too. I wondered if the previous evening's events had scared Sam into staying away that day. Or maybe she was just busy supervising the police work going on outside.

"Hello?" I called softly. I gave a quick look around, but no one seemed to be on duty at the moment. I pursed my lips together, spying the ledger book I knew Sam had used on previous occasions to find guests' room numbers. I did a quick angel-shoulder-devil-shoulder thing, but the devil hardly had to make a case to win this one.

I quickly stepped around the counter and scanned my index finger down the list until I came to the names of Edward and Meredith Somersby. They were in room 7A.

I jumped back around the counter, feeling my pulse quicken with guilt, and took the stairs two at a time up toward the guest rooms. I reached the top landing and found a door labeled 1A. One down from it was 2A. I continued following them until I reached a bend in the hallway, where I stopped short.

At the end of the second floor hallway stood Natalie Weisman.

Her back was turned toward me as she leaned against one of the doors, jiggling the handle.

I ducked back around the corner again as she sent a gaze over her shoulder, as if making sure that she was alone. I paused a moment, then peeked my head back around. She was still jiggling the handle. It was clear she was trying to get into the locked room…and just as clear that she didn't have a key. She had some small object in the keyhole, but she was doing a lot of wiggling and a little cursing as she tried to get the door to open. After a few more seconds of trying, the knob finally turned in her hand. She wasted no time, slipping into the room and closing the door behind her.

Had I just witnessed Natalie break into the room of another guest?

To my immediate left was a glass-paned door that led out onto a large balcony overlooking the garden. Making a split-second decision, I walked out onto the porch and carefully shut the door behind me so as not to make any noise. Then I tiptoed past the first two windows, coming to a stop beside the third.

I pressed my body against the side of the house and leaned in, squinting as I tried to see through the thin, gossamer curtain. I could make out Natalie's dark hair and her slim frame as she moved about the room, opening and closing drawers and stooping to pull a suitcase out from under the four-post canopy bed.

Through the open closet door, I recognized the cream-colored dress that Juliet had worn on the day of the wedding rehearsal.

Natalie was going through Juliet's things.

I watched the dark-haired woman place the luggage on the bed. She began to rifle through it, pulling blouses out of the little pink suitcase and tossing them aside. She was definitely searching for something.

Whatever it was, she didn't find it in the luggage, and I watched her frown as she turned to a tall chest of drawers then systematically went through each one. After a minute, she paused and removed a purple silk pouch from the third one down, and her expression immediately brightened. She opened the small bag and peered inside. Reaching her hand in, Natalie retrieved something too small for me to see at a distance. She dropped it in her pocket and began to stuff Juliet's clothes back into the suitcase.

"What are you doing?" A man's voice sounded close behind me.

I jumped, bumping my head against the window in the process.

Whirling around, I found Justin Hall standing behind me on the balcony. His hands were on his hips, and a scowl stretched across his lean face. I'd been so engrossed in watching Natalie as she plundered through Juliet's possessions that I must not have heard him approach.

"Why are you spying on Juliet?" he demanded.

"I wasn't!" I said quickly.

"Then what are you doing looking in her window?"

"Uh..." I flicked a glance back through the window and saw that Natalie had disappeared. The room was now empty. *Crap.* She must have heard us and gotten spooked.

I swallowed and turned back to face Justin. "I was just... I was looking for the Somersbys," I said, sticking as close to the truth as possible. "I have a bill that still needs paid."

"That's Juliet's room."

"Uh, is it?" I glanced back through the window. "I...I don't suppose you've seen her?" I asked, knowing full well he had.

"Juliet's not here," Justin told me, the suspicion in his eyes not waning. "She left." His jaw twitched.

"Oh. Uh, you don't happen to know where I could maybe find Juliet's father, do you?"

He paused a beat, probably still not sure if he should trust me. Finally he said, "Downstairs. On the side porch."

"Right. Great. Thanks!" I gave him a big smile.

One that he did not return as I quickly side-stepped past the man. I could feel his eyes on me as I practically ran inside and back down the stairs.

My heart rate had almost returned to normal when I reached the front doors again and followed the front porch as it wrapped around the south side of the building. Stepping out into the sunlight, I shaded my eyes with my hand as I spotted both Edward and Meredith Somersby seated in a pair of chairs facing a white picket fence brimming with morning glory vines still awaiting their spring buds. While the setting was serene, the expressions on the couple's faces were not. If I had to guess, this was round number two of the altercation I'd witnessed in the parking lot the day before—only this round was much quieter and filled with restrained tension rather than outright anger.

I paused, wondering if I should intrude.

As I glanced around, I noticed Andrew a few paces away, sipping from a cup of coffee as he watched the police proceedings at the back of the house from a distance. To my left, I spied Baker on a small patch of lawn below the porch, cell phone to his ear as he chatted with someone. He looked up and saw me, giving a short nod of recognition before turning his attention back to his conversation.

Considering I had at least two witnesses within earshot, I sucked in a deep breath and approached the Somersbys.

Edward spotted me first, a frown pulling his mouth down in a way that created deep rivets in his skin on either side.

"Miss Oak," he said, his courteous tone sounding forced. "What brings you here?"

"I was hoping to speak to you," I replied. "Uh, about a financial matter."

Meredith's expression tightened at my words.

Edward shook his head. "Now is not a good time."

"When would be a good time?" I pressed.

His frown turned into a downright scowl. "In light of the recent events, I would imagine your bill could wait."

I swallowed, trying not to lose my nerve in the face of his obvious displeasure. "Perhaps," I agreed, though really it couldn't wait all *that* much longer. "But there's another matter I'd actually like to discuss with you."

His bushy eyebrow went up, and his wife turned a questioning gaze my way as well.

I licked my lips. "About your art collection?"

The scowl froze on Edward's face as the color drained from his skin in a way that told me Ava and I had been right about the Miscetti.

Meredith, on the other hand, still looked confused. "I don't understand. Our art collection?"

"Uh, maybe you and I should talk in private," Edward told me, quickly recovering himself. He rose from his chair, and I couldn't help but notice that his balance was a bit unsteady.

"Edward, what is this about?" Meredith asked.

But he waved her off. "Don't worry. I'll handle it."

I suppressed a shudder at that wording. It was the same he'd used before taking off for Justin's art studio the day before—and possibly bashing me on the head. Which made me slightly reluctant as he motioned for me to follow him down the steps toward the lawn.

"Let's take a walk, shall we," he said. Clearly a demand and not a suggestion.

I bit my lip, glancing around. Both Andrew and Baker were still within eyesight. I supposed as long as there were witnesses...

I complied, following him until we were far enough out of Meredith's earshot for him to feel comfortable. He turned to face me as we came up against the fence full of vines.

"Alright. What do you know about my art collection?" he asked, challenging me as he crossed his arms over his chest.

"I know you're selling some of it."

His nostrils flared, telling me I'd hit a nerve, even though he said nothing.

"You have a Miscetti up for auction next week, in fact," I continued.

"So what if I do?" he spat out. "It's my art. I can sell it whenever I want to."

"And you want to now?"

"I-I I'm tired of looking at it."

I couldn't help the *get real* look that escaped me. "It's worth almost half a million dollars. You can't tell me that its value is purely decorative to you."

He blinked at me, probably trying to figure out how much I already knew before amending his lie. "Fine. I'm liquidating a few assets. Exactly what business is this of yours?"

I ignored his question, answering it with one of my own. "Why are you selling this particular painting?"

"Excuse me?"

I took a deep breath and went for broke. "Is it because you had Justin Hall paint a replica?"

Edward's eyes snapped to me and flashed with anger. "That's preposterous," he said, voice rising.

"You were at Justin Hall's studio yesterday though, weren't you?" I asked, wondering how far I could push him.

"H-how did you know…" He trailed off, looking flustered. "Have you been following me, Miss Oak?"

Yes. But if he'd been the one to hit me on the head, he already knew that.

"Justin Hall had a perfect replica of *Sunlit Pasture* at his studio. I saw it."

His jaw clenched. "What that degenerate paints is no concern of mine."

"Was it a concern of Freddie's?"

"Freddie?" His eyes narrowed.

"Or should I say Frank?" I asked, watching his reaction.

The flustered looks vanished and were instantly replaced with one that was hard and suddenly menacing.

I glanced around again for my witnesses and noticed to my dismay that Baker had apparently finished his call and left. Andrew too seemed to have vacated the scene. I could see Meredith a few paces away, but I wasn't sure she'd be any match for whatever her husband had in mind as he took a step toward me.

"Be careful what you say, Miss Oak," he warned, his voice low and unmistakably threatening.

Instinctively I took a step backward, feeling myself come up against the fence.

"You wouldn't want to offend the wrong person," he finished.

He stared me down for a beat, eyes hard and threatening the type of violence that could leave a person bleeding to death on a sunny terrace.

Then he abruptly turned and walked stiffly across the lawn, leaving me alone.

I let out a breath I hadn't realized I was holding as I watched him ascend the steps to the porch again, rejoining his wife. He leaned down to say something into her ear.

I could only guess what it was, but Meredith Somersby went rigid. She cut a dark look my way before rising from her seat and following her husband through the back door of the bed and breakfast and disappearing inside.

I took a moment to get my breath under control before I trusted my shaky legs to walk me back to the parking lot. I retrieved my keys from my purse as I did, grateful to be in the familiar protection of my Jeep as I slid behind the driver's seat.

I was still doing deep yoga style breaths when my phone jarred me by buzzing with an incoming text. I pulled it out of my purse, trying to shake the nervous energy, as I checked the screen. It was from Juliet. I swiped to read it.

I need to talk to you.

I stared at the words, wondering what it was she wanted to talk about. Did it have something to do with her altercation I'd witnessed with Justin? Or perhaps the accusation I'd just thrown her father's way—could she have found out about it that quickly? Or maybe the grieving almost-widow was just taking me up on the offer of a shoulder to cry on.

I'm at the B&B now. Meet me here? I sent back. Justin had mentioned that she'd left, but maybe she was still nearby.

However, as her answer came back a moment later, that idea was shot down.

Can't get away now. I'll come to your winery later. 9pm.

I glanced at my dash clock. It was just past five now. Whatever she needed could apparently wait. I wanted to ask just what she was doing that she couldn't get away—not to mention inform her that I had just caught Natalie going through her things!—but that felt like a conversation better had in person. The last thing I wanted to do was upset her or interrogate her. I'd done that to enough of her family already that day.

I'll be there, I told her.

CHAPTER EIGHTEEN

———

I left the B&B, and before heading home to the winery, I stopped by Silver Girl to fill Ava in on my confrontation with Edward. I caught her between customers, and she had much the same reaction I'd had to Edward in person, minus the near heart attack—that he was definitely not acting like an innocent man. I was almost certain he was guilty of trying to sell a forged painting. And considering the disdain he already had for Freddie, I didn't see murdering his future son-in-law as a big leap.

Unfortunately, Ava had a private client coming in that evening, so I left her with a promise of a call tomorrow to let her know what Juliet's request to chat was about. The sun had already sunk into the hill as I made my way home, the sky turning from deep purples streaked with pastel pinks and then to an inky black dotted with thousands of pinprick stars as I pulled up to Oak Valley.

I got out of my car and tried Grant's number again but again got voicemail. Instead of leaving another one, I shot him a quick text.

Call me when you're free.

I traversed the driveway, gravel crunching beneath my feet, and was unlocking the winery's front entrance in anticipation of Juliet's arrival when a response buzzed in.

Everything ok?

While it was short and to the point, I couldn't help smiling at just how quickly it had come.

Fine, I typed back. *Just found out*—I paused, trying to come up with a way that was both truthful about how I'd learned of Edward's involvement with Justin and the forgery as well as seemingly not interfering. Finally I settled on, *an interesting rumor you might want to hear.*

There. That sounded benign and totally innocent. Ish.

I flipped on lights in the tasting room and set my purse on the bar before his response came in.

Stuck in autopsy. Will call later.

I grimaced as I imagined him texting me over the remains of poor Bridget McAllister. I quickly shot back, *No rush. Not an emergency.*

While I was honestly dying to tell him about Edward, the truth was, it really wasn't urgent. Grant had already given the Somersbys the order not to leave town, and even if he hadn't, it wasn't as if Edward felt like a flight risk. His roots in the Bay Area ran deeper than the oak trees dotting the property. And the Miscetti wasn't scheduled to be auctioned off for another week.

I glanced at the time on my phone. 8:43. With a few minutes before Juliet was scheduled to arrive, I stuffed my phone back into my purse and perused the selection of wine Jean Luc had left in the chiller behind the bar. Whatever Juliet had to discuss, it would likely be better done over a glass of Chardonnay. I'd just selected one and stood on tiptoe to grab a couple of glasses from the overhead cupboards, when something outside the back window caught my eye.

A flash of movement between the trees.

I froze, blinking out into the darkness.

Had it been an animal? A person? Or just my overfueled imagination?

I set the bottle down on the counter and moved closer to the window, squinting out into the night.

There it was again. A flash of something dark, moving between the trees again.

I swallowed hard, my mind racing. I grabbed the wine bottle by the neck, holding it like a club as I stepped to the back door and opened it a crack, listening.

Crickets chirped among the vines, and the wind rustled the leaves in the trees, almost sounding like the ebb and flow of waves crashing on the shore. I strained, trying to catch any sound that felt out of place—anything that would break the sleepy serenity of the quiet vineyard.

Nothing.

I licked my lips. "Hello?" I called, my eyes scanning. "Juliet?"

I thought I heard a rustle to my left, but it could have just been the wind.

"Juliet? Is that you?" I asked again. The answering silence only made my nerves more raw, adrenaline pumping in my ears.

I was a second away from jumping back inside, bolting the door, and calling 9-1-1 purely on a suspicious feeling in the creepy darkness.

Then I saw it.

A deer bounded across the meadow where the wedding gazebo still stood as a silent hulking skeleton.

I let out a sigh, the adrenaline rushing out of me. Deer were regular nuisances at the vineyard—I should have guessed that was what my nighttime visitor had been. Unfortunately, they were almost as bad as whatever else I'd been imagining, being the number one pest to pillage a crop of grapes before it could be harvested. In the spring, we often mixed up homemade deer repellant and employed nets to keep them away. At this time of year, there was little for them to nibble, but once they found a spot they thought would yield, it was almost impossible to get them to go without force. And as much as I needed a good harvest, I couldn't bring myself to actually harm any of them. I'd seen *Bambi* too many times.

"Shoo!" I yelled, hoping to scare the creature off. I ran toward the gazebo, still wielding the wine bottle as a weapon above my head. "Scram!"

The deer lifted its head, showing an impressive set of antlers in the moonlight that gave me pause. My wine bottle would be no match against those if he decided to charge.

"Go! Shoo!" I yelled again.

He was still a moment.

Until a sound more menacing than my raised voice startled him.

A loud crack cut through the air, frightening the deer into motion, causing it to scamper away up the hill in a rustle of leaves and rushing limbs.

It had much the same effect on me, as I intuitively ducked, eyes darting around to find the source of the sound.

Then it happened again, the loud crack closer, and I saw a chunk of the wooden post beside me go flying.

I blamed the darkness and the near miss with the deer that my brain was slow to realize what was going on. But as a third shot rang out, this one hitting the wine bottle in my hand and shattering it into tiny shards of glass that rained down on me in a torrent of wasted Chardonnay, it finally became clear.

Someone was shooting at me.

Instinct kicked in, and before I could even make the conscious decision to do so, I was running. The shots had come from somewhere to my right—near the winery buildings. So I ran left, out of the gazebo, and sprinted toward the rows of grapevines. Another shot ripped through the night, and the dirt near my heels flew up in tufts that were so close I heard myself whimper in fear. I nearly lost my balance as I propelled myself down the steep hillside behind the meadow, glad at least I hadn't opted for heels that day as my boots sank into the soft soil.

I struggled to regain my footing as another shot exploded from somewhere behind me, followed by the sound of heavy footsteps. Whoever was shooting at me was moving closer. And their aim would only get better.

I picked up my pace, ducking under the first row of dormant vines. I ran as fast as I could down the rows, weaving in and out where I could in an effort to throw the footsteps behind me off my trail. Even though that seemed futile, as they pounded the dirt louder and louder until I could hear panting accompanying them.

Whoever was behind me was gaining on me.

A sharp cramp tore through my side, and I realized I was not going to outrun my attacker. The best I could do was hope to hide.

My mind was racing as I spied a wheelbarrow that someone had left behind. I ducked behind it, crouching low, trying to figure out who was chasing me. Had I pushed Edward too far that afternoon? Had Natalie seen me spying on her as she'd stolen that mystery item from Juliet's room? Or had Justin seen through my lie about coming to the bed and breakfast to see

Juliet? Perhaps he'd spoken with Edward and had learned that I knew about their art forgery scheme. Could one of the two men have come to the winery to silence me before I told someone else about their plans?

I'd been wrong when I'd told Grant it wasn't an emergency that he know about Edward's plan for the Miscetti—I only prayed not *dead* wrong.

I sucked in a deep breath and held it for what felt like an eternity, straining to hear my attacker's footsteps over the sound of my heart pounding in my ears. Only now the vineyard was eerily silent. I stayed crouched low, breathing in shallow spurts to stay quiet as I strained against the chill in the air to hear anything.

A twig snapped nearby. The noise sounded as if it had come from the next row over.

Still crouching close to the ground, I moved as quietly as I could toward the end of the row and peeked my head around the grapevines, trying to get a look at my attacker.

A figure stood perfectly still at the opposite end of the row, poised as if listening for me to make a sound and give away my hiding spot. It was too dark to make out more than a silhouette, but from the bulky frame, I was almost certain it was a man.

I flinched when my hand accidentally brushed dry leaves, causing them to rustle. I backed up a few steps, ready to retreat into the next row.

But it was too late.

He had heard the noise. He whipped around, and my breath caught in my throat as his face was illuminated in the slim sliver of moonlight.

I'd been wrong. It wasn't Edward Somersby. And it wasn't Justin Hall.

Standing over me, a shiny black handgun pointed at my chest, was the best man.

Baker Evans.

CHAPTER NINETEEN

———

"Don't move," he directed, the gun in his hand much more steady than I felt.

I did as told, freezing on the spot, even though my mind was moving at an alarming rate. Of all the people I might have put in the role of shooter as I'd run through the vineyard, Baker Evans had not even been on my list.

A mistake that suddenly felt very grave.

"Wh-what are you doing?" I asked, even though the gun in his hand kind of made it clear he wasn't there to taste my Pinot Grigio.

"Taking care of loose ends," he replied in a chilling monotone.

Being considered a loose end was never good. "I-I don't understand," I told him truthfully.

"Don't you?" He took a step forward, and I felt my legs moving backward, despite my orders not to move, fear propelling them without a single say-so from me.

"Don't play the dumb blonde, Ms. Oak," he continued. "I overheard you talking to Somersby."

My eyes pinged from the gun barrel up to his face, something clicking. "About the Miscetti?"

He frowned. "About *Frank*," he clarified. "You should have kept your mouth shut about that."

I wholeheartedly agreed in that moment.

"Edward already knew," I blurted out. "He hired a PI to follow Freddie."

Baker's eyes narrowed. "So that's how you knew." He shook his head. "I told Freddie he was getting too sloppy. That his ego was going to get us in trouble. I told him to just stick to the plan."

"The plan to marry Juliet for her money?" I guessed. "You *did* know about it all along."

"Know about it?" He took a step forward, the menace in his voice turning into a growl. "I created it. It was *my* plan."

"Yours?" I breathed out, hearing the shock evident in my voice.

"You thought Freddie came up with this?" He threw his head back and laughed out loud.

The sudden change in his emotions was unnerving. I felt my eyes darting from side to side, looking for any means of escape. All that I could see on either side of me was more rows of vines. The winery buildings were at least a hundred yards away now—way farther than I thought I could get before his gun went off.

"Freddie was an idiot," Baker spat out. "Spent money faster than anyone could make it, and thought he was God's gift to women."

"But he was your friend," I said, still trying to shuffle pieces around in my head to make them fit.

Baker sneered. "Sure. Some friend. You know what he used to call me in high school?"

I shook my head.

"His sidekick." He scoffed. "Without me, Freddie would have been nothing. He wouldn't have even made it through the tenth grade. And still he always thought he was better than me. That he was the star and I was just some poor schlub he let ride his coattails."

"That sounds terrible," I said, trying to appease him.

"Yeah well I was used to that. I could have lived with that, you know? Everyone thinking it was the Freddie show and I was just poor Baker along for the ride. Even though I was the one who did all the hard work. I came up with the ideas. I put everything in motion. It was my plan. And what does he do? Screw it all up over some girl. Some stupid, stupid girl."

I was trying hard to play catch up. "You mean Bridget?"

"What?" Baker shook his head. "No. Juliet."

I paused, a sudden thought occurring to me. "You know, she'll be here any minute. Juliet. She's supposed to meet me at the winery, and when I'm not there, she'll call the police and..." I trailed off as I saw Baker's menacing grin widen into something akin to amusement.

"You women really are gullible, aren't you?" he asked, shaking his head.

I licked my lips. "What have you done with Juliet?" I asked softly, suddenly fearing for her life as well as my own.

"Nothing," he replied, his lips still twisted in a sinister smile. "Don't worry, the princess is fine. Let's just say I *borrowed* her cell earlier today to make sure you'd be here."

My heart sank. Baker had sent the texts. Juliet had never been coming to meet me. No one was. I was alone. "She'll see the texts," I protested feebly.

He shook his head. "You think I'd go through all that trouble just to leave the texts behind on her phone?"

No. Of course he'd have deleted them. He'd covered his tracks. "And you killed Freddie," I said, kind of stating the obvious at that point. But if no one was coming—if I was truly on my own—I had to stall for time to come up with something to save my skin.

He nodded slowly. "You just now putting that together, Einstein?"

"But why?" I asked. "I mean, you said this was all your idea—Freddie marrying Juliet for her money. Didn't you need Freddie for that?"

His eyes narrowed. "Freddie was my puppet. He did what I told him—charmed the women I pointed him at like a trained dog."

"So, you chose the woman. The marks for your con?"

He laughed out loud again. "Wow, someone has been watching too many crime dramas. Our *marks*." He shook his head. "Very dramatic. But, yes, I found wealthy women in need of companionship. I did my research on them—found out their likes, dislikes, soft spots. I groomed Freddie to be exactly what these women wanted—whatever that may be. A Boy Scout for some, a bad boy for others."

"And Juliet?" I asked, trying to keep him talking as I glanced around the vineyard for anything I could use as weapon. Dry leaves and dormant vines were all that stared back at me. "You were planning to con her out of her money too?"

"Juliet wanted a knight in shining armor," he said, his tone mocking. "Fitting for a pampered princess, no? Freddie played the part to a tee. God bless him, he really could turn on the charm when he wanted."

"Then why kill him?" I asked again, having a hard time taking my eyes off the gun. "It sounds like everything was going according to your plan."

"Oh it was," he said. "Until Freddie decided to change it."

"Change it?" I asked.

Baker's eyes went dark, his jaw hard. "I should have watched him more carefully. I should have seen the signs."

"Signs of what?"

"Love!" He spat the word out like it made him sick. "The fool fell in love with her."

I blinked at him. That had been the last thing I'd expected him to say. "Wait—are you saying Freddie actually was in love with Juliet?"

Baker sneered, seeming to barely hear me as he continued talking. "All he was supposed to do was get in and get out. We'd done it half a dozen times before. Charm her, get your hands on her cash, then disappear and do it all over again somewhere else. We were good at it. A team. I was the brains, and he was the face. We were making out like bandits."

"Like you did with Natalie?" I asked.

The wicked grin snaked across his face again. "I don't know how you figured it out about her not being Freddie's cousin, but you did, didn't you?" He wagged his gun at me like he was chastising a naughty child.

I couldn't help my eyes bobbing up and down with it, riveted to the muzzle with some kind of hypnotic fear. I bit my lip to keep from yelling at him to be careful with that thing.

"Yes, we played our little game with Natalie," he confessed, though contrite was the last thing he sounded. "She'd just been through a nasty divorce—easy pickings."

I felt a sudden pang of sympathy for her. "I'm guessing her and Freddie's whirlwind romance in Vegas was not chance?"

"Ha!" Baker barked out the word. "No, it was all by design. *My* design. I found Natalie at a bar one day. Listened to her sad story. Heard how she'd taken her ex for all he was worth—just under a cool million. Then I gave Freddie his script and let his charming face do the rest."

"And once he married her, he took everything," I said, remembering how the PI had told me he'd cleaned out her bank accounts.

"*We* took everything. *We.* You're not getting it. It was my idea, my accounts, my setup." Baker shook his head. "And it was working great until Freddie started getting sloppy."

"You mean, how Natalie tracked Freddie down under his new name."

"I told Freddie to get rid of her. She was going to blow our biggest payday yet."

"But Freddie didn't get rid of her."

"No." Baker shook his head. "He just said he could handle it. That he'd keep her in line until we took off again. He was so sure of his charm, that cocky fool." His eyes narrowed at the memory.

"Whose idea was it for Natalie to be his cousin?"

"Mine, of course," he snapped. "I told you, it was all my idea. Until Freddie deviated from the plan."

"To be with Juliet," I guessed.

Baker turned a menacing look on me, as if I'd had something to do with it. "She was too good. Too sweet. She had him under this spell. This perfect little angel. It should have been so easy—I handpicked her, you know."

"Did you?" I asked. Not that I cared at that point, but the longer I could keep him talking, the longer he'd be not-shooting.

"Daddy's little princess, always got everything she wanted. I knew she'd be an easy target. All Freddie had to do was smile in her direction and the girl practically fell in his lap. And that family of hers." He chuckled, though the sound held more disdain than humor. "They were loaded. Had been forever. All Freddie had to do was string the princess along long enough to get access to her accounts, and we be set. Juliet was so trusting."

"What happened?" I licked my lips, glancing to my right. I knew a row over was where the wheelbarrow sat. I racked my brain, trying to think what I could do with a wheelbarrow, but any way you sliced it, in wheelbarrow vs. gun, gun would win.

"I told you what happened!" Baker snapped. "He fell in love. The moron actually fell for the pampered princess. He said he wasn't going to leave this one. He figured he could have a nice tidy life enjoying Juliet's trust fund for many years."

"Which left you high and dry," I said.

Though, in hindsight, maybe I should have kept that thought to myself, as his face contorted with rage and his gun wobbled in my direction again.

"I was *not* going to let him do that to me. Not after I made him. He would have been nothing without me."

"So you killed him," I said, wondering how I'd missed just how crazy Baker was. Apparently Freddie hadn't been the only one of the pair who had been good at hiding his true self.

"He was getting sloppy." Baker's voice rose, and if we'd been anywhere but an abandoned vineyard late at night, I might have had hope someone would hear us. "First Natalie tracked him down, and then that Bridget trash showed up at the wedding. I told him. On the terrace, after she left. I told him he had to be more careful. That we couldn't go on like this. And you know what he said?"

I licked my lips. "What?"

"He said *we* weren't going on. That he didn't need me anymore. He had Juliet, *and* he had that family of hers eating out of the palm of his hand. And he was going to ride that gravy train for a long time." He took deep ragged breaths, his eyes taking on almost a sad quality as he shook his head. "He didn't need me anymore."

He dragged in air and let out a long, cleansing breath down toward the earth. And when he raised his eyes again to meet mine, the sadness had drained, and it was replaced by a dark, flat quality that was almost scarier than his emotional outburst had been.

"So I had to kill him," he said flatly.

I swallowed hard. "A-and Bridget?" I almost hesitated to ask. "Did you have to kill her too?"

He nodded very slowly. "She knew too much. She showed up at the Belle Inn and threatened to tell the police everything if I didn't pay her to keep quiet. That was a huge mistake on her part."

He took a menacing step toward me.

"Bad things happen to people who try to get in my way," he said, his eyes glittering in the moonlight. "You should have just left it alone, Emmy."

Yep. I should have. And every warning Grant had ever given me to leave all this alone rang in my ears now. Oh, how I longed to live to hear him gloat with an *I told you so.* I shoved that thought down, trying to stave off panic and keep Baker talking.

"Is that why you attacked me?" I asked.

He nodded slowly again. "When you came to me about Freddie's previous marriage, I knew you were getting too close to the truth. That it would only be a matter of time before you realized Freddie hadn't acted alone. So, I decided to send you a little warning."

"You followed me to the studio from the B&B," I said, mentally working it out.

"I really did try to send you a warning," he said, as if he'd been doing me a favor by knocking me out cold. "I wish you had taken it."

Me too. More than just about anything right then. I could feel the chill in the air slapping against my face, the panic in my stomach growing that I was out there, alone. With no way to fight back.

With a mad man who had already killed two people.

"What about the feathers?" I asked, grasping for ways to stall.

Baker looked confused. "Feathers?"

"From Juliet's dress. The police found them on the terrace near Freddie's body."

Baker tipped his head back and laughed again. "Is that why the police were so focused on poor little Juliet?" He shook his head. "I honestly haven't the foggiest." He paused. "Maybe Saint Juliet *is* keeping some secrets from us after all, huh?"

I doubted that, but I had a strict policy to not argue with men who had me at gunpoint.

"And the Miscetti?" I asked, feeling my time running out. I took a small step backward, but came up against the vines. There was nowhere to go. I was trapped.

Baker shook his head. "I wish Freddie had consulted me before he did that. I would have told him it was a bad idea. Too greedy."

"He found out about Edward's plan to sell the forgery?"

"He did," Baker confirmed. "Thought he could hold it over the old man's head to keep him in line. If I'd known, I would have stopped him. Men like Somersby don't take kindly to that sort of thing. But Freddie thought he could handle it all. Charm all of them into doing whatever Freddie wanted. Stupid, cocky fool," he snarled. "He should have just kept his mouth shut."

He paused, his eyes meeting mine. "You should have too."

"Me?" I squeaked out, my heart thumping in my chest so hard that it hurt.

He took a step forward. "You should have left it alone, Emmy. You should have just let the Somersbys handle their mess. They had enough money. Juliet never would have gone to jail over it."

He was right. On so many levels. But mostly that I should have left it alone. Freddie's scheme had been unraveling before his eyes, even before he'd died, and it was only a matter of time now before it all came out. Grant was a good cop. He would have figured Baker out.

Only now, it might not be before Baker took a third victim.

"Look, I won't tell anyone," I said, knowing how feeble those words sounded even to my own ears.

Baker gave me a condescending smile. "Nice try."

I swallowed hard. "You won't get away with this," I said, trying another tactic. "The police will figure out it was you."

He shrugged. "Maybe. Eventually. But I don't plan to stick around Wine Country any longer. I'll be halfway to Mexico by the time anyone even finds your body, Emmy."

I felt my breath come fast at the way he was already talking about me as if I were a dead body. Tears pricked the back of my eyes as I realized he could be right. No one knew I was with him. It would be morning before anyone even missed me. Maybe hours later before they'd come looking for me. No one would have any reason to think I'd be in the vineyard. With the vines dormant, it could even be days before anyone came out here. Days before I was found. Plenty of time for Baker to drive the length of California and slip away into the anonymity south of the border.

"Please," I heard myself say as a last ditch effort to appeal to some humanity within him. I suddenly wondered if Bridget had pleaded too. If she'd begged for her life as Baker had strangled the last breath out of her.

"I'm sorry, Emmy," Baker said, though the look on his face held no hint of sympathy. In fact, the way his eyes suddenly lit up and the gun in his hand was rock steady, I had a sick feeling that he was almost enjoying the moment. Feeling some sort of rush at me being so completely at his mercy.

The tears leaked from my eyes, though I couldn't tear them away from the muzzle of the gun as Baker slowly raised it to aim at my head. He took a step forward, and I watched the small hollow metal barrel come closer. My focus blurred so it was the only thing in my world. I could almost feel its cool, deadly touch.

I shivered—from fear, the cool night air, the desperate sadness of everything that would be left behind.

I closed my eyes and steeled myself for the inevitable.

A shot rang through the air—loud, brief, and sharp enough to make me jump.

I stopped breathing, and it took me a moment to realize I wasn't dead.

I opened my eyes, sucked in air, and watched the world sway in front of me.

Wait—no, it wasn't the world that was swaying. It was Baker.

My heart pounded as I watched him blink in surprise, his mouth moving up and down wordlessly. His body teetered back and forth on his feet in precarious balance before he finally keeled forward with a crash that made me jump again.

I tore my eyes from the bright red spot spreading across his back to look upward, across the field. Two rows over I saw a figure outlined in the moonlight and the faint whiff of smoke rising from a gun in its hands.

For a brief moment fear was renewed, thinking I'd just traded one gunman for another, before the figure called out.

"Emmy! Are you okay?"

I cried out in relief as I recognized the voice. Grant.

"Emmy?" Apparently my cry did nothing to alleviate his concern, as he crashed through the rows of vines toward me.

Before I could attempt to answer him again, he was at my side, arms wrapped tightly around me, as I cried into his shoulder.

"It's okay," he said, his hand in my hair, lips whispering at my temple. "You're safe now. Everything is going to be okay."

And for the first time in days, I actually believed that.

CHAPTER TWENTY

———

"Please tell me *that* is not an option tonight?" Eddie gaped at me as I held up a little black dress that I had thought was actually kind of cute. Ruffled hem, long sleeves, cowl neck.

"What's wrong with this?" I asked, smoothing down the skirt.

"Nothing," Eddie said, eyes wide as he shook his head. "If you're a nun going to a funeral."

Ava snorted. "He's right. Show some skin, girl."

I reluctantly put the LBD back into my closet. "It's January. My skin will freeze," I mumbled.

It had been just over a week since my altercation with Baker in the vineyard, and Grant had finally closed the file on Freddie Campbell, aka Frank Campbell, aka Alfred Camptown—whose *real* name turned out to be Alfred Campbell Clark—and Grant had asked me to dinner to celebrate. I had, of course, said yes. When I hadn't bargained for was the entourage who had insisted they needed to help dress me for my "hot date." (The entourage's words—not mine.)

When Grant had called to let me know the case was officially closed, it had been the first time we'd really had a chance to talk since the shooting—both of us having been caught up in various forms of damage control immediately afterward. Grant had finally given me his version of the events of that evening that ended in my vineyard. He'd told me that as soon as he'd finished attending Bridget McAllister's autopsy, he'd decided to make a personal visit to the winery instead of calling me back. He'd arrived just in time to hear gunshots and had finally found us in the vineyard, catching the very tail end of Baker's confession before discharging his own gun.

While Grant's timing could not have been better, the fact that Baker had been killed ensured that not only were police, crime scene techs, and the medical examiner swarming my winery in a matter of minutes afterward, but Internal Affairs had also gotten involved, doing a thorough investigation of Grant having shot someone in the line of duty. Again.

I'd felt a whole host of emotions about that, ranging from relief to guilt to fear over what might happen to him next. The first time he'd killed someone on the job, he'd been transferred to Wine Country. Luckily, as of yesterday, IA had deemed his use of force as necessary, and Grant was off the hook. At least professionally. Personally, I wasn't sure how it all sat with him.

Though, the fact that he'd asked me out to dinner that night was a positive sign.

"What about red?" Ava asked, pulling a low cut red number from my closet. "This dress would look fab on you."

"*That* is a shirt," I told her, taking the hanger from her and holding the item up to my chest. The hem hit just a smidgeon below my booty.

"With the right boots, it's a dress to die for," Eddie decided.

"How about the right boots *and* a pair of leggings," I asked, going for a compromise.

My gruesome fashion twosome must have realized that was the best they were going to get out of me, as Eddie nodded and Ava reluctantly agreed with, "Fine. But we're leaving the top two buttons undone."

"Deal," I said, mentally crossing my fingers behind my back. Hey, I could always button them back up again as soon as Grant picked me up.

Clothing decided upon, I let Eddie advise on the right boots (thigh high with three-inch heels) and Ava advise on the jewelry (simple earrings and a large pendant to—as she put it—draw the eye to the cleavage). I topped it all off with a smoky eye thing and lot of hair product and blow drying, and the end result was pretty darn good. Even if there was a little more of my cleavage showing than felt totally comfortable.

I grabbed my purse, and the three of us made our way from my cottage to the tasting room, where Grant had said he'd meet me.

I spotted him right away at the bar sipping a glass of Pinot Noir, and, I kid you not, my heart actually did a little flutter. He was dressed in casual jeans and a button down, minus the blazer, that showed off just how nicely his biceps filled out a dress shirt. The sleeves were rolled up, exposing tanned forearms, and he was sans tie, the top button on his shirt undone, giving him a softer, more casual feel. His hair looked damp, as if fresh from a shower, his face was clean shaven, and I caught the faint hint of his musky aftershave from a few paces away. I almost felt a little regret at the fact we were going out that night. Suddenly I could think of a whole lot of fun we could have staying in.

I blamed the hormone rush that it took me a moment to realize he was not alone.

I watched Jean Luc fill a second glass and slide it across the bar to Grant's companion—David Allen. In contrast to my date, David looked like he'd come straight from a daylong binge of playing video games and smoking pot—his jeans torn, his black T-shirt just a little too loose, and his dark hair pulled back in a messy man bun. He laughed at something Grant said as he took a long swig of his wine, and I wondered what they were talking about. Usually when law enforcement appeared, the card shark took that as his cue to leave.

David was the first to look up as we entered the room. "Wow," he said, setting his glass down as he gave my outfit a once-over. "Someone is looking to get lucky tonight." He grinned at Grant and gave him a wink.

My cheeks suddenly felt as red as my low cut shirt. I self-consciously buttoned it back up one. "David," I said, glancing at his glass. "Here for the free wine again?"

"And the company. I was just having a lovely chat with your detective here."

I was about to protest that he wasn't *my* detective, but with how good he looked—and smelled now that I was up close—I was rethinking that issue.

"Hey," Grant said, rising from his barstool to give me a quick peck on the cheek.

"Hey yourself," I replied.

"You look lovely." His eyes strayed only the slightest to the cleavage-highlighting pendant Ava had loaned me. I made a mental note to later thank her with a bottle of wine from our special section of the cellar.

"Thanks," I said, still blushing.

"Is it weird to invite you to join us for a glass of wine at your own winery?" Grant asked, indicated the barstool next to him as he gave me a crooked grin.

"Not at all," I told him. He could have invited me to go to Mars right then, and I would have been delighted.

Jean Luc pulled a glass down for me, adding another one for Ava as she sat next to David. Eddie walked around the bar and grabbed his own, which earned him a scowl from Jean Luc, but it was hardly a deterrent.

"I was telling Detective Grant, here," David said, "that I've just come from an auction at San Francisco Bay Auctions."

"Oh?" I asked, tearing my eyes off the hunk of man beside me to give David my attention. "The Pablo Miscetti?"

David nodded. "Uh-huh."

"How much did it end up going for?" Ava asked, sipping from her glass.

"Four hundred and seventy-two."

Eddie did a low whistle. "Wow. Let's hope that helps the Somersbys pay their bill now." He nodded in my direction.

After the truth about Freddie had come to light, and law enforcement had once again swarmed the B&B with questions for the wedding party, Edward Somersby had broken down and admitted that, yes, he had been selling off his art collection. At first, as he'd told me, he'd just been looking to liquidate a few items to pay off creditors. Turns out that while the Somersbys' holdings were plentiful, their debts were just as large. I wasn't the only person Edward Somersby had been putting off paying. In fact, he'd been in such serious need of cash, he'd started skimming from other accounts—including his and his wife's retirement accounts. Which had actually been the missing money I'd overheard Meredith arguing with him about when I'd eavesdropped in the parking lot. Edward had been hoping to "handle it" and replace the money by selling the Miscetti.

That's when he'd thought of Juliet's ex-boyfriend, Justin Hall.

We'd been right in assuming Edward had commissioned Justin to paint *Sunlit Pasture* for him. According to Justin—who had been more than cooperative with police once they'd told him Edward was spilling everything—Edward had planned to auction the painting, swap it out for a fake, then resell the original again on the black market—essentially collecting twice for the same painting.

Luckily for the pair of them, Edward had yet to make the switch. The fake painting had still been sitting in the back storage room of Justin's art studio. So no crime had been committed—only planned. Both Edward and Justin had been let off with warnings, and according to Juliet, Edward and Meredith were downsizing their lifestyle while he tried to liquidate more assets to pay off their debts. Legally this time.

"One can only hope my bill is near the top of his pile," I said, mentally making a note to put in a call to him tomorrow.

"Well, I will tell you one thing," David added, lifting his glass to his lips. "That fake *Sunlit Pasture* was good. I mean, scary good. I'm not sure I would have been able to tell them apart."

"Justin finally gave you a look at it?" I asked.

David nodded. I knew he'd been to visit the Art Imitative a couple of times since Justin had been cleared of any suspicion. "He did. Not really my cup of tea, artistically speaking, but the kid has some serious talent."

"His original work was thought provoking," Ava added.

I had to agree, even if the dark sort of thoughts they provoked were not ones I wanted running around in my head. "Maybe you two should do a show together," I suggested to David.

He shrugged. "The thought crossed my mind." He paused. "Of course, it will have to wait until after he and Juliet get back from Cancun."

"Wait—Juliet and Justin?" Eddie asked.

I nodded, realizing I hadn't filled him in yet on that development. "He and Juliet decided to give things another try. She's taking him to Mexico to get away from everything for awhile at one of her family's resorts."

The morning after my confrontation with Baker, I'd called Juliet at the B&B, sure that news of everything—Baker's death, Freddie's con, and Bridget's relationship with her fiancé— had reached her by that point. I'd been surprised at how well she'd taken it. Of course she'd been devastated to learn she'd been conned and angry that Freddie had lied to her...but the fact that he'd been willing to leave that whole lifestyle behind for her and that he had truly loved her, at least as much as Freddie had the capacity to love anyone, had been something of a comfort. She'd confessed to me that even while she'd fallen for Freddie's charm, part of her had been unable to stop thinking about Justin and what might have been.

Apparently Justin had felt the same way—he'd gone to the rehearsal dinner that night to ask her to give him one last chance, but he'd only gotten as far as the parking lot before Freddie had waylaid him and they'd come to blows. When I'd overheard Justin and Juliet arguing at the B&B in the parlor, he'd been trying once again to convince her to give their relationship another chance. At the time, Juliet had been mourning the death of a man she thought had been devoted to her. When the truth came out about Freddie, Juliet said it somehow freed her to leave that part of her life behind and start anew with Justin. And this time, she said her father had no say in the matter.

"I'm happy for her," Ava said, licking a stray drop of Pinot off her lower lip.

I nodded in agreement. "With everything she's been through, she deserves some happiness."

"And what's more fun than a hot, brooding artist?" Ava joked.

David Allen's eyebrows rose as he swiveled in his seat to grin at her.

I mentally moved having a chat with Ava about flirting with David to the top of my to-do list, as I watched her wink back at him.

"What I want to know," Eddie said, breaking into my thoughts, "is did you ever find out what Natalie was after in Juliet's room?"

"Juliet's engagement ring," Grant jumped in, fielding that question. "According to Natalie, it was the same one Freddie had given her. He'd taken it when he'd disappeared."

"And he used the same ring to propose to Juliet?" Ava scrunched up her nose. "What a jerk."

"Chances are he'd used it before," I told her, remembering how Baker had referred to the half dozen times his scheme had worked just fine before Freddie had screwed it up. While I knew the police had a good lead on where to start unraveling Freddie's many identities, thanks to a warrant for PI Sean Carter's records, I had a feeling it would be some time before they tracked down all of Baker and Freddie's victims.

"You didn't arrest Natalie for stealing the ring, did you?" Ava asked Grant.

He shook his head. "Juliet decided not to press charges. After she learned everything Natalie had been through, she gave her the ring. Said it was the least she could do."

"Saint Juliet strikes again," David said, raising his glass. Though I wasn't entirely sure if he was giving her a compliment or being sarcastic—his own lifestyle falling several sins short of sainthood.

"And what about the feathers?" Ava asked Grant. "The ones found at the crime scene. Did you ever find out where they came from?"

Grant grinned, but cocked his head to me. "You want to take that one, Emmy?"

"They were there from Edward Somersby."

"No!" Ava set her glass down on the bar with a clink. "So he *did* lie about seeing Freddie the day he died?"

I nodded. "Before the ceremony. He actually headed Freddie off in the parking lot, catching him as soon as he set foot on the grounds, confronting him with what the PI had found out about his past wives. He told Freddie that if he didn't call off the wedding, he'd expose him as a fraud."

"But Freddie didn't call it off," Eddie pointed out.

I shook my head. "According to Edward, Freddie laughed at him. He threatened that if Edward told Juliet about his past wives, Freddie would tell her about Edward's forgery scheme. In fact, Edward said that Freddie tried to tell him they were 'cut from the same scheming cloth' and he looked forward to many more years of working with his 'dad.'"

Ava snorted. "I bet Edward loved that."

"I'm surprised he didn't kill Freddie then," David added.

I shrugged. "Who knows. If he'd been near a bottle of champagne, he might have cracked."

"So that was where he was for the twenty minutes that were unaccounted for," Ava mused.

I nodded.

"Typical blue blood," David said.

I frowned at him. "He was only trying to protect his daughter."

David shook his head. "He could have saved his daughter a lot of grief if he'd just told the police where the feathers had come from before they set their sights on interrogating her." He glanced to Grant. "No offense."

Grant cleared his throat. "Actually, we were never seriously considering Juliet as a suspect."

I blinked at him. "Wait—what?"

He shrugged. "I tried to tell you that. Every time you asked about Juliet."

I thought back to the conversations we'd had. He was right. While I'd pushed him to tell me what he had on Juliet, he'd never confirmed she was a suspect. I'd just assumed at the time that he'd been stonewalling me.

"Then why did you haul her down to the station?" I asked.

"We were actually focused on Edward Somersby at the time. We were hoping to get Juliet to give something away."

Mental forehead smack. "You thought Edward did it?"

Grant shrugged, sipping from his glass.

"So did we," Ava confessed, pointing to David and herself.

"Me too," I admitted.

David laughed, raising his glass to the group in a mock salute. "Well, here's to being wrong, and living to tell the tale of it!"

"Amen to that," I said, shoving aside thoughts of just how close to *not* living to tell of it I'd been.

I tipped my glass back to sip the last of my Pinot, when I felt Grant's hand at the small of my back.

"If we're going to make our reservation, we'd better get going."

I shivered at his touch and nodded, the both of us saying our good-byes to Ava, David, Eddie, and Jean Luc before I grabbed my purse and walked with him out into the chilly evening. I followed Grant to his SUV, where he held the door open for me. But before I could climb inside, he stopped me, one hand going around my waist to spin me toward him.

"That is a very nice dress," he said, his voice low, his breath warm on my cheek, and his eyes dark with all sorts of wicked promises dancing in them.

I licked my suddenly dry lips. "It's a shirt," I said lamely.

His lips curled into a slow smile. "Then it's a very nice shirt." His eyes strayed down to the one button still undone just below my silver pendant.

Despite the cool night, a wave of heat rushed through me as his gaze slowly moved upward again, taking its time to linger on my lips.

"We're going to miss our reservation," I said, my brain suddenly foggy.

His smile widened into a practically wolfish grin as he leaned down, his lips whispering over mine.

"Then maybe we should just stay in."

Oh boy. All five million of my hormones just died and went to heaven.

RECIPES

————

Lobster Tails Thermidor

2 lobster tails (fresh or frozen)
⅔ cup olive oil
2 tablespoons butter
1 shallot, finely chopped
1 ⅜ cups fresh fish stock
¼ cup white wine
¼ cup double cream
½ teaspoon dry mustard
1 tablespoon fresh lemon juice
1 tablespoon tarragon
2 tablespoons chopped fresh parsley
salt and freshly ground black pepper to taste
¼ cup freshly grated Parmesan

Preheat oven to 400°.

With a sharp chef's knife, split the lobster tails in half lengthwise. Brush the lobster with olive oil and bake in the oven for 15 minutes. When cooked and cooled enough to handle, remove the lobster meat from the shells, cut into pieces, and return to the shells.

Melt the butter in a large skillet over medium heat. Add the shallot and sauté until tender. Mix in the fish stock, white wine, and double cream. Bring to a slow boil and cook until reduced by half. Mix in the mustard, lemon juice, tarragon, 1 tablespoon parsley, salt and pepper.

Preheat your oven's broiler.

Place the lobster halves in a shallow baking pan or lipped sheet. Spoon the sauce over the lobster meat in the shell then sprinkle with parmesan cheese. Broil for 3–4 minutes, just until golden brown. Garnish with remaining parsley.

Makes two decadently delicious lobster tails!

Wine Pairings
Best served paired with rich white wines that complement the rich sauce, like a Viognier, Chardonnay, or white burgundy. Some of Emmy's suggestions: Calera Mt. Harlan Viognier, Maison Champy Mâcon Villages, Rebuttel Chardonnay

Brie and Baby Spinach Omelet with Toasted Ciabatta Bread

ciabatta bread
½ cup olive oil
3 large eggs
¼ cup whole milk
salt and freshly ground pepper
1 tablespoon butter
handful of baby spinach
2 oz Brie cheese, thinly sliced

Preheat the oven to 375°.

Slice your ciabatta bread into ½-inch thick slices and lay out on a baking sheet. Brush olive oil on each slice then place the sheet into the oven. Cook for 12–15 minutes.

While your bread is cooking, separate the egg whites and yolks into two bowls.

In one bowl, whisk together the egg yolks, milk, and a small amount of salt and pepper.

In the second bowl, use a handheld mixer to beat the egg whites until they are stiff peak, about 1–2 minutes. Use a spatula to gently fold the egg whites into the egg yolk mixture, just until combined. Don't over fold—it's better to still see some egg whites than over mix.

In your omelet pan, melt 1 tablespoon of the butter over medium heat. Add the egg mixture, evenly distributing it across the pan. Let it cook—without moving it or stirring it—until the middle just starts to set, roughly 4 minutes. Then add the spinach and Brie to one half of the omelet, cover the skillet, and cook until the cheese begins to melt. Carefully fold the empty side over the filled side to enclose and cook for another 1 minute.

Remove the pan from the heat and slide the omelet onto a plate with the toasted ciabatta bread.

Makes one omelet, though it can be large enough to share!

Tips!
Use a 10–12-inch nonstick skillet for your omelet pan—10 if you like them thicker, 12 if you prefer more thin. When adding ingredients to the omelet, leave about an inch between the cheese and edges all around so it doesn't ooze out when you fold the omelet over.

Wine Pairings
Best served paired with acidic white wines that cut through the fatty eggs and cheese, like champagne, Sauvignon Blanc, or a Chardonnay. Some of Emmy's suggestions: Dry Creek Vineyard Sauvignon Blanc, Poco a Poco Chardonnay, Argyle Oregon Brut Sparkling Wine

Crustless Vegetable Quiche

6 eggs
1 cup milk
½ cup grated cheddar cheese
½ cup grated swiss cheese
2 tablespoons parmesan cheese
salt and pepper to taste
⅓ cup chopped broccoli
⅓ cup chopped spinach
⅓ cup chopped green onions
1 tomato, thinly sliced

Preheat your oven to 350°.

In a large bowl, whisk together the milk, egg, cheese, and salt and pepper. Gently stir in the broccoli, spinach, green onions.

Pour the egg mixture into a pie dish and bake uncovered for about 25–30 minutes, or just until the top layer is set. Arrange the thinly sliced tomatoes on the top—in any pattern that looks pleasing to you! Return to the oven for an additional 15–20 minutes until the egg mixture is no longer jiggly and is fully set. Slice and enjoy!

Wine Pairings
As with the omelet, this is best served paired with acidic white wines that cut through the fatty eggs and cheese, like sparkling wines or dry white wines. Some more of Emmy's suggestions that also compliment the vegetables: LaMarca Prosecco, The White Knight Pinot Grigio, Pacific Peak Pinot Grigio

Roasted Eggplant Mozzarella with Homemade Basil Marinara Sauce

4 tablespoons extra virgin olive oil
1 medium yellow onion, peeled and chopped
3 cloves garlic, minced
28 ounce can San Marzano crushed tomatoes
¼ cup freshly chopped basil
1 tablespoon tomato paste
1 teaspoon granulated sugar
1 teaspoon salt
1 large eggplant
2 teaspoons salt
8 ounces mozzarella cheese

For the Sauce:
In a large pot, heat 2 tablespoons of olive oil over medium low heat. Add the onion and sauté until softened and translucent, about 8–10 minutes. Add the garlic and sauté an additional minute then add the crushed tomatoes, basil, tomato paste, sugar, and salt. Stir to combine and simmer uncovered over low heat for 20–30 minutes.

For the Eggplant:
Preheat oven to 375°.

Slice eggplant into about ½-inch slices. Sprinkle with salt and set aside for roughly 20 minutes, to draw out the moisture. Then arrange on a baking sheet and drizzle with olive oil. Bake for 15 minutes or until lightly browned.

In a shallow baking pan, spread a few spoonfuls of the marinara sauce along the bottom. Then arrange the roasted eggplant slices in the pan. Add the remaining marinara sauce then cover with mozzarella cheese. Return to the oven and bake an addition 20–25 minutes, until dish is bubbling and cheese is golden brown.

Makes about 4 hearty servings!

Shortcut!
If you're short on time or ingredients, jarred marinara sauce can be substituted for homemade. For a brighter flavor, stir in some chopped, fresh basil to your jarred sauce before heating. If you're not a fan of eggplant (which even Emmy knows is a hit and miss vegetable), you can substitute zucchini.

Wine Pairings
Best served paired with a rich, bold red to counteract the acidic tomato sauce, like a Cabernet, Pinot Noir, or Merlot. Some of Emmy's suggestions: Titus Cabernet Sauvignon, Menage a Trois Pinot Noir, Duckhorn Vineyards Merlot

French Onion Soup with Sherry

5 tablespoons butter
4 tablespoons vegetable oil
4 medium onions, thinly sliced
1 teaspoon salt
½ teaspoon freshly ground black pepper
½ teaspoon granulated sugar
1 ½ cups dry white wine
6 cups beef broth
1 tablespoon fresh thyme
2 bay leaves
1 baguette
1 garlic clove, cut in half lengthwise
2 teaspoons sherry
4 ounces Gruyère cheese, grated

In a large pot, melt 3 tablespoons butter over medium heat. Add 2 tablespoons of olive oil and onions, cooking until the onions are until softened. Add the salt, pepper, and sugar and continue to cook, stirring occasionally, until onions caramelize, roughly 30–40 minutes. Once caramelized, add wine and raise heat to high to cook off the alcohol, roughly 7–9 minutes. Add broth, thyme, and bay leaves to pot. Bring to a boil then reduce heat to simmer for roughly 30 minutes. Remove from heat then remove the bay leaves and whisk in remaining 2 tablespoons butter.

While the soup is simmering, preheat your oven's broiler.

Slice the baguette into ½-inch slices and place them on a rimmed baking sheet and brush with remaining 2 tablespoons of olive oil. Toast in oven until crisp and dry but not overly browned, about 1 minute per side. Rub one side of each toast with the garlic clove and set aside.

Place ramekins or oven safe bowls on a rimmed baking sheet, add ½ teaspoon of sherry to the bottom of each. Ladle soup into bowls. Top each serving of soup with toast—depending on the size of your bowl, you may need two slices. Divide the grated cheese among the servings, covering the bread and some of the soup. Carefully transfer baking sheet to oven and broil until cheese is melted and bubbling, roughly 5–9 minutes.

Makes about 4 melty servings!

Tips!
You can make the soup ahead and refrigerate, warming later and adding the toast and cheese. The soup can even be frozen for up to 6 months!

Wine Pairings
Best served paired with a rustic Pinot Noir or a rich white Pinot Gris to accentuate the buttery flavors in the cheese and crouton. Some of Emmy's suggestions: Hartford Court Pinot Noir, Jules Taylor Pinot Gris, Thomas Fogarty Santa Cruz Mountains Pinot Noir

Maple Bacon Pancakes

1 lb. bacon, frozen
2 cups all-purpose flour
2 tablespoon baking powder
1 teaspoon salt
3 tablespoons dark brown sugar
2 eggs
1 tablespoon vanilla
1 ¼ cup milk
½ cup maple syrup (plus extra for drizzling)
5 tablespoon butter, melted

Slice frozen bacon into thin slivers and add to a heated skillet. Cook until crispy then drain on a paper towel and set aside.

In a large bowl, whisk the flour, baking powder, and salt.

In another bowl, combine the dark brown sugar, eggs, vanilla, ½ cup maple syrup, milk, and butter.

Add the wet ingredients to the dry ingredients bowl and stir just until combined. Don't over stir or you will break the air bubbles in your pancake batter that make it light and fluffy. Then add in half of the bacon and gently combine.

Heat a lightly oiled griddle or large nonstick skillet over medium-low. Then add about ¼ cup of your batter to the griddle at a time, creating your pancakes. When bubbles begin to form in the batter—roughly 3–5 minutes—flip to the other side. Cook until lightly browned on each side then remove.

To serve, sprinkle a little bit of reserved bacon on each pancake and drizzle with maple syrup.

Tips!
By freezing the bacon before use, it makes slicing it into slivers that crisp up to perfect much easier than with raw bacon.

Shortcut!
Short on time but still craving this salty sweet goodness? Use a pancake mix and decrease the wet ingredients (water or milk) slightly, substituting ½ cup maple syrup until you get the right consistency. Add in bacon and cook as above!

Wine Pairings
Bacon forward dishes are best served with tannic red wines, like a Malbec or Syrah. Some of Emmy's suggestions: Big Basin Santa Cruz Mountains Syrah, Riccitelli Republic Malbec Wine, Recuerdo Malbec

Or, if having this dish earlier in the day, try pairing with the light brunch sangria below!

Brunch Sangria

1 orange, thinly sliced
½ lemon, thinly sliced
20 large strawberries, sliced
1 cup orange juice
1 750ml bottle sweet white wine, like a Riesling
1 750ml bottle champagne or sparkling wine

Place all fruit and orange juice in a large pitcher or bowl, add wine, and allow to sit in the refrigerator for at least 4 hours, though it's best overnight. Right before serving, add champagne.

ABOUT THE AUTHOR

Gemma Halliday is the #1 Amazon, *New York Times & USA Today* bestselling author of several mystery and suspense series. Gemma's books have received numerous awards, including a Golden Heart, two National Reader's Choice awards, a RONE Award for best mystery, and three RITA nominations. She currently lives in the San Francisco Bay Area with her large, loud, and loving family.

To learn more about Gemma, visit her online at www.GemmaHalliday.com

The Wine & Dine Mysteries

www.GemmaHalliday.com

CPSIA information can be obtained
at www.ICGtesting.com
Printed in the USA
BVHW031313070222
628302BV00008B/82